政大英文系 **陳超明** 教授／著　**郭惠菁**／整理

全球英語文法

GLOBAL
ENGLISH
GRAMMAR

目錄

　　我認為這是第一本為了全球英語（Global English）所寫的文法。過去的文法書都是從結構的概念來寫，針對所謂 Native Speaker（母語人士）所學的英語（包括英式英語和美式英語），將文法分為許多詞性及固定的規則，從最基本的文法到最高深的文法一一進行分析。但 Global English 是從「功能性」的概念出發，是以全球溝通為主的文法概念。

Global English 的定義

　　首先我們要先定義 Global English。我認為 Global English 的發展有三個階段。第一個階段是 19 世紀。當時大英帝國在世界各地進行殖民，英式英語自然而然成為經濟、貿易、殖民等活動的主要溝通語言。在當時，「講英式英語」這件事就如同標示了一個人的社經地位一樣，成為上流社會的語言。第二個階段是在一次世界大戰之後。當時美國挾帶著貿易、政治、軍事實力崛起，美式英語就成了全球的語言，主導了一切。不過相較於英式英語，美式英語因為美國多元族群的特色，接收了許多外來的影響，語言變得比較彈性、比較多元。後來好萊塢電影更加強美式英語的發展。例如電影《酷斯拉》中，法國情報頭子甚至說他的英文是學貓王的英文！可見美國影視力量更推廣了美式英語在全球的發展。然而，自 2003 年開始，英語進入了另一個發展時期。由於網路和全球化的關係，全球人才在世界各地移動，英語再度逐漸成為主要的溝通語言。不過這次的英語是以 Non-native speaker 為主。None-native speaker 將英語當作溝通的工具。所以在前兩個階段，不管是學英式英語還美式英語，兩種語言都挾有強烈的文化性，講英語主要是跟英文母語人士（英國人、美國人）溝通。但在第三個階段，英語已經脫離了英、美的文化性，成了工具，英語的重要性落在「溝通」這件事上，也就是英語脫離了母語人士的獨攬地位，成為非母語人士、母語人士間的重要溝通媒介。這階段的英語，多位研究英語文發展史的學者與專家，如 David Graddol 或前法國 IBM 行銷副總 Jean-Paul Nerriere，稱之為全球英語（Global English）。

Global English 的特色

　　Global English 有幾個特色：語言不受意識形態影響，溝通直接，以語意為主，規則只用來服務語意等。簡單來說，Global English 就

Grammar for
Global English
前言

是 "a simplified version of native speaker's English without native speaker's cultural influence"，是一種不受母語文化影響的簡化的英語。它的文法很簡單：第一，它是功能性，目的是用來溝通；第二，它是描述性的概念，沒有對錯。文法是告訴你英語大概是怎麼溝通的，而不是規定你一定要怎麼用才對。

Global English 只有溝通順暢與否的問題，沒有對錯的問題。舉例來說，我跟外國人確定時間，如約九點十五分，我可以說 "I will meet you at nine, one-five." 輔以手勢，外國人也聽得懂我們約在九點十五分見面，不一定要說：at nine fifteen。有時甚至 at 也省略了。只要溝通的目的達成了即可。但是過去的文法規則會告訴你這是錯的。

但是要溝通，當然語言一定要有 common ground（共識），比方說大家都要對同一個單字的意思有共同的理解，不能我說 apple 是蘋果，你說 apple 是橘子。不過單字也有簡化的趨勢，新創的字都是組合字。比方 text 這個字，就被用作「簡訊」或「傳簡訊」。大家不再創造過多新單字，而是擴充舊單字的意思。Global English 另外一個特色，就是使用者會非常頻繁的再確認（reconfirm），確定雙方有一致的理解。

使用全球英語是種學習過程，而非語言學習的終極目標！

不過，有些人可能會質疑，那全球英語不就有很多不合標準英語的文法規則或修辭原則，好的或漂亮英文表達豈不是被污染了？這種說法，其實忽略了語言的功能性，只強調語言的純粹性。不過，我們在此不是要否定美式、英式等母語人士的英文，也不是要摧毀英美文學作品中優美的文字與用法。我們只是提出，全球英語是非母語人士學習語言的一個過程（process），不是終極目標（end）。有人只是希望能使用直接、簡單的語言溝通，達到其專業（如商務）的目的，有的人希望英語能達到母語人士的語言精準度，閱讀理解狄更斯（Charles Dickens）的作品。因此語言學習有層次性、階段性與目的性。個人要是覺得 Global English 無法滿足你，當然可以更進一步去鑽研優美的、好的英語表達方式。但是如果，你的目的只是生活的、日常溝通的，實在沒有必要去學高深、複雜的文法結構與修辭方式！

Global English 的文法

因此對 Global English 來說，不影響語意的文法規則都不重要，比方假設法，就幾乎不用，因為不夠直接；此外，如 a/an 的分別；我們也不用 cannot help but... 這種雙重否定的英文，而直接用 we have to... 這樣肯定、簡單易懂的英文，也不計較到底是要用原形動詞還是 V-ing。

以修辭為主的語法結構會減少，取而代之的是字序、時態等最基本的概念。所以這本書講的就是溝通中最需要知道的「基本語法結構」。

在這本書中，我替 Global English 的文法做了簡單的歸納。重要的概念只有三點：

1. 影響語意：Global English 最重要的是作為國際溝通。不影響語意的文法不用刻意去記憶。除了最基本的文法概念以外，我統整出最常使用的十大句法，只要掌握基本概念和十大句型，與外國人溝通就綽綽有餘。
2. 字序（word order）：字序是最基本的概念之一。本書教你如何使用字序理解句意。
3. 功能性：本書教你捨棄結構式的文法概念，改以了解文法的功能性為重點，也提出在何種狀況下使用該語法或文法觀念，如何影響語意。

不過在附錄我還是放了傳統文法需要的東西，當作一種過渡，幫助讀者適應新的學習方式。

本書特色

相較於以往的傳統文法書，我們不教你文法規則，我們只談文法怎麼「用」。我們用規則，不學規則。所以章節後面的練習請大家一定要實際操作，透過操作才能理解使用英文的基本學習方式。

如何使用本書？

1. 先看例句，從例句中尋找自己的障礙與重要的文法觀念。
2. 看規則，學怎麼用。每章都有許多來自 real life（真實生活經驗）或考試的實例，請跟著實例的解說步驟，學習新的理解方式。
3. 練習實際應用。每章的結尾都有練習題。跳脫以往挖空格「代換」的傳統，請各位實際練習如何使用文法。

透過實際練習，很多訴諸文字的解說都會變得輕鬆易懂。實際練習也可以幫助學習者將文法的使用方法深深印入腦中。因此，請大家務必要實際操作，如此必可提升英文程度，與外國人（母語人士或非母語人士）用互相都使用的文法來溝通，並不是難事！

Grammar for Global English
前言

文法術語說明

　　許多人在學習英文的過程中，常會被各式各樣的「術語」（如助動詞、關係代名詞等）搞得暈頭轉向，好像不搞懂這些術語，就不叫學英文。可是其實這類術語對一般的語言使用者來說並不那麼重要。它們只是輔助說明，我們只需要了解各種字詞的角色，並能正確使用，就已足夠。

　　文法術語只有兩種，一種是「詞性」，另一種是「功能」。「詞性」術語包括名詞、動詞、形容詞等等，作用在替字詞作分類；「功能」術語包括主詞、動詞、受詞等，作用是解釋字詞在句子中擔任的角色與作用。

　　為了方便說明，這些術語有時會出現在本書的內容中，但請讀者切記不需要強記這些術語的定義，理解才是重點。

★詞性

「詞性」就是字詞的分類，通常每種詞性都有一定的功能。

◎名詞 Nouns (N)

　　舉凡任何有關人、事、物的字詞，都叫名詞。通常名詞的功能是當主詞或受詞（動詞所受的人事物）使用，告訴讀者或聽者這個句子談論的主角是哪個人、事、物。

> Ex) **Playing in the water** / is lots of fun on a hot summer day. 　　（98 年第一次學測）
> 　　　　　　N
> 玩水 / 在炎熱的夏天很有趣

◎動詞 Verbs (V)

　　舉凡任何牽涉到行為、狀態的字詞，都叫動詞。動詞又分 Be 動詞和一般動詞，告訴讀者或聽者哪個人、事、物做了什麼事，或是處於什麼狀態中。

Ex) Dad / always **tells** me / not to study only for tests.　　　（98 年國中第一次基測）

V

爸爸 / 總是**告訴我** / 別只為了考試念書

Ex) Tomorrow / **is** / Mom's birthday.　　　（98 年國中第一次基測）

Be 動詞

明天 / 是 / 媽媽的生日

◎形容詞 Adjectives (Adj)

　　舉凡任何用來描述某個名詞的外表、心情、狀態等的字詞，都叫形容詞。形容詞通常用來告訴讀者或聽者哪個人、事、物看起來如何。

Ex) Your hat / looks / so **comfortable**!　　　（98 年國中第一次基測）

Adj

你的帽子 / 看起來 / 如此**舒適**

◎副詞 Adverbs (Adv)

　　舉凡任何用來加強描述某個動詞或形容詞的字詞，都叫副詞。副詞通常用來說明讀者或聽者某個動作、狀態（如時間、地點、方式等）。

Ex) At dinner time, / I / **often** enjoy / telling Mom everything happened at school.

Adv　　　　　　　　　　（98 年國中第一次基測）

在晚餐時間 / 我 / **常常很喜歡** / 告訴媽媽學校發生的每一件事情

Ex) Sue : Your hat / looks / so comfortable!

Ann : It's / **more than** / comfortable. / If you wear a hat like this, / you won't feel

Adv

cold / on a windy day.　　　（98 年國中第一次基測）

蘇：你的帽子 / 看起來 / 如此舒適

安：它 / 不只是 / 舒服而已 / 如果你戴一頂像這樣的帽子 / 你也不會覺得冷 / 在有風
　　的日子

◎介（系）詞 Prepsitions (Prep)

介（系）詞通常是用在某個動詞和某個名詞之間，以表示兩者間的關係或某個方位。

Ex) Candy / has decided to / move <u>**to**</u> Taipei next year.　　　（98 年國中第一次基測）
　　　　　　　　　　　　　　　　 Prep

凱蒂 / 已經決定要 / 明年搬去台北

★關係詞

◎連接詞 Conjuctions (Conj)

連接詞分成連接詞 (conjunctions) 和連接副詞 (conjuctive adverbs)，兩者都是用來表示兩個句子間的特定邏輯關係。

Ex) My brother enjoys having cold drinks, / **so** he always puts his Coke in the
　　　　　　　　　　　　　　　　　　　　　 Conj

refrigerator / before he drinks it.　　　　　　　　　　（98 年第一次學測）

我哥哥喜歡喝冷飲 / 所以他總是把他的可樂擺在冰箱裡 / 在他喝之前

Ex) Marsha thought her friends would do something special to celebrate her birthday;

/ **however**, they just gave her a little card.　　　　（改寫自 99 年國中第一次基測）
　 Conj Adv

瑪莎以為她朋友會做些特別的事情來幫她慶生 / 然而他們只有給她一張小卡片

◎助動詞 Auxiliary Verbs (Aux V)

助動詞是輔助動詞的動詞，用來表示動詞的時態、狀態（肯定或否定）等。

Ex) What <u>**can**</u> we learn from the dialogue?　　　　　（98 年國中第一次基測）
　　　 Aux V

我們可以從這對話中學到什麼？

★功能

所謂「功能」就是字詞在句子中的角色，通常每個角色都有一定的功能。

◎主詞 Subjects (S)

主詞就是一個句子中的主角，可能是談論的對象，也可能是行使動作的那個人、事、物。

> Ex) **You** / can't miss / Tasty Bakery's meat pie!　　　　（98 年國中第一次基測）
>
> 　　 S
>
> 你 / 不能錯過 / 美味麵包店的肉派

◎動詞 Verbs (V)

動詞是一個句子中的靈魂，指出主詞行使了什麼動作，或處於什麼狀態之中。

> Ex) She / **wanted to feel** the grass / with her feet.　　　　（98 年國中第一次基測）
>
> 　　　　　　 V
>
> 她 / 想要感受這片草地 / 用她的腳

◎受詞 Objects (O)

受詞指的是接受某種動作的名詞，通常用在動詞之後。

> Ex) Let's buy some flowers / for **her**.　　　　（98 年國中第一次基測）
>
> 　　　　　　　　　　 O
>
> 我們買些花 / 給她

Grammar for Global English
文法術語說明

◎ 關係代名詞 Relative Pronouns

關係代名詞指的是具有連接詞功能的代名詞,通常用來修飾前面的名詞。

Ex) Peter Jackson / <u>**who**</u> adapted *The Lord of the Rings* into a movie / made a hit.

        Relative Pronoun

彼得‧傑克森 / 將小說《魔戒》改編成電影的那個人 / 一炮而紅

◎ 關係副詞 Relative Adverbs

關係副詞 where / why / when / how 的作用是引導副詞子句(Adv Clause),用來補充說明某些狀況、原因、方式等。

Ex) <u>**When**</u> she studies in an art school there, / she lived with her aunt for five months.

        Relative Adverb   (98 年國中第一次基測)

當她在那邊念藝術學校的時候 / 她和她阿姨一起住了五個月

文法解析篇

文法解析篇

1. 主詞與動詞結構

　　大部分的人在學英文的時候，總覺得英文好難：文法規則這麼多、這麼複雜，要怎麼記？坊間的文法書又總是厚厚一本像字典一樣，看前面忘後面、看後面忘前面，讓人眼花撩亂。

　　可是學英文真的不難。學任何一種語言都一樣，以練習為主。文法錯了沒關係，熟能生巧，重點在於能溝通就好，不會有人拿著一本文法書，糾正你口語中的每一個錯誤。語言是活的，而不是紙上談兵。除非是要做深入的閱讀或是寫作，才必須要掌握較高深的文法規則。若是在一般日常生活中使用語言，則只要掌握幾點基本要素即可。

　　以英文為例，英文文法最強調的其實是「字序」（word order），尤其是「主詞＋動詞」的次序。閱讀的時候只要找出句子裡的主詞和動詞，就可以抓到句子的大致意義；在口語中也只要先提出主詞、再說出動詞，就可以開口說英文了。現在，就讓我們來練習尋找句子的主詞和動詞，你將發現學英文其實是件愉快又有成就感的事。

◎ **I see you.** – *Avatar*

◎ **Everybody loves stories.**

◎ **No cake for a birthday is kind of sad.**

◎ **It is an important thing to respect others.** （respect：尊重）

◎ **It is parents' job to serve various foods to their children.**

文法解析

★主詞與動詞結構

在英文句構中，「主詞＋動詞」是最主要的結構，只要將句子中的主詞、動詞找出來，就可以大致抓到句子的意思。

◎ I / see / you.

   S   V

我 / 感覺到 / 你　　　　　　　　　　　　　　　　　　　　（電影《阿凡達》）

※ 主詞 I 搭配 see 這個動作，即意為「我感覺到～」。

◎ Everybody / loves / stories.

       S   V

每個人 / 喜愛 / 故事

※ 主詞 Everybody 搭配動詞 loves，即意為「每個人都愛～」。

◎ Fresh fruits / have / a higher water content.

      S   V

新鮮的水果 / 有 / 更高的水含量

※ 主詞 Fresh fruits 搭配動詞 have，意為「新鮮水果有～」。

◎ We / closely followed / the advice in your article.
     S   V

我們 / 完全遵守 / 您文章中的建議。   （98 年大學指考）

※ 主詞 We 做出 follow 這個動作，意為「我們遵守～」。

★主詞的三種變化

「主詞」有不同的變化。除了一般名詞（人名、地名、物品名等）之外，抽象的概念也可以拿來當作主詞。

◎ No cake for a birthday / is / kind of sad.
             S   V

生日沒有生日蛋糕 / 是 / 有一點讓人傷心

※1. 主詞 No cake for a birthday 這個名詞片語被當作一個整體（一件事）來看。

    2. 搭配 Be 動詞 is，即意為「生日沒有生日蛋糕（這件事情）是～」。

◎ To respect others / is / an important thing.
        S   V

尊重他人 / 是 / 一件重要的事

※1. 主詞 To respect others 這個片語被當作一個整體（一件事）來看，也是一種抽象概念。

    2. 搭配 Be 動詞 is，即意為「尊重他人（這件事情）是～」。

◎ Taking care of a baby / is / so tiresome.
          S   V

照顧嬰兒 / 是 / 如此累人

※1. 主詞 Taking care of a baby 這個動詞片語被當作一個整體（一件事）來看。

    2. 搭配 Be 動詞 is，即意為「照顧嬰兒（這件事情）是～」。

Grammar for
Global English
主詞與動詞結構

1

如果覺得主詞太長，也可以用 "It" 來代替：

◎ It / is / kind of sad / to have no cake for a birthday.
　　S　V

　這件事情 / 是 / 有一點讓人傷心的 / 生日沒有生日蛋糕

※1. It 代表「這件事情」，真正的主詞為 to have no cake for a birthday，接上 Be 動詞 is，
　　意思為「這件事情是～」。
　2. 因為 It 沒有解釋「這件事情」是什麼，它的內容是空的，所以稱為「虛主詞」。
　3. 後方的 to have no cake for a birthday 用來補充說明「這件事情」的內容，才是主詞真
　　正的內容。

現在了解了嗎？我們再來看看其他例子：

◎ It / is / an important thing / to respect others.
　　S　V

　這件事情 / 是 / 一件重要的事 / 尊重他人

※1. 虛主詞 It 代表「這件事情」，接上 Be 動詞 is，意思為「這件事情是～」。
　2. 後方的 to respect others 用來補充說明「這件事情」的內容，也就是主詞的真正內容。

◎ It / is / so tiresome / to take care of a baby.
　　S　V

　這件事情 / 是 / 如此累人的 / 照顧嬰兒

※1. 虛主詞 It 代表「這件事情」，接上 Be 動詞 is，意思為「這件事情是～」。
　2. 後方的 to take care of a baby 用來補充說明「這件事情」的內容，才是主詞的真正內容。

★動詞的變化決定句子的意義

「動詞」幾乎可說是英文句子的靈魂。一個動詞可以有多種用法，而每種變化都
會替句子帶來新的涵義。請看下面的例子：

◎ I / walk.
　 S 　 V
　 我 / 走路

※ 主詞 I 搭配上動詞 walk，即意為「我走路」。

◎ I / walk to / the post office.
　 S 　 V
　 我 / 走到 / 郵局

※ 當 walk 加上介系詞 to，即代表「走到～」，而這個句子的意思就變為「我走路到～」。

此外，動詞的不同用法也決定了句子的不同意義：

◎ Children / like / to adventure.
　　 S 　　 V
　 小朋友 / 喜歡 / 冒險

※ 主詞 Children 搭配動詞 like，即意為「小朋友喜歡～」。

◎ Children / are likely to / adventure.
　　 S 　　　 V
　 小朋友 / 很可能會 / 冒險

※1. 當動詞 like 換成了形容詞用法 likely，其意思即變成「很可能會～」。
　 2. 搭配主詞 Children，本句意思轉變為「小朋友很可能會～」，句子意思就與上句不同。

★英文單一動詞的觀念

　　一個句子裡只會有一個動詞。當一個句子中出現兩個以上的動詞時，主要動詞（主詞的動作）不變，其餘動詞皆會弱化，改以其他形式（Ving, Ved, to V）出現，避免搶走主要動詞的重要性。

Grammar for
Global English
主詞與動詞結構

1

◎ Jolin / likes / singing.

       S   V   Ving

Jolin / 喜歡 / 唱歌

※1. 主詞 Jolin 搭配動詞 like，即意為「Jolin 喜歡～」。

  2. 為避免混淆重要性，動詞 sing 改以 Ving 型態出現，轉變成名詞用法。

  3. singing 亦可改為動詞片語 to sing，只要不搶走主要動詞 like 的重要性
     就可以了。

讓我們再看一例：

◎ Some teachers / reject / to allow foods in class.

         S   V   to + V

有些老師 / 拒絕 / 允許學生在課堂上吃東西

※1. 主詞 Some teachers 搭配動詞 reject，即意為「有些老師拒絕～」。

  2. 既然動詞 reject 是專門給主詞用的，它就是本句的主要動詞，並且決定了這一句話的
     意思。

  3. 為了避免混淆重要性，主要動詞 reject 所連接的 to allow foods in class 中，
     動詞 allow 即改以 to allow 出現。

再加上主詞的變化：

◎ It / is / parents' job / to serve various foods to their children.

    S V   to + V

這 / 是 / 父母的責任 / 提供不同的食物給他們的小孩

※1. 虛主詞 It 搭配 Be 動詞 is，即意為「這件事是～」。

  2. 因為 Be 動詞 is 是專門給主詞用的，它就是本句的主要動詞，並且決定了這一句
     話的意思。

  3. 為了避免混淆重要性，補充說明虛主詞 It 的內容 to serve various foods to their
     children 中，動詞 serve 即改以 to serve 出現。

重點整理

◎ 先抓出句子中的主詞及動詞就對了！

◎ 抽象概念（如片語等）和虛主詞（It）也是主詞的一種喔。

◎ 動詞是句子的靈魂，動詞的變化決定了句子的不同意義。

◎ 一個句子裡只會有一個動詞！主詞所採取的動作就是主要動詞；其它動詞
皆會以弱化形式（Ving, Ved, to V）出現。

常見錯誤用法：

I am believe that this is not going to work. (X)

Are you believe that this is not going to work? (X)

She was not work late for overtime pay. (X)

練習

第 1 題到第 4 題：請判斷畫線部分的詞性，分辨哪個是主詞，哪個是主要動詞。

第 5 題和第 6 題：請標示主詞和主要動詞。

範例：The project needs at least US$ 20 millions.

　　　主詞：The project　　主要動詞：needs

1. Number of injured hits 25.

　　主詞：_____　　主要動詞：_____

2. Newspapers tried many ways to collect news.

　　主詞：_____　　主要動詞：_____

3. The government works to stop the disease.

　　主詞：_____　　主要動詞：_____

Grammar for
Global English
主詞與動詞結構
1

4. Making bread and washing cars are their ways to make money.

   主詞：_____　　主要動詞：_____

5. It is cruel to cheat on others.

   主詞：_____　　主要動詞：_____

6. More than 150 people died in the tsunami.

   主詞：_____　　主要動詞：_____

作業

第 1 題到第 4 題：請將括號中的字詞放入適當的位置。第 5 題和第 6 題：請將字詞重新排列成完整的句子。

範例：a worldly-famed film. (Titanic / is)

Titanic is a worldly-famed film.

1. _____ _____ in the Pacific Ocean. (typhoons / occur)

   _____

2. _____ _____ surprising to see him laugh. (it / isn't)

   _____

3. _____ _____ under the threat of extinction. (are / many animals and plants)

   _____

4. _____ _____ difficult for women in Afghanistan. (life / is)

_____

5. wiped out / were / bedbugs / in the 1950s

_____

6. troublesome / so many refugees / it / to arrange / is

_____

Grammar for Global English
主詞與動詞結構
1

2. 肯定句、否定句、疑問句

　　掌握了最基本的句型結構（主詞＋動詞），我們接著就要來釐清最基本的文法概念：肯定句、否定句、疑問句。還記得當初學英文時，被一堆術語搞得七葷八素的樣子嗎？其實學英文沒那麼難，只要想想我們在什麼樣的情況之下會說出什麼樣的句子，就可以很容易理解英文句子的用法。所謂的術語只是用來分類句型幫助理解，並不需要死記活背。文法的重要性不在於教你對錯，而是教你如何應用。

句型範例

◎ **Just do it.** – Nike 廣告標語

◎ **Ice sculpting is a difficult process.**（ice sculpting：冰雕）

◎ **The music isn't pleasing to ears.**

◎ **Are you sure this is going to work?**

◎ **Do you believe in this rumor?**（rumor：謠言）

文法解析

★肯定句

　　表示意義的肯定或是敘述一個事實、情境、觀念等，其語意及句法皆與中文句子雷同。想想你在述說一件事情、一個想法的時候肯定的樣子，就足以解釋為什麼叫「肯定句」了。

◎ Just do it.

　　做就對了

※ 這句話表現了一個觀念「做就對了」，因此為肯定句。

◎ Ice sculpting / is / a difficult process.
　　　　S　　　　V

　　冰雕 / 是 / 一個困難的過程

※ 這句話說明 Ice sculpting 這件事的特質，是一個事實，即肯定句的一種。

★否定句

　　相反的，否定句就是在表達否定（not）的概念，通常表示：不、沒有、不曾、不能、無法等。其用法有兩種：

☆ am/ are/ is/ was/ were + not

◎ The music / **isn't** / pleasing to ears.
       S   V

這音樂 / 並不 / 悅耳

※ 這句話認為這音樂一點也「不」悅耳，因此為否定句。

◎ The Paralympics / **isn't** / for the ordinary.
        S   V

殘障奧運 / 並不是 / 讓普通人參加的

※ 這句話提出殘障奧運會「並不是～」，因此為否定句。

☆ 其他動詞的用法：助動詞 + not + 動詞

如 : do/ does not + 動詞
     can/ could not + 動詞
     has/ have not + 動詞 ed (PP)

◎ Children / **don't** trust in / unfamiliar tastes.
      S   V

小朋友 / 不信任 / 不熟悉的味道

※ 這句話表示小朋友往往「不信任～」，因此為否定句。

◎ You **can't** understand / unless / you experience it.
   S   V

你不會明白 / 除非 / 你親身經歷

※ 這句話認為一個人「並不能／不會～」，因此為否定句。

Grammar for
Global English
肯定句、否定句
疑問句
2

★疑問句

表示詢問別人意見或事情的句子，中文的疑問句通常會在字尾加個「嗎？」或是提高尾音。英文則有以下兩種表示方式：

☆ Is/ Am/ Are/ Was/ Were + 主詞 + 名詞（或修飾主詞的字詞）... ?

◎ Are you / sure / this is going to work?
　　S 　　　　　　　　　N

你 / 確定 / 這個行得通嗎？

※ 這句話在詢問別人的意見，想確定某事（第二個底線部分）「能夠～嗎？」；故為疑問句。

◎ Is it / possible / that all seniors fail to pass the exam?
　　S 　　　　　　　　　　　N

這件事 / 有沒有可能 / 所有高年級學生都沒有通過考試？

※ 這句話表達疑惑，懷疑所有高年級學生都不及格「～是可能的嗎？」；故為疑問句。

☆助動詞（如 Do, Does, Did, Can, Could, Have, Has, etc) + 主詞 + 動詞 ...?

◎ Do you / believe in / this rumor?
　　　S 　　　V

你 / 相信 / 這個謠言嗎？

※ 這句話在詢問某人「相信～嗎？」；故為疑問句。

◎ Should / Taiwan / have the fourth nuclear power plant?
　　　　　S 　　　V

應該 / 臺灣 / 要有第四座核電廠嗎？

※ 這句話在表達疑惑，想知道臺灣「應該～嗎？」；故為疑問句。

◎ Can / chefs / convince kids / to eat the vegetables?
　　　　　 S　　　 V

能夠 / 廚師 / 說服孩童 / 吃蔬菜嗎？

※ 這句話在疑惑廚師「能夠～嗎？」；故為疑問句。

　重 點 整 理

◎ 表達事實、情境、觀念的句子即為肯定句；表達否定的概念即為否定句；
　 詢問他人意見（表達心中疑惑）的句子即為疑問句。
◎ 否定句中字的排列次序：
　 ＊ am/ are/ is/ was/ were + not
　 ＊ 助動詞 + not + 動詞
◎ 疑問句中字的排列次序：
　 ＊ Am/ Are/ Is/ Was/ Were + 主詞 + 名詞（或修飾主詞的字詞）...？
　 ＊ 助動詞 + 主詞 + 動詞 ...?

練習

　　請依上下文語意判斷其句型為肯定句、疑問句，或否定句；並依括號內的提示，
填入適當的動詞變化，以完成句子。

範例：Some schools ＿＿＿＿＿ allow junk foods for health's sake. (does)
　　　本句型為 否定句 。括號內助動詞應改為 doesn't 。

1. She ＿＿＿＿＿ plastic surgeries to become prettier. (take)

　　　本句型為 ＿＿＿＿＿ 句。括號內動詞應改為 ＿＿＿＿＿ 。

Grammar for
Global English
肯定句、否定句
疑問句
2

2. _____ you want to change yourself and your life overnight? (does)

本句型為 _____ 句。括號內助動詞應改為 _____ 。

3. Even scientists _____ know how many creatures live in the world's oceans. (can)

本句型為 _____ 句。括號內助動詞應改為 _____ 。

4. _____ CNN News provide trustful world news? (does)

本句型為 _____ 句。括號內助動詞應改為 _____ 。

5. _____ there water on the moon? (is)

本句型為 _____ 句。括號內 Be 動詞應改為 _____ 。

6. The accurate picture of ocean life _____ help scientists notice changes. (can)

本句型為 _____ 句。括號內助動詞應改為 _____ 。

請依中文語意判斷句子的型態（肯定句、疑問句或否定句），並填入適當的動詞、助動詞及其變化。

範例：幾百萬隻蜜蜂在過去幾年中消失殆盡。

    Millions of honeybees <u>disappeared</u> over the past few years.

1. 每個人都不是完美的。

    Every person _____ perfect.

2. 時間管理真的能夠增進學習效率嗎？

    _____ time management really enhance one's learning efficiency?

3. 臺灣的氣象預報一向都很準確嗎？

    _____ the weather forecast in Taiwan always accurate?

4. 不隨波逐流是很不容易的事。

    It _____ easy not to follow the trends.

5. 為了變得更好，Yahoo Mail 做了它最大的改革。

    Yahoo Mail _____ a huge revamp to make it better.

6. iPhone 引發新潮流這件事讓你感到驚訝嗎？

    _____ it surprise you that iPhone leads a new trend?

Grammar for
Global English
肯定句、否定句
疑問句

2

3. 十大句法

　　有了對文法的初步認識後，我們接下來就要嘗試更豐富的變化。

　　就像說中文一樣，為了吸引聽眾注意，我們會在句子裡加上很多細節，或是改變不一樣的說法，好讓我們呈現的內容更有變化。英文也是一樣。大家常被英文顛三倒四的語法搞得頭昏腦脹，但其實英文句法的變化一直都謹守「主詞＋動詞」的概念，只是會在不同的地方插入一些補充，讓句子看起來不一樣。

　　將英文句法的眾多變化整理出來，大多不脫以下十大句法。只要將複雜的句子適當分段，你會發現原來理解英文句子是這麼簡單！

◎ **Marilyn Monroe, the famous actress, is a legend.**（legend：傳說）

◎ **(Being) a black, President Obama changes history.**

◎ **I stand here today, humbled by the task before us.** –《歐巴馬就職演說》

◎ **With a higher water content, fresh onions tastes sweeter and milder.**

◎ **Thanks to the weather, the fireworks successfully ended.**

◎ **Plato once said, "Every man is a poet when he is in love."**

◎ **The report says that all the department stores are on anniversary sale.**

◎ **If parents go on a diet, children tend to pick foods more.**

◎ **Peter Jackson who adapted *The Lord of the Rings* into a movie made a hit.**

◎ **There comes Tom Cruise.**

文法解析

★句法一：S + (...) + V

雖然「主詞＋動詞」是最基本的句型結構，為了使句子變得更豐富、完整，主詞和動詞之間往往會插入一個片語或子句，對主詞作補充說明。

◎ Marilyn Monroe /, the famous actress, / is a legend.

          S   V

瑪麗蓮夢露 / 那位有名的女演員 / 是個傳奇

※ 1. 主詞 Marilyn Monroe 搭配 Be 動詞 is，即意為「瑪麗蓮夢露是～」。

  2. 中間的名詞 the famous actress 用來對主詞作補充，說明瑪麗蓮夢露的身分。

  3. 補充說明中的主詞與本句的主詞是同一個人，此即為「同位語」概念。

◎ Pacific islands /, like Easter Island and Tahiti, / are hot resorts.

          S   V

太平洋群島 / 例如復活節島和大溪地 / 是熱門觀光景點

※ 1. 主詞 Pacific islands 搭配 Be 動詞 are，即意為「太平洋群島是～」。

  2. 中間的插入句 like Easter Island and Tahiti 用來對主詞作舉例說明，並不影響全句語意。

◎ President Obama / , who is black, / changes history.
　　　　　　　S　　　　　　　　　　　　　　V

歐巴馬總統 / 身為黑人 / 改變歷史

※ 1. 主詞 President Obama 搭配動詞 changes，即意為「歐總統巴馬改變～」。

  2. 中間的插入句 who is black 用來對主詞作補充說明，強調歐巴馬總統的黑人血統，對
     比出這個改變的重要性。

★句法二：Ving (Ved) (To V)..., S + V

補充說明也可以擺在基本句構「主詞＋動詞」之前。如果補充說明中的
動詞是主動的，就用 Ving；如果表示被動，則用 Ved，表示目的的則用 to V。

◎ (Being) a black, / President Obama / changes history.
　　　　　　　　　　　　　　S　　　　　　V

身為黑人 / 歐巴馬總統 / 改變歷史

※ 1. 主詞 President Obama 搭配動詞 changes，即意為「歐巴馬總統改變～」。

  2. 歐巴馬總統天生身為黑人，因此補充說明中的 Be 動詞改以 Ving 形式出現（Being 放
     在句首通常可省略，因此以括號表示）。

◎ Breaking seven world records, / Michael Phelps / wins / eight gold medals.
　　　　　　　　　　　　　　　　　　　S　　　　　V

打破七項世界紀錄 / 麥可‧菲爾普斯 / 贏得 / 八面金牌

※ 1. 主詞 Michael Phelps 搭配動詞 wins，即意為「麥可‧菲爾普斯贏得～」。

  2. 因為是 Phelps「打破」世界紀錄，所以補充說明中的動詞 break 改以
     Ving 型態出現，表示主動。

Grammar for Global English
十大句法
3

◎ Injured in the car accident, / he / could barely move / his legs.
                                    S   V

在車禍中受傷 / 他 / 幾乎不能移動 / 他的雙腿

※ 1. 主詞 he 搭配動詞和副詞 could barely move，即意為「他幾乎不能移動～」。

2. 因為車禍「造成」主詞受傷，所以補充說明中的 injure 改以 Ved 型態出現，表示被動。

★ 句法三：S + V...(to V), Ving (Ved)

補充說明 Ving、Ved 和 to V 也可以擺在基本句構「主詞＋動詞」之後，表示前面的主要句子動作，造成後面 Ving、Ved、to V 的結果。

◎ I stand here today /, humbled by the task before us.
  S   V

我今天站在這裡 / 為我們眼前的任務感到謙卑   （《歐巴馬就職演說》）

※ 1. 主詞 I 搭配動詞 stand，即意為「我站在～」。

2. 補充句 humbled by the task before us 用來對主詞作補充，說明歐巴馬站在臺上的心境。

3. 因為眼前的任務「使」歐巴馬感到謙卑，因此動詞 humble 是用 Ved 型態出現，表示被動。

◎ Lin Yu Chun / conquers "American Idols" / with the song "I Will Always
       S   V

Love You," / becoming a celebrity.

林育群 / 征服《美國偶像》/ 藉著 "I Will Always Love You" 這首歌 / 成為一個名人

※ 1. 主詞 Lin Yu Chun 搭配動詞 conquers，即意為「林育群征服～」。

2. 補充句 becoming a celebrity 用來對主詞作補充，說明林育群征服《美國偶像》之後的成就。

3. 因為是林育群自己造就了這樣的成就，所以動詞 become 是以 Ving 型態出現，表示主動。

★句法四：With / Without + N + (Ving or Ved)..., S + V 或
S + V, with / without + N + (Ving or Ved)

以 with 或 without 引導的補充說明，通常有「造成」主要句構的暗示。

◎ With a higher water content, / fresh onions / tastes / sweeter and milder.
                                              S   V

有更高的水含量 / 新鮮洋蔥 / 嘗起來更鮮甜而不嗆辣

※ 1. 主詞 fresh onions 搭配動詞 tastes，即意為「新鮮洋蔥嘗起來～」。
　　 2. With 引導的名詞則是用來補充說明，解釋是什麼原因造成新鮮洋蔥嘗起來比較鮮甜而
　　　 不嗆辣。

◎ With a sharp sensation, / animals / are capable of / predicting earthquake.
                                    S   V

有敏銳的知覺 / 動物 / 能夠 / 預測地震

※ 1. 主詞 animals 搭配動詞片語 are capable of，即意為「動物能夠～」。
　　 2. With 引導的名詞則是用來補充說明，解釋是什麼原因讓動物能夠預測地震。

也可以有否定的用法：

◎ Without hesitation, / the woman / gives her water to the thirsty man.
                             S   V

一點都不猶豫 / 那個女人 / 把她的水給了那個口渴的男人

※ 1. 主詞 the woman 搭配動詞 gives，即意為「那個女人把～給～」。
　　 2. Without 引導的名詞則是用來補充說明，強調在一點也「不」猶豫的情況之下，那女
　　　 人把她的水給了那個口渴的男人。

★句法五：(Phrase), S + V

「片語」也可以拿來當句子的開頭，對主要句構進行各種補充說明。

Grammar for Global English
十大句法

3

◎ Thanks to the weather, / the fireworks / successfully ended.

　　　　　　　　　　　　　　　S　　　　　　　　　　V

幸虧天氣（好）/ 煙火大會 / 順利結束

※ 1. 主詞 the fireworks 搭配動詞 ended，即意為「煙火大會～結束」。

　 2. Thanks to 帶出的片語則是對主要句構進行補充，說明是什麼原因讓煙火大會順利結束。

◎ According to popular folklore, / many animals / are smarter than they appear.

　　　　　　　　　　　　　　　　　S　　　　V

根據流傳的民間傳說 / 許多動物 / 都比牠們看起來的樣子更聰明。

（98 年大學學測）

※ 1. 主詞 many animals 搭配動詞 are，即意為「許多動物都是～」。

　 2. According to 帶出的片語則是對主要句構進行補充，說明「許多動物都比牠們看起來的樣子更聰明」這個說法是從哪裡來的。

★句法六："...," says SB 或 SB says, "..."

這個句型就是中文常用的「某人說了某事」。動詞 say 也可以改成其他動詞，例如 tell（告訴）、cry（大叫）等等。

◎ Plato / once said, / "Every man is a poet when he is in love."

　　S　　　　V

柏拉圖 / 曾經說過 /「每個戀愛中的人都是詩人」

※ 1. 主詞 Plato 搭配動詞 said，即意為「柏拉圖曾說～」。

　 2. 引號（""）內的句子即為柏拉圖說話的內容。

◎ "To be, / or not to be, / that is a question," / meditates / Hamlet.

　　　　　　　　　　　　　　　　　　　　　　　　V　　　　S

「存在 / 不存在 / 這是個兩難的問題」/ 沉思著 / 哈姆雷特

（莎士比亞《哈姆雷特》）

※ 1. 主詞 Hamlet 搭配動詞 meditates，即意為「哈姆雷特沉思著～」。

　　2. 引號（＂＂）內的句子即為哈姆雷特沉思的內容。

如果不曉得某句話、某個消息是從哪裡來的，也可以這樣說：

◎ It is said that / "First love is only a little foolishness and a lot of curiosity."

　　S 　 V

　　據說 /「初戀就是一點點笨拙外加許許多多好奇心」

※ 1. 虛主詞 It 搭配動詞 is said，即意為「據說～／有人說～／人們說～」。

　　2. "It is said" 也可改為 "People say"。

　　3. 引號（＂＂）的句子即為這句話的內容。

★句法七：S + V + that + (noun clause)

這種句型多半會用在闡述某件事，或是陳設某個觀點的情境之中，例如我認為 "I think that..."（我認為～），或 "The study claims that..."（研究指出～）。

◎ The report says that / all the department stores are on anniversary sale.

　　　S 　　 V

　　報導說 / 各大百貨公司都在周年慶

※ 1. The report 搭配動詞 says，即意為「報導說～」。

　　2. that 帶出的名詞子句則解釋了報導的內容。

◎ Recent research finds that / children will try new food / if they fix meals.

　　　　 S 　　 V

　　最近的研究發現 / 孩童會嘗試新食物 / 如果他們動手做飯

※ 1. 主詞 Recent research 搭配動詞 finds，即意為「最近的研究發現～」。

　　2. that 帶出的子句則說明了研究內容。

Grammar for
Global English
十大句法

3

★句法八：Adv clause, Main clause 或 Main clause, Adv clause

原因、時間、條件等副詞子句也可對主要句構進行補充說明。

◎ If parents go on a diet, / children / tend to / pick foods more.
                            S   V

如果父母節食減肥 / 孩子們 / 容易 / 更為挑食。

※ 1. 主詞 children 搭配動詞 tend to，即意為「孩子們容易～」。

  2. If 帶領的副詞子句則是對主要句構進行補充，說明在什麼條件之下孩子們更容易挑食。

◎ When dogs sense danger, / they / erect their ears and show their tooth.
                           S   V   V

當狗察覺危險時 / 牠們 / 豎起耳朵並且露出牙齒。

※ 1. 主詞 they 搭配動詞 erect...and show...，即意為「牠們豎起～並且露出～」。

  2. When 帶出的時間子句則是對主要句構進行補充，說明在什麼樣的情況之下狗會做出
     這些反應。

◎ Since Ma Ying-jeou become the President, / jogging / has become / one of
                                              S   V
the most popular exercises in Taiwan.

自從馬英九當選總統 / 慢跑 / 已經成為 / 臺灣最流行的運動之一

※ 1. 主詞 jogging 搭配動詞 has become，即意為「慢跑已經成為～」。

  2. Since 帶出的原因子句則是對主要句構進行補充，說明從什麼時候開始，慢跑已經成
     為台灣最流行的運動之一。

★句法九：S, Adj clause, V

形容詞子句（Adj clause）可以插在主詞和動詞之間，就近對主詞進行補充說明或
修飾。

◎ Peter Jackson / who adapted *The Lord of the Rings* into a movie / made a hit.

        S   V

彼得‧傑克森 / 將小說《魔戒》改編成電影的人 / 一炮而紅

※ 1. 主詞 Peter Jackson 搭配動詞片語 made a hit，即意為「彼得‧傑克森一炮而紅」。

    2. who 所帶領的子句用來對主詞進行補充，說明彼得‧傑克森的身分。

> 補充說明：主詞為人，用 who 或 that 來引導；如為物，則用 which 或 that。

◎ Young children / that are exposed to big cities / are more likely to be sick.

        S   V

年幼的孩童 / 接觸大都市 / 是較容易生病的

※ 1. 主詞 Young children 搭配 Be 動詞 are，即意為「年幼的孩童是～」。

    2. that 所帶領的形容詞子句用來對主詞進行補充，說明在哪裡生長的幼童較容易生病。

★句法十：Adv + V + S（倒裝句：Sentence Inversion）

在英文中，為了強調句子的重要性，往往會顛倒主要句構的次序，將動詞或助動詞搬到主詞之前，以達到強調的效果。

◎ (From) There / comes / Tom Cruise.

        Adv   V   S

（從）那邊 / 來了 / 湯姆‧克魯斯

※ 1. 本句正常型態應為 "Tom Cruise comes from there."

    2. 主詞 Tom Cruise 搭配動詞 comes，即意為「湯姆‧克魯斯來了」。

    3. 為了強調這句話的重要性，主詞與動詞的順序對調，則成了 "(From) There comes Tom Cruise."

    4. 介系詞 From 放在句首可以省略，故為 There comes Tom Cruise.

◎ Never can / a human being / live alone.

    Adv +Aux V   S   V

絕不可能 / 一個人類 / 獨自生存

Grammar for
Global English
十大句法

3

※ 1. 本句正常型態應為 "A human being can never live alone."

2. 主詞 A human being 搭配頻率副詞和助動詞 never can，即意為「人類絕不可能～」。

3. 為了強調人類絕對不可能獨自生存，故將頻率副詞及助動詞 Never can 移到主詞之前。

4. 以頻率副詞 Never 為首的句子，一定是倒裝句。

◎ The feud between the Red Sox and the Yankees / does / the Curse of the

Aux V   S

Bambino / fuel.

V

紅襪隊和洋基隊的世仇 / 貝比魯斯的詛咒 / 點燃

※ 1. 本句正常型態應為 "The Curse of the Bambino does fuel the feud between the Red Sox and the Yankees."

2. 主詞 the Curse of the Bambino 搭配助動詞和動詞 does fuel，即意為「貝比魯斯的詛咒點燃～」。

3. 為了強調貝比魯斯詛咒造成的效果，故將助動詞 does 挪到主詞之前。

 重 點 整 理

◎ 英文的基本句構為「主詞＋動詞」(S + V)，其他插入句皆是用來作為補充說明。

◎ 若補充句放在主詞和動詞之間，那一定是用來對主詞作補充說明。

句法一：S + (...) + V

句法九：S, Adj clause, V

◎ 若補充說明中的主詞和基本句構的主詞相同，則視情況使用 Ving 型態、Ved 型態或 to V 型態，對主詞作補充說明。

句法二：Ving (Ved) (To V)..., S + V

句法三：S + V (to V)..., Ving (Ved)

◎ 補充句也可用來對主要句構進行補充，說明事情發生的情境、條件、原因。

句法四：With / Without + N + (Ving or Ved)..., S + V

或 S + V, With / Without + N + (Ving or Ved)

句法五：(Phrase), S + V

句法八：Adv clause, Main clause 或 Main clause, Adv clause

◎ 陳述想法、表達意見、表示觀點等等，可以使用下列兩種句型：

　　句法六：" …," says SB 或 SB says, " …"

　　句法七：S + V + that + (noun clause)

◎ 如果要強調句子的重要性，那就用倒裝句吧！

　　句法十：Adv + V + S（倒裝句：Sentence Inversion）

練習

第 1 題到 7 題，請依照畫線部分的提示，分辨這些句子各是哪種句法。第 8 題到第 10 題，請自行判斷。

範例：<u>In order to</u> write a report on stars, <u>we</u> <u>decided</u> to observe the stars every night.

　　　　　　　　　　　　　　　　　　　S　　V

　　此句法為句法五 (Phrase) + S + V

1. <u>Shared</u> by Jim Carrey and Bernie Mac, <u>a sense of humor</u> <u>makes</u> them success.

　　　　　　　　　　　　　　　　　　　S　　　　　V

　　此句法為 _____

2. "<u>Necessity is the mother of invention</u>," <u>it</u> <u>is</u> said.

　　　　　　　　　　　　　　　　　　S　V

　　此句法為 _____

3. <u>For the sake of</u> convenience, <u>Julie</u> <u>bought</u> a notebook.

　　　　　　　　　　　　　　　S　　V

　　此句法為 _____

4. <u>My grandmother</u>, <u>who</u> likes to surprise people, never <u>tells</u> before

　　　　S　　　　　　　　　　　　　　　　　　　　　V

her visits.

　　此句法為 _____

Grammar for
Global English
十大句法

3

5. I heard that many scholars will be invited to attend this yearly conference.
   S   V

   　　此句法為 _____

6. The organic food products, with no additional flavors added, are made of
   　　　　　　　　　　　S   V

   natural ingredients.

   　　此句法為 _____

7. Never should life rest on a single hope.
   　　　　　　S   V

   　　此句法為 _____

8. When an election comes, the streets are overwhelmed with ugly flags.

   　　此句法為 _____

9. With the sudden force of desire, shopaholics just can't stop purchasing.
   （shopaholics : 購物狂）

   　　此句法為 _____

10. It rains all week, causing landslides and flooding in the mountain area.

   　　此句法為 _____

作業

以下字詞皆按照主詞／動詞／插入句的型態分類。請按照句法提示，將字詞重新組合成完整的句子。

範例：<u>Nelson</u> / his mobile phone anymore / <u>forgetting to pay his phone bills</u> /
　　　　S　　　　　　　　　　　　　　　　　　　　　　　　　　插入句

　　　couldn't use（句法二：Ving (Ved) (to V)..., S + V）

　　　<u>Forgetting to pay his phone bills, Nelson couldn't use his mobile phone</u>
　　　<u>anymore.</u>

1. <u>a boat</u> / <u>will stand by</u> / in the cross-lake swimming race / in case of any
　　　S　　　　　　V

　emergency.（句法五：(Phrase), S + V）

　_____ .

2. <u>had a debate</u> with President Ma / <u>Tsai Ing-wen</u> / in 2010 / the head of DPP
　　　　　V　　　　　　　　　　　　　　　　　　S

　（句法一：S + (...) + V）

　_____ .

3. of the city / <u>Ai River</u> / <u>recovers</u> its beauty / with the great efforts
　　　　　　　　　　S　　　　　V

　（句法四：With / Without + N + S + V）（Ai-River: 愛河）

　_____ .

Grammar for Global English
十大句法

3

4. <u>a search</u> / whenever a Dalai Lama died / for his reincarnation / <u>began</u>
      S   V

   （句法八：Adv clause, Main clause 或 Main clause, Adv clause）

   （incarnation: 轉世）

   _____ .

5. <u>people</u> <u>say</u> that / has the ability to identify / a Dalai Lama / his previous self
      S   V

   （句法七：S + V + that + (noun clause)）

   _____ .

6. <u>build</u> / parodying Hollywood / <u>Bollywood movies</u> / its own features
     V   S

   （句法二：Ving (Ved) (To V)…, S + V）

   _____ .

7. that / <u>is said</u> / "Failure is the mother of success" / <u>it</u>
            V   S

   （句法六："…," says SB 或 SB says, "…"）

   _____ .

8. <u>stir</u> / <u>stories about aliens</u> / readers' imaginations / which are believed to exist
    V   S

   （句法九：S, Adj clause, V）（stir: 激發）

   _____ .

9. a person / never / try to climb Taipei 101 / did
     S   V

（句法十：Adv + V + S 倒裝句：Sentence Inversion）

_____ .

10. part of the truth / the news / leaving spaces for doubts / only tells
                    S   V

（句法三：S + V... (to V), Ving（Ved））

_____ .

Grammar for Global English
十大句法
3

45

4. 十大句法的實戰練習：
閱讀報章雜誌

在學習英文的過程中，大家最感棘手的大概就是英文長句的理解了。看到一串落落長的句子，任誰都想舉白旗投降。但只要善加運用基本句構「主詞＋動詞」及十大句法，任何人都可以輕而易舉將英文長句變得簡單而易於理解。本課將示範如何活用這兩項利器，來擊破英文長句。

在開始之前，提醒各位四大祕訣：

一、觀察句型，找出主要結構與次要結構，並找出相對應的十大句法

二、找出主要結構中的主詞及動詞

三、依照語法結構將長句切成小單元，有助於了解語意

四、依照英文句法邏輯理解語意，而不要硬從中文邏輯去理解

請先閱讀下列這個句子：

　　After Dad died ten years ago, you had to work in a supermarket in the daytime and in a restaurant at night.

（99 年國中第一次基測）

　　接著使用上述四個祕訣來理解語意：

1. 觀察句型，發現 After 帶領的時間子句是對應句法八：Adv clause, Main clause。因此可以知道前半句為補充說明，後半句才是主要子句。

2. 在主要句子中，主詞 you 搭配動詞 had to work，即意為「你必須工作～」。

3. 依照語法結構分別將兩個句子切成小單元，變成：

　　After / Dad / died / ten years ago,
　　　　　　　S　　　V

　　在～之後 / 爸爸 / 死亡 / 十年前

　　You / had to work / in a supermarket / in the daytime/ and in a restaurant /
　　　S　　　　V

　　at night.

　　你 / 必須工作 / 在一家超市裡 / 白天的時候 / 還有在一家餐廳裡 / 晚上的時候

4. 其實到了步驟三，這句話的意思就很清楚。只要稍加以邏輯排列，即可得知全句語意為「十年前爸爸過世之後，你必須白天在超市上班，晚上在餐廳工作」。

　　分析單一句子比較簡單，讓我們試試一次分析多個句子：

請請先閱讀下列這個段落：

The word "prom" was first used in the 1890s, referring to formal dances in which the guests of a party would display their fashions and dancing skills during the evening's grand march. In the United States, parents and educators have come to regard the prom as an important lesson in social skills. Therefore, proms have been held every year in high schools for students to learn proper social behavior.

（99 年大學學測）

接著使用上述四個祕訣來理解語意：

1. 觀察句型，發現第一句對應句法三：S + V... (to V), Ving (Ved)；第二句及第三句皆對應句法五：(Phrase), S + V；因此可得知其句型分別為：

a. <u>The word "prom" was first used in the 1890s</u>, <u>referring to ... grand march.</u>
           主要子句   補充說明

b. <u>In the United States,</u> <u>parents and educators have come to regard ... skills.</u>
  補充說明（地方）   主要子句

c. <u>Therefore,</u> <u>proms have been held ... social behavior.</u>
    副詞   主要子句

2. 進一步找出主要子句中的主詞及動詞，可得知其句意分別為：

a. <u>The word "prom"</u> / <u>was</u> first <u>used</u> / in the 1890s,
        S   V

主詞 The word "prom" 搭配動詞 was used，即意為「『正式舞會』這個字被使用～」。

b. ..., <u>parents and educators</u> / <u>have come to regard</u> the prom <u>as</u> / an important
                  S   V

lesson / in social skills.

主詞 parents and educators 搭配動詞 have come to regard...as...，即意為「父母和教育學家將～視為是～」。

c. ..., <u>proms</u> / <u>have been held</u> / every year / in high schools / for students / to
         S   V

learn proper social behavior.

主詞 proms 搭配動詞 have been held，即意為「正式舞會被辦在～」。

3. 若覺得句子太長導致句意不夠明確，則可分別進一步分析：

a. <u>The word "prom"</u> / <u>was</u> first <u>used</u> / in the 1890s, / <u>referring to</u> / formal
       S   V   V

dances / in which / <u>the guests of a party</u> / <u>would display</u> / their fashions /
                               S   V

and dancing skills / during the evening's grand march.

「正式舞會」這個字 / 第一次被使用 / 在 1890 年代 / 指的是 / 正式的舞會 / 在這樣的舞會中 / 舞會的客人 / 能夠展現 / 他們的服裝 / 和舞蹈技巧 / 在晚間的盛大遊行

b. In the United States, / <u>parents and educators</u> / <u>have come to regard</u> the
                                S   V

prom as / an important lesson / in social skills.

在美國 / 父母和教育學家 / 將正式舞會視為 / 一個重要課程 / 在社交技巧方面

c. Therefore, / proms / have been held / every year / in high schools / for
　　　　　　　　 S　　　　V

students / to learn proper social behavior.

因此 / 正式舞會 / 被舉辦 / 每年 / 在高中 / 讓學生 / 學習適當的社交行為

4. 依照英文的語意邏輯，即可得知：

a. The word "prom" / was first used / in the 1890s, / referring to / formal
　　　　 S　　　　　 V　　　　　　　　　　　　　　 V

dances / in which / the guests of a party / would display / their fashions /
　　　　　　　　　　　　　　 S　　　　　　　 V

and dancing skills / during the evening's grand march.

「正式舞會」這個字 / 第一次使用 / 在 1980 年代 / （「正式舞會」這個字）
指的是 / 正式的舞會 / 在（這樣的正式）舞會中 / 舞會的客人 / 能夠展現 / 他
們的服裝 / 和舞蹈技巧 / 在晚間的盛大遊行

b. In the United States, / parents and educators / have come to regard the
　　　　　 Phrase　　　　　　　　 S　　　　　　　　　　 V

prom as / an important lesson / in social skills.

在美國 / 父母和教育學家 / 將正式舞會視為 / 一個重要的課程 / （在哪方
面？）在社交技巧方面

c. Therefore, / proms / have been held / every year / in high schools / for
　　　　　　　　 S　　　　V

students / to learn proper social behavior.

因此 / 正式舞會 / 被舉辦 / 每年 / 在高中 / （為了誰？）讓學生 /
（目的是）學習適當的社交行為

誠如我們在範例一所發現的，其實在進行到第三個步驟時，句子的語意往往就已經呼之欲出；第四個步驟只是再進一步確定句意而已。除非是想要將句子翻譯成漂亮的中文，否則如果只是單純要了解語意，前三個步驟即已綽綽有餘。

接下來的兩個範例，我們會稍稍加快分析的節奏。

範例三

請先閱讀下列這個段落：

"It's a slippery slope," Susan Linn, director of the Campaign for a Commercial-Free Childhood, says of determining which ads are permissible in schools. "It is really better to draw the line at none, because schools are going to be constantly weighing the impact."

（Time Magazine）

一樣使用上述四個祕訣來理解語意：

1. 觀察句型，並立即分析主詞：

   a. "It's a slippery slope," **Susan Linn**, director of the Campaign for a
   　　　　　　　　　　　　　　　　S
   Commercial-Free Childhood, **says** of determining which ads are permissible
   　　　　　　　　　　　　　　　　V
   in schools.

   此句融合了句法六："...," says SB 及句法一：S+(...)+ V。

   分析完句型結構後，即可立即對主要子句進行主詞和動詞的分析：

   主詞 Susan Linn 搭配動詞 says，即意為「蘇珊琳說～」。

   b. "It is really better to draw the line at none, because schools are going to be
   　S V
   constantly weighing the impact."

此為簡單句 S＋V；後面接上連接詞 because，即意為「這件事～，因為～」。

分析完句型結構後，即可立即對主要子句進行主詞和動詞的分析：

虛主詞 It 搭配動詞 is，即意為「這件事～」。注意這句話有引號（" "），即代表這是蘇珊琳的發言。

2. 將整個長句分成小單位，幫助理解句意；若有分析困難的地方，則以英文語意的邏輯更進一步分析：

a. "It / is / a slippery slope," / Susan Linn, / director of the Campaign / for a
   S   V   S
   Commercial-Free Childhood, / says / of determining / which ads are
                                 V   S   V
   permissible in schools.

補充說明：slippety slope 指的是連續事件的開始，如一開始某件事就會導致嚴重的後果。

「這 / 是 / 一個連續事件」/ 蘇珊琳 /（是誰？）這個運動的領導者 /（什麼樣的運動？）為了一個無廣告汙染的童年 / 說 /（邊說邊如何？）邊決定 / 哪些廣告可以在校園播放

b. "It / is / really better/ to draw the line / at none, / because schools /
   S   V   S
   are going to be constantly weighing / the impact."
           V
「這 / 是 / 真的會比較好 / 去設定界線 /（將界線設定為）零的狀態 / 因為學校 / 總是會持續權衡 / 影響（什麼樣的影響？得視前後文決定）」

請先閱讀下列這個段落：

A survey of young people's music ownership has found that teenagers and college students have an average of more than 800 illegally copied songs each on their digital music players. Half of those surveyed share all the music on their hard drive, enabling others to copy hundreds of songs at any one time. Some students were found to have randomly linked their personal blogs to music sites, so as to allow free trial listening of copyrighted songs for blog visitors, or adopted some of the songs as the background music for their blogs. Such practices may be easy and free, but there are consequences.

（98 年大學指考）

一樣使用上述四個祕訣來理解語意：

1. 觀察句型，並立即分析主詞：

a. <u>A survey of young people's music ownership</u> <u>has found that</u> teenagers and
                        S   V

college students have an average of more than 800 illegally copied songs each on their digital music players.

此句為句法七：S＋V＋that＋(noun clause)，因此可知 A survey...has found 為主要子句。

分析完句型結構後，即可立即對主要子句進行主詞和動詞的分析：

主詞為名詞片語 A survey of young people's music ownership，搭配動詞 has found，即意為「一項關於年輕人音樂擁有權的調查發現～」；後方 that 子句則補充說明發現的內容。

b. <u>Half of those surveyed</u> <u>share</u> all the music on their hard drive, enabling

              S   V

others to copy hundreds of songs at any one time.

這句為句法三：S + V...(to V), Ving (Ved)，因此 Half of...hard drive 為主要子句。

分析完句型結構後，即可立即對主要子句進行主詞和動詞的分析：

主詞為名詞片語 Half of those surveyed，搭配動詞 share 即意為「有一半的受訪者分享～」；後方 enabling 帶出的子句則補充說明這件事造成的影響。

c. **<u>Some students</u> <u>were found to have</u>** randomly **<u>linked</u>** their personal blogs to

     S   V

<u>music sites</u>, so as to allow free trial listening of copyrighted songs for blog visitors, or adopted some of the songs as the background music for their blogs.

此句為句法五：(Phrase), S + V（或 S + V, (Phrase)，因此
Some students...to music sites 為主要子句。

分析完句型結構後，即可立即對主要子句進行主詞和動詞的分析：

主詞 Some students 搭配動詞 were found to have linked...to...，即意為「有些學生被發現將……連結到……」；so as 帶出的子句則補充說明這件事的目的。

d. **<u>Such practices</u> <u>may be</u> easy and free**, but there are consequences.

         S   V

本句為簡單句 S + V，以 but 連接兩個句子，則為 S + V, but...

分析完句型結構後，即可立即對主要子句進行主詞和動詞的分析：

主詞 Such practices 搭配動詞 may be，即意為「這種行為也許是～，但是～」。

2. 將整個長句分成小單位，幫助理解句意；若有分析困難的地方，則以英文語意
   的邏輯更進一步分析：

   a. A survey of young people's music ownership / has found that / teenagers
      　　　　　　　　　　S　　　　　　　　　　　　　　V　　　　　　　S

      and college students / have / an average of more than 800 illegally copied
      　　　　　　　　　　　　V

      songs / each on their digital music players.

      一項關於年輕人音樂擁有權的調查 / 發現 /（發現什麼？）青少年和大學生 /
      有 / 平均超過八百首盜版的歌曲 / 在他們每個人的數位音樂播放器

   b. Half of those surveyed / share / all the music on their hard drive, / enabling
      　　　　　S　　　　　　　　　V　　　　　　　　　　　　　　　　　　　　V

      others to copy / hundreds of songs / at any one time.

      有一半的受訪者 / 分享 / 他們硬碟中的所有音樂 /（分享硬碟這件事）幫助其
      他人複製 / 數百首歌 / 在任一時刻

   c. Some students / were found to have randomly linked their personal blogs to
      　　　S　　　　　　　　　V

      music sites, / so as to allow / free trial listening of copyrighted songs / for blog
      　　　　　　　　　　　V

      visitors,/ or adopted / some of the songs / as the background music for their
      　　　　　　　V

      blogs.

      有些學生 / 被發現任意將他們的個人部落格連結到音樂網站 / 為了要允許 /
      （允許什麼事？）免費試聽正版的歌曲 /（允許誰？）為了他們部落格的訪
      客 / 或者是採用一些（是哪些？）正版的歌曲 / 當作他們部落格的背景音樂

d. Such practices / may be easy and free, / but / there are consequences.
           S   V

這樣的行為 / 也許很方便又不用錢 / 但是 / 必需承擔後果

 重 點 整 理

◎ 先觀察句型，找出主要結構及次要結構，看看有沒有符合的句法可以使用。

◎ 接著找出主要子句中的主詞及動詞，先了解大致的句意。

◎ 耐心將長句子切成小單元，可以幫助消化句意。

◎ 以英文的句法邏輯思考，就可以輕鬆理解句子！

練習

以下段落已有句法（底線）及主、動詞（粗體字）提示，請按照提示，將剩下的部分作適當的切割。語意的部分可以自行嘗試釋義，之後再參考解答。

範例：**Newspapers have tried** many things to stop a seemingly nonstop decline in readers.

（99 年大學指考）

主詞為 ___Newspapers___，動詞為 ___have tried___。

此句句法為 ___S + V + to V___，可切割為：

Newspapers / have tried / many things / to stop a seemingly nonstop decline / in readers.

Grammar for Global English
十大句法的實戰練習
閱讀報章雜誌

4

請嘗試接下來的段落內容：

Now __France is pushing forward__ with a novel approach: giving away papers to young readers in an effort to turn them into regular customers.　　（99 年大學指考）

主詞為 ＿＿＿＿＿＿＿＿＿＿＿，動詞為 ＿＿＿＿＿＿＿＿＿＿＿。

此句句法為＿＿＿＿＿＿＿＿＿＿＿，可切割為：

＿＿＿＿＿＿＿＿＿＿＿＿＿＿＿＿＿＿＿＿＿＿＿＿＿＿＿＿＿＿＿＿＿

＿＿＿＿＿＿＿＿＿＿＿＿＿＿＿＿＿＿＿＿＿＿＿＿＿＿＿＿＿＿＿＿＿

__The French government__ recently __detailed__ plans of a project called "My Free Newspaper," under which 18- to 24-year-olds will be offered a free, year-long subscription to a newspaper of their choice.　　（99 年大學指考）

主詞為 ＿＿＿＿＿＿＿＿＿＿＿，動詞為 ＿＿＿＿＿＿＿＿＿＿＿。

此句句法為＿＿＿＿＿＿＿＿＿＿＿，可切割為：

＿＿＿＿＿＿＿＿＿＿＿＿＿＿＿＿＿＿＿＿＿＿＿＿＿＿＿＿＿＿＿＿＿

＿＿＿＿＿＿＿＿＿＿＿＿＿＿＿＿＿＿＿＿＿＿＿＿＿＿＿＿＿＿＿＿＿

　　接下來的段落沒有任何提示，請自行標示出主要子句的主詞及動詞，並將句子做適當的切割。語意的部分可以自行嘗試釋義，之後再參考解答。

　　Every celebrity Muggle in New York City showed up for the Nov. 15 premiere of *Harry Potter and The Deathly Hallows: Part 1*, from Sarah Jessica Parker and Sandra Lee to Melissa Joan Hart, best known as *Sabrina, the Teenage Witch*, all of whom walked down the red carpet.

As for the crowd of shrieking girls, they just had one thing to say: "OMG OMG OMG OMG OMG OMG!" Most of them also came carrying posters that read MOODBLOODS ❤ EMMA, NYC WIZARD ROCK, and I ❤ THE BOY WHO LIVED. "It always amazes me how enthusiastic they are after all these years," says Rupert Grint, who plays Ron Weasley. "It's really great!" So are all these secrets that we plucked from the film's leading actors.

（想知道《哈利波特》有哪些祕密嗎？請翻閱 *Newsweek*，2010/11/16）

5. 主要結構與次要結構

　　在前四章中,我們探討的是基本的句法概念,教的是如何抓出句子的主要涵義,以求快速了解句子大致內容。在這一章中,我們要更深入談論句子的結構,教你句子是如何組成,以及如何拆解。

　　在英文的句法中,「階層」是個很重要的觀念:除了主要子句之外,英文還可以使用許多次要的補充說明來拉長句子;前者我們稱為「主要結構」,因為它包含了句子的主詞、動詞,進而決定了句子的主要涵義;後者我們稱之為「次要結構」,目的在於對主要結構作補充說明,重要性較弱。

　　因此,在拆解英文長句的時候,不妨可以將長句想像成交通網:主要結構是幹道,提供最直接的交通路徑,直達目的地;次要結構則是支線,將主要道路連到其他地區。我們要做的就是分析哪條是主要幹道、哪些是支線,進而去判斷要選取哪一條路才能抵達我們最想去的地方。

　　第一課「主詞與動詞結構」已說明了主要幹道的組成;因此在本章中,我們將以支線為主,為各位說明這些支線的用途及分辨方法。值得一提的是,坊間的文法書大多以複雜的專有名詞來解釋各種次要結構的組成;本書則回歸次要結構的本質,以「用法的不同」來教你輕鬆分辨各種次要結構。

　　最後,要分析、理解長句子,不妨試試以下三個步驟:

1. 找出主要結構,理解句子的主要涵義
2. 判斷次要結構是片語還是子句
3. 理解次要結構的涵義,再與主要涵義作結合

句型範例

◎ One of his two cooks ran away with some money.

◎ He kept singing, louder and louder.

◎ I put fish in the ice box to keep it fresh.

◎ Stanley was surprised that the water felt warm.

◎ The pants I bought last year are too small now.

◎ When I heard my baby girl say her first word, my heart was filled with joy.

（以上例句皆取自 99 年國中第一次基測）

文法解析

★找出主要結構

當一個子句包含的主詞及動詞決定了句子的主要涵義時，我們稱這個子句為「主要結構」。首先，找出句中的所有主詞和動詞，接著再以邏輯推理，就可以分辨何者為主要結構、何者為次要結構了。

◎ **One of his two cooks ran away** / with some money.　（99 年國中第一次基測）
　　　　　S　　　　　　　V

他兩個廚師的其中一個跑掉了 / 帶著一些錢

※1. 在本句中，很明顯主詞和動詞都各只有一個，因此這句子本身只有一個子句。

　2. 主詞 One of his two cooks 搭配動詞 ran away，即意為「兩個廚師中的一個跑掉了～」，是主要結構。

　3. 依邏輯判斷，後方的片語 with some money 用來對主要結構作補充說明，因此是次要結構。

◎ **He kept singing**, / louder and louder.　　　　　（99 年國中第一次基測）
　　S　　V

他持續唱歌 / 愈來愈大聲

※1. 在本句中，很明顯主詞和動詞都各只有一個，因此這句子本身只有一個子句。

　2. 主詞 He 搭配動詞 kept singing，即意為「他持續唱歌～」，是主要結構。

　3. 依邏輯判斷，後方的片語 louder and louder 用來對主要結構作補充說明，因此是次要結構。

◎ **I / put / fish in the ice box** / to keep it fresh.　（99 年國中第一次基測）
　S　V

我 / 放 / 魚在冰桶裡 / 為了保持新鮮

※ 1. 在本句中，很明顯主詞和動詞都各只有一個，因此這句子本身只有一個子句。

　2. 主詞 I 搭配動詞 put，即意為「我把～放在～」，是主要結構。

　3. I put fish in the box 即為一個完整的主要結構；後方的片語 to keep it fresh 用來補充說明把魚放進冰桶的目的，因此是次要結構。

◎ **Stanley was surprised** that // the water felt warm.　（99 年國中第一次基測）
　　　S　　V　　　　　　S　　V

史丹利很驚訝 // 水感覺起來很溫暖。

※ 1. 仔細觀察這個句子，可以發現共有兩個主詞和兩個動詞，因此有兩個句子結構。

　　Stanley was surprised (that...). →子句 1

　　The water felt warm. →子句 2

　2. 子句 1 的主詞 Stanley 搭配 Be 動詞 was，即意為「史丹利是～」；

　　子句 2 的主詞 The water 搭配動詞 felt，即意為「水（摸起來）感覺～」。

　3. 依邏輯判斷，子句 2 為子句 1 的原因，用來補充說明史坦利為什麼感到驚訝，因此判斷子句 1 為主要結構，子句 2 為次要結構。

◎ **The pants** / I bought last year / **are** too small now.　（99 年國中第一次基測）
　　S　　S　　V　　　　　V

那條褲子 / 我去年夏天買的 / 現在太小了

※ 1. 觀察這個句子可發現，共有兩個主詞和兩個動詞，因此有兩個句子結構。

　　The pants...are too small now. →子句 1

　　I bought last year. →子句 2

Grammar for Global English
主要結構與
次要結構

5

2. 子句 1 的主詞 The pants 搭配 Be 動詞 are，即意為「那條褲子是～」；

　　子句 2 的主詞 I 搭配動詞 bought，即意為「我買～」。

3. 依邏輯判斷，子句 1 主導了句子的主要意思，為主要結構；

　　子句 2 用來補充說明那條褲子是怎麼來的，為次要結構。

◎ When I heard / my baby girl say her first word, // my heart was filled with joy.
　　　　S V　　　　S　　 V　　　　　　　　　　　　　　 S　　　　　 V

（99 年國中第一次基測）

當我聽見 / 我的寶貝女兒說出她第一個字 // 我的心充滿喜悅

※ 1. 這個句子共有三個主詞和三個動詞，由此可知本句有三個子句

　　When I heard... →子句 1

　　My baby girl say her first word. →子句 2

　　My heart was filled with joy. →子句 3

　　┌───┐
　　┊ 補充說明：say 為原形是因為感官動詞（heard）＋受詞（my baby girl）＋原形動詞（say）。┊
　　└───┘

2. 子句 1 的主詞 I 搭配動詞 heard，即意為「我聽見～」；子句 2 的主詞 my baby girl

　　搭配動詞 say，即意為「我的寶貝女兒說～」；子句 3 的主詞 my heart 搭配動詞 was

　　filled with，即意為「我的心充滿～」

3. 依邏輯判斷，子句 3 掌握了句子的主要涵義，為主要結構；子句 1 解釋了子句 3 的原因，

　　因此為次要結構；子句 2 又補充子句 1 的內容，因此為次要結構中的次要結構。

 重 點 整 理

◎ 先找出句子中所有的主詞和動詞就對了！

◎ 依邏輯判斷哪一組主詞和動詞構成的子句決定了句子的主要涵義，就能夠
　分辨出主要結構和次要結構。

◎ 次要結構是可以不斷增加的！除了句子本身有主要結構和次要結構的分別
　之外，在主要結構和次要結構之中，亦可以穿插更多的次要結構。

◎ 用標點符號（尤其逗號、破折號）來與子句作區隔的片語或子句，通常是
　次要結構。

★片語的概念

如果一個次要結構並不能單獨成句，這個次要結構就稱為「片語」。依用法的不同，片語可分為名詞片語、形容詞片語，以及副詞片語。

☆名詞片語

凡是當作「名詞」使用的片語，皆稱為名詞片語。

◎ **One of his two cooks** <u>ran away</u> / with some money. （99 年國中第一次基測）
　　　　　 S　　　　　　　 V

他兩個廚師的其中一個跑掉了 / 帶著一些錢

※ 1. 已知主要結構為 One of his two cooks ran away，次要結構為 with some money
　　　（請參考「找出主要結構」）。

　　2. One of his two cooks 這個片語當作主詞使用，具有名詞功能，因此是名詞片語。

　　3. 片語 with some money 用來描述廚師逃跑的狀態，作副詞用，因此是副詞片語。

◎ **Using a heating pad or taking warm baths** / <u>can</u> sometimes <u>help</u> / to relieve
　　　　　　　　　　　 S　　　　　　　　　　　　　 V

pain in the lower back.　　　　　　　　　　　　　　　（99 年國中第一次基測）

使用電熱墊或是洗熱水澡 / 有時候可以幫助 / 消除下背部的疼痛

※ 1. 在本句中，很明顯主詞和動詞都各只有一個，也沒有其他附加的說明，因此這句子本
　　　身就是主要結構。

　　2. 主詞 Using a heating pad or taking warm baths 搭配動詞 can help，即意為「使用電
　　　熱墊或是洗熱水澡可以幫助～」。

　　3. Using a heating pad or taking warm baths 這個片語當作一件事看待；也就是說，這
　　　個片語當作「名詞」使用，因此是名詞片語。

　　4. 如第一章所說，名詞片語通常會拿來當主詞使用。

Grammar for Global English
主要結構與
次要結構
5

☆形容詞片語

凡是當作「形容詞」使用的片語，皆稱作形容詞片語。

◎ The most effective way / **to keep fit** / is to eat healthy.
              S   V

最有效的方法 / 保持身材 / 就是吃得健康

※ 1. 主要結構是 The most effective way is to eat healthy.

    2. to keep fit（維持身材）就是用來形容這個 the most effective way 的目標。

       因此為形容詞片語。

◎ The girl / **with long hair** / is waiting for the bus.
      S   V

這女孩 / 留著長髮 / 正在等公車

※ 1. 主要結構是 The girl is waiting for the bus. 這女孩正在等公車。

    2. 是怎樣的女孩呢？我們用 with long hair 來說明她是一位長髮女孩。

       因此 with long hair 作形容詞片語使用，修飾 the girl。

◎ She is a woman / **in a black jacket**.
      S V

她是一位女人 / 身穿著黑夾克

※ 1. 已知我們要說明的對象是一個 woman。

    2. 用 in a black jacket 來說明這位女人是身穿黑夾克的女人。因此 in a black jacket 在這

       邊是形容詞片語，用以修飾 a woman。

◎ Harry Potter is a boy / **with a scar on his forehead**.
             S   V

哈利波特是個男孩 / 額頭上有一道疤痕

※ 1. 主要結構是 Harry Potter is a boy. 哈利波特是個男孩。

    2. 用 with a scar on his forehead 這個形容詞片語修飾 the boy，來說明這個男孩是額頭

       上有一道疤痕的男孩。

☆副詞片語

凡是當作「副詞」使用的片語，提供時間、地點、條件、原因等說明，皆稱作副詞片語。

◎ **Due to inflation**, / prices for daily necessities / have gone up / and / we / have
　　　　　　　　　　　　　　　S　　　　　　　　　V　　　　　　S　　V
to pay more / for the same items now.　　　　　　　　　　　（99 年大學學測）

因為通貨膨脹的緣故 / 日常用品的價格 / 已經上漲 / 並且 / 我們 / 必須付更多錢 / 現在為了買相同的商品

※ 1. 觀察發現 prices...have gone up 以及 we have to pay...items now 皆包含了主詞、動詞；因此得知 Due to inflation 為片語，prices 一句與 we 一句分別為獨立的子句。

2. 連接詞 and 連接 prices 和 we 這兩個句子，因此判斷 prices 和 we 同為這個句子的主詞。

3. Due to inflation 這個片語解釋了原因，說明在如何的條件之下會造成主要結構的內容，作副詞用，因此是副詞片語。

◎ **With / a DJ playing various kinds of music / rather than just rap, / and a mix of clothing labels / designed more for taste and fashion / than for a precise age**, / department stores / have managed to appeal to / successful
　　　　　　　　　　　　　　S　　　　　　　　V
middle-aged women / without losing their younger customers.

（99 年大學學測）

藉著 / 一個 DJ 播放各種音樂 / 而不是只有饒舌音樂 / 還有提供各種品牌的服飾 / 設計更有品味及時尚 / 而不是僅提供給單一年齡層 / 百貨公司 / 能夠吸引 / 事業有成的中年女性 / 同時避免年輕顧客的流失。

※ 1. 只有後半句 department stores...their younger customers 包含主詞、動詞，可單獨成句；因此得知 With...a precise age 為片語，是次要結構；department stores 一句為主要結構。

2. 主詞 department stores 搭配動詞 have managed to appeal to，即意為「百貨公司成功吸引～」。

3. With 帶領的片語解釋了百貨公司成功吸引顧客的條件，因此作副詞用，是副詞片語。

**Grammar for
Global English**
主要結構與
次要結構
5

67

★子句的概念

如果一個次要結構可以單獨成句,這個次要結構就稱為「子句」。依用法的不同,子句可分為名詞子句、形容詞子句,以及副詞子句。

☆名詞子句

凡是被當作「名詞」使用的子句,皆稱為名詞子句。

◎ Stanley was surprised that // **the water felt warm**. (99 年國中第一次基測)
　　 S 　　　 V 　　　　　　 S 　 　 V

史丹利很驚訝 // 水很溫暖

※ 1. 已知 Stanley was surprised 為主要結構,the water felt warm 為次要結構。
　　(請參考「找出主要結構」)
　 2. that 帶領的子句 the water felt warm 說明是哪件事讓 Stanley 感到驚訝,作名詞用,
　　　因此是名詞子句。

◎ What the researchers found / after about a year of testing / was **that** // **the**
　　　　　 S 　　　　　　　　　　　　　　　　　　　　　　　 V 　　　　　 S

drug / **appeared to cut** /male-to-male HIV transmission / by 44%.
　　　　 V 　　　　　　　　　　　　　　　　　　　　　　　 (BBC News)

研究人員發現(什麼事?)/ 在約一年的測試之後 /(那件事)就是 // 那種藥品
/ 似乎能夠減少 / 愛滋病毒在男性之間的散播 / 44% 的機率。

※ 1. 這個句子中共有兩個主詞和兩個動詞,因此有兩個子句。
　 2. 子句 1 的主詞 What the researchers found 搭配 Be 動詞 was,即意為「研究人員發現(什
　　　麼事)~」;子句 2 的主詞 the drug 搭配動詞 appeared to cut,即意為「(那件事就是)
　　　那種藥品似乎能夠減少~」。
　 3. 依邏輯判斷,子句 2 為子句 1 的詳細內容,即意為「研究人員發現那種藥品能夠減
　　　少~」;因此判斷子句 1 決定了句子的主要涵義,為主要結構;子句 2 用來補充說明,
　　　為次要結構。

4. 若要再細分，可在子句 1 中發現 after about a year of testing 這個片語指出了這項研究結果的條件（經過約一年的測試後得知），為補充說明，因此是子句 1 中的次要結構。

5. 記得虛主詞的概念嗎？ What 的作用就像虛主詞一樣，代表「某件事」；而那件事的內容就是 the drug...by 44%。

→ What (the researchers...of testing) was that (the drug...by 44%.)

6. 由此得知，What 帶領的子句被當作一件事看待，作名詞用，因此為名詞子句。

◎ They're worried // that / "sloppy" habits / gained while using textese /
    S   V   S

will result in / students' growing ignorance / of proper spelling, grammar
    V

and punctuation.

（99 年大學指考）

他們擔心（擔心什麼？）//（擔心）那件事 /（那件事是）「散漫的」習慣 /（哪樣的習慣？）在使用簡訊用語的時候（獲得的習慣）/ 將會導致 / 學生愈來愈無知 / 關於正確的拼字、文法及標點符號的用法

※ 1. They're worried 和 sloppy habits...punctuation 皆包含了主詞、動詞，皆可單獨成句。

  2. 子句 1 的主詞 They 搭配動詞 are worried，即意為「他們擔心～」；子句 2 的主詞 "sloppy" habits 搭配動詞 will result in，即意為「散漫的習慣將會導致～」。

  3. 依邏輯判斷，子句 2 應為子句 1 的內容，意即是「他們擔心散漫的習慣將會導致～」；因此子句 1 為主要結構，子句 2 為次要結構。

  4. that 帶領的子句可當作一件事（他們擔心的事），作名詞用，因此是名詞子句。

  5. 在 that 子句中，又發現 gained while using textese 這個片語是拿來形容 "sloppy" habits 是「以哪種方式形成的」，作形容詞用；因此是形容詞片語。

  6. 因此，在 that 這個次要結構中，又包含了另一個更小的次要結構。

Grammar for
Global English
主要結構與
次要結構
5

☆形容詞子句

凡是當作「形容詞」使用的子句，皆稱作形容詞子句。

◎ The pants / **I bought last year** / are too small now. （99 年國中第一次基測）
    S   S   V   V

那條褲子 / 我去年夏天買的 / 現在太小了

※ 1. 已知子句 1 The pants...are... 為主要結構，子句 2 I bought last year 為次要結構。
    （請參考「找出主要結構」）
   2. 子句 2 I bought last year 用來說明那條褲子是去年夏天買的，當形容詞用，因此是形容詞子句。

◎ Girls // **who are highly educated** // are required to have larger dowries /
    S   S   V   V

because they usually marry more educated men. （98 年大學指考）

女孩子 //（那些）有較高教育程度的（女孩子）// 被要求有更多嫁妝 / 因為她們通常嫁給教育程度更高的男人

※ 1. 這個句子中共有兩個主詞和兩個動詞，因此有兩個子句。
   2. 子句 1 的主詞 Girls 搭配動詞 are required，即意為「女孩子被要求～」；子句 2 的主詞 who 搭配 Be 動詞 are，即意為「那些女孩子是～」。
   3. 依邏輯判斷子句 2 為子句 1 的內容，即意為「女孩子（那些～的女孩子）被要求～」；因此判斷子句 1 決定了句子的主要涵義，為主要結構；子句 2 用來補充說明及修飾，為次要結構。
   4. 子句 2 who are highly educated 用來解釋是哪樣的女孩子會被要求有更多嫁妝，作形容詞用，因此是形容詞子句。

◎ Many satellites in space / are equipped with / large panels // **whose solar**
                 S   V   S

cells / transform sunlight directly into electric power. （99 年大學指考）
       V

很多外太空的衛星 / 都裝上了 / 大型的 / 面板 //（那些衛星的）太陽能板 / 直接將太陽能轉換成電力

※ 1. 這個句子中共有兩個主詞和兩個動詞，因此有兩個子句。

2. 子句 1 的主詞 Many satellites in space 搭配動詞 are equipped with，即意為「很多外太空的衛星都裝上～」；子句 2 的主詞 whose 搭配動詞 transform...into...，即意為「那些衛星的～能夠將～轉換成～」。

3. 依邏輯判斷子句 2 為子句 1 的內容，即意為「很多外太空的衛星都裝上了（面板），而那些衛星的（面板／太陽能板）～能夠將～轉換成～」；因此判斷子句 1 決定了句子的主要涵義，為主要結構；子句 2 用來補充，為次要結構。

4. 子句 2 whose 一句解釋了這些面板有「什麼樣」的功能，作形容詞用，因此為形容詞子句。

☆副詞子句

凡是當作「副詞」使用的子句，提供時間、地點、條件、原因等等說明，皆稱作副詞子句。

◎ **When I heard / my baby girl say her first word**, // my heart was filled with joy.
     S V   S V   S   V

（99 年國中第一次基測）

當我聽見 / 我的寶貝女兒說出她第一個字 // 我的心充滿喜悅

※ 1. 已知主要結構為子句 3 my heart was filled with joy（請參考「找出主要結構」）。

2. 子句 1 When I heard... 解釋是因為什麼原因造成我的心充滿喜悅，因此為副詞子句。

3. 子句 2 my baby girl say her first word 又說明 I 聽見了「哪件事」，作名詞用，因此是名詞子句。

◎ **Since the orange trees / suffered / severe damage / from a storm / in the**
                  S   V

summer, // the farmers / are expecting / a sharp decline / in harvests / this
             S   V

winter.

（99 年大學學測）

Grammar for
Global English
主要結構與
次要結構
5

因為 / 那些柳橙樹 / 遭受 / 嚴重的傷害 / 在一場暴風雨中 / 在夏天 //
農民們 / 預期 / 銳減 / 收成 / 今年冬天

※ 1. 這個句子中共有兩個主詞和兩個動詞,因此有兩個子句。

2. 子句 1 的主詞 the orange trees 搭配動詞 suffered,即意為「那些柳橙樹遭受~」;子句 2 的主詞 the farmers 搭配動詞 are expecting,即意為「農民們預期~」。

3. 依邏輯判斷,子句 1 解釋子句 2 的發生原因,整句話的邏輯為「因為那些橘子樹遭受~,所以農民們預期~」;因此子句 1 當作補充說明,是次要結構;子句 2 則為主要結構。

4. 因為 Since 一句解釋造成農夫們如此預期的原因,作副詞用;因此判斷 Since 一句為副詞子句。

◎ **When** / <u>**the cockroaches**</u> / <u>**were trained**</u> / **at night**, // <u>they</u> / remembered /
                 S   V   S   V

the new associations / (peppermint = sugar water; vanilla = salt water) /

for up to 48 hours.　　　　　　　　　　　　　　　　　　　（99 年大學指考）

當 / 蟑螂 / 被訓練 / 在晚上 // 牠們 / 記得 / 新的連結關係 / (薄荷糖=糖水;香草=鹽水) / 至少 48 小時

※ 1. When...at night 和 they remembered...48 hours 這兩個句子皆包含了主詞、動詞,皆可單獨成句。

2. 比對十大句法,發現此句為句法八:Adv clause, Main clause,因此可知 they remembered...48 hours 為主要結構(Main clause),When...at night 為次要結構。

3. 亦可依常理判斷,When 一句解釋在什麼樣的條件之下會造成 they remembered...48 hours,因此是對 they 一句進行補充說明;由此得知 When 一句為次要結構,they 一句為主要結構。

4. 因為 When 一句提供導致主要結構的情況與條件,作副詞用;因此判斷 When 一句為副詞子句。

重點整理

◎如果次要結構不能單獨成句，稱為「片語」；可以單獨成句的話，則稱為「子句」。

◎不論是片語或是子句，次要結構只有三種用法：當名詞用、當形容詞、當副詞用。

◎根據用法的不同，即可判斷某次要結構為「名詞片語／子句」、「形容詞片語／子句」或是「副詞片語／子句」。

◎在次要結構中，別忘了下列字詞的用法：

　who →代稱「人」：**Girls who are highly educated...**

　whose →代稱「所有格」：**Many satellites...whose solar cells...**

　which →代稱「事、物」：**...the pain which happens in the lower back.**

　that →代稱「人、事、物」：**They're worried that...**

練習

　　第 1 題到第 6 題，請按照提示判斷何者為主要結構、何者為次要結構；第 7 題和第 8 題，請自行找出句子中的主詞及動詞，並判斷何者為主要結構、何者為次要結構。以下例子皆選自 98 年大學指考。

範例：Children who experienced parental neglect often grew up with low
　　　　　S　　S　　　　V　　　　　　　　　　　　　　　V

　　　self-esteem.

主要結構為：Children...often grew up with low self-esteem

次要結構為：who experienced parental neglect

1. There was a time when Whitney didn't have a lot of friends.
　　　S　　V　　　　　　　　S　　　　V

主要結構為：＿＿＿＿＿＿＿＿＿＿＿＿＿＿＿＿＿＿＿＿＿

次要結構為：＿＿＿＿＿＿＿＿＿＿＿＿＿＿＿＿＿＿＿＿＿

Grammar for Global English
主要結構與
次要結構
5

2. In all cultures and throughout history <u>hair</u> <u>has had</u> a special significance.
                                          S   V

主要結構為：_____

次要結構為：_____

3. <u>The idea of long hair</u> as a symbol of male strength <u>is</u> even mentioned in the Bible.
         S   V

主要結構為：_____

次要結構為：_____

4. <u>The only person</u> <u>who</u> <u>knew</u> his secret <u>was</u> Delilah.
         S   S   V   V

主要結構為：_____

次要結構為：_____

5. <u>You</u> <u>will love</u> how <u>you</u> <u>feel</u> after helping others.
      S   V   S   V

主要結構為：_____

次要結構為：_____

6. <u>Camille and other children</u>, volunteering thousands of hours annually, <u>can fill in</u>

                  S   V

some of the gaps.

     主要結構為：_____

     次要結構為：_____

7. "I just wanted to save some money and I always thought the threat was just a
   scare tactic."

     主要結構為：_____

     次要結構為：_____

8. The organization that files lawsuits against illegal downloaders, states that
   suing students was by no means their first choice.

     主要結構為：_____

     次要結構為：_____

下列兩個句子中都有不只一個次要結構，請試著將所有的次要結構分析出來。以下例子皆選自 98 年大學指考。

範例：The program's official website states that the program was changed in order to provide both boys and girls with opportunities to explore careers at an age when they are more flexible in terms of gender stereotyped roles.

<u>The program's official website states</u> <u>that the program was changed</u> in order to
        主要結構   名詞子句

provide both boys and girls with opportunities to explore careers at an age
<u>when they are more flexible in terms of gender stereotyped roles.</u>
    名詞子句中的副詞子句

主要結構：The program's official website states (...).
句子的次要結構：that the program...stereotyped roles（名詞子句）
次要結構中的次要結構：when they are...stereotyped roles（副詞子句）

1. The NFW developed the project more than a decade ago to address the self-esteem problems that many girls experience when they enter adolescence.

2. According to research, kids who start volunteering are twice as likely to continue doing good deeds when they are adults.

6. 時態

　　了解句法概念之後,學習英文的第二重點就是時態。除了表示時間的字詞(如 yesterday, two months ago 等)之外,英文也會利用動詞的變化或者加上一些補助字詞,來表示時間狀態。

　　一般而言,最常用的時態包含「現在式」、「過去式」,以及「未來式」,分別用來表示現在的事實或狀態、過去發生的事情或狀態,以及未來即將發生的事情或狀態。在這三種時態之外,還有「進行」及「完成」兩種時態,分別表示當下正在進行的動作,以及在一段時間之內持續的狀態。

　　要理解這五種常用時態其實並不困難,只要畫條時間線就很清楚:

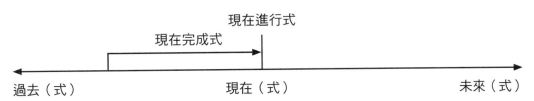

◎ **Beatrice loves to draw apples.**（99 年國中第二次基測）

◎ **The little boy jumped up and down happily.**（99 年國中第二次基測）

◎ **We are going to the Food Festival this weekend.**（99 年國中第二次基測）

◎ **Tension is running high on the Korean peninsula, in Asia.**

（Tension：緊張的氛圍；peninsula：半島）（*Time for Kids*）

◎ **I've lived with Eric for more than five years.**（99 年國中第二次基測）

● 文法解析

★現在式（V, V-s, V-es 或 V-ies）

凡是表示事實或是狀態的句子，一律用現在式。如果主詞為第三人稱單數，則在動詞後方加上 -s, -es, -ies。

◎ Beatrice / **loves** to draw apples.（99 年國中第二次基測）
　　　S　　　　V

碧翠絲 / 喜愛畫蘋果

※ 1. 主詞 Beatrice 搭配動詞 loves to draw，即意為「碧翠絲喜愛畫～」。

　 2. 因為主詞是第三人稱單數，因此在動詞 love 後方加 -s。

◎ The Paralympics / **are** / Olympic-style games/ for athletes with a disability.
　　　　　S　　　　　V　　　　　　　　　　　　　　（99 年國中第二次基測）

殘障奧運 / 是 / 仿擬奧運形式的比賽 / 為殘障運動員舉辦

※ 1. 主詞 The paralympics 搭配 Be 動詞 are，即意為「殘障奧運是～」。

　 2. 因為本句在描寫一個事實，所以用現在式。

◎ When people **feel** uncomfortable or nervous, / they / **may fold** their arms /

                                                        S   V

across their chests / as if to protect themselves.　　　　（98 年大學學測）

當人們感到不舒服或是緊張時 / 他們 / 可能會交疊他們的手臂 / 交叉在胸前 / 彷彿要保護他們自己

※ 1. 主詞 they 搭配動詞 may fold，即意為「他們可能會交疊～」。

   2. 因為本句在描寫一般大眾的行為，是一種事實，因此用現在式。

   3. 注意助動詞 may 亦是使用現在式。

◎ We / **hope** / that there **will be** no war in the world / and that all people **live**

  S   V

in peace and harmony with each other.　　　　　　　　（98 年大學學測）

我們 / 希望 / 世界將不會有任何戰爭 / 並且人們都能夠彼此和平與和諧相處

※ 1. 主詞 We 搭配動詞 hope，亦即為「我們希望～」。

   2. 因為是希望將來不會發生任何戰爭，所以用 will be 來表示。

   3. and 之後的 that 子句其實應該寫為 that all people will live...，只是因為前一個 that 子句已經有了助動詞 will，為了不讓句子太冗長，所以將這邊的 will 省略。

★過去式（V-ed 或不規則變化）

凡是表示發生在過去的事情或是狀態的句子，一律用過去式。動詞變化有規則變化以及不規則變化兩種。

◎ The little boy / **jumped** up and down / happily.　　　　（99 年國中第二次基測）

          S   V

那個小男孩 / 蹦蹦跳跳 / 很開心地

※ 1. 主詞 The little boy 搭配動詞 jumped up and down，即意為「那個小男孩蹦蹦跳跳～」。

Grammar for Global English
時態

6

2. 過去式動詞 jumped 暗示這件事發生在過去，小男孩剛剛或以前蹦蹦跳跳的，現在已經沒有了。

◎ The pineapple/, long a symbol of Hawaii, / **was** not a native plant.
　　　　S　　　　　　　　　　　　　　　　　　　　　　V　　　　　（98 年大學學測）

　　鳳梨 / 長久以來一直是夏威夷的象徵 / 以前並不是本土植物

※ 1. 主詞 The pineapple 搭配 Be 動詞的否定型態 was not，即意為「鳳梨以前並不是～」。
　　2. was 暗示這件事是發生在過去，而現在已經不再是這樣了。換句話說，鳳梨以前並不是本土植物，但現在是了。

◎ The mirror / **slipped** out of the little girl's hand, / and the broken pieces /
　　　S　　　　V　　　　　　　　　　　　　　　　　　　　　　　S

scattered all over the floor.　　　　　　　　　　　　（98 年大學指考）
　　　V

　　那鏡子 / 從那小女孩的手中滑出 / 然後碎片 / 散了一地

※ 1. 主詞 The mirror 搭配動詞 slipped，即意為「那鏡子滑出～」。
　　2. 注意動詞皆以過去式的型態呈現，即暗示這件事情已經結束了。
　　3. 注意連接詞 and 連接的兩個句子時態必須一致。

◎ Steve's description of the place / **was** / so vivid / that / I / **could** almost
　　　　　　　　　　S　　　　　　　　　V　　　　　　　　　　S　　V

picture it / in my mind.　　　　　　　　　　　　　　（98 年大學學測）
　　V

　　史提夫對那地方的描述 / 是 / 如此生動 / 以至於 / 我 / 幾乎能夠想像畫面 / 在我心中

※ 1. 主詞 Steve's description of the place 搭配 Be 動詞 was，即意為「史提夫對那地方的描述是～」。
　　2. 注意前面的 was 和後方的助動詞 could 時態一致，皆為過去式。

★未來式（will / shall + V 或 am / is / are + going to + V）

　　凡是表示未來發生的事情或是狀態的句子，一律用未來式。通常以助動詞 will / shall + V 表示，亦可以用（am / are / is）+ going to + V 表示。

◎ We / **are going** to / the Food Festival / this weekend.（99 年國中第二次基測）
　 S　　　V

　我們 / 將要去 / 美食節 / 這個週末

※ 1. 主詞 We 搭配動詞 are going，即意為「我們將要去～」。
　 2. 因為 this weekend 還沒到來，又動詞是 go，所以使用現在進行式 are going，表示即將要去。
　 3. are going 亦可用 will go 代換。

◎ You'**ll need** the store receipt / to show proof of purchase / if you **want to**
　 S　　V

　return any items you bought.　　　　　　　　　　　　　　（98 年大學指考）

　你將需要店家收據 / 證明你的購買行為 / 如果你想要退回你購買的任何貨品

※ 1. 主詞 You 搭配動詞 will need，即意為「你將需要～」。
　 2. will need 以未來式呈現，表示是未來的行為。
　 3. 但是「想退貨的話需要收據證明購買行為」這是一般常識，所以 if 子句維持現在式。

◎ "The new design / **will roll out** gradually / and **reach** all users / by early next
　　　　　 S　　　　V　　　　　　　　　　　　 V

　year," / Facebook **said** Sunday in a blog post / describing the changes.
　　　　　　 S　　　 V　　　　　　　　　　　　　　　（*CNN News*）

　「新設計 / 將會逐漸推行 / 並且抵達每位使用者手中 / 在明年初」 / Facebook 星期天在部落格發文表示 / 描述這項改變

※ 1. 主詞 Facebook（臉書）搭配動詞 said，即意為「Facebook 說～」。
　 2. 因為這項改變將會在未來產生影響，所以用未來式 will roll out... and (will) reach。
　 3. 但因為這篇文章已經在星期天發布，所以用過去式 said。

★現在進行式 (am / is / are + Ving)

凡是表示現在當下正在發生的事情或是狀態的句子，一律用現在進行式；以 am / are / is + Ving 表示。

◎ Tension / **is running** high / on the Korean peninsula, / in Asia.
    S   V   （*Time for Kids*）
緊張的氛圍 / 正逐漸升高 / 在韓國半島上 / 在亞洲

※ 1. 主詞 Tension 搭配動詞 is running，即意為「緊張的氛圍正逐漸～」。
    2. 現在進行式 is running 除了用來強調這件事正在發生以外，還暗示這個現象可能會持續一段時間。

◎ In South Korea, / English-teaching robots / **are helping** some students /
                                S   V
learn English.   （*Time for Kids*）

在南韓 / 英語教學機器人 / 正在幫助一些學生 / 學習英文

※ 1. 主詞 English-teaching robots 搭配動詞 are helping，即意為「英語教學機器人正在幫助～」。
    2. 現在進行式 are helping 除了強調這件事正在發生以外，還暗示這個現象可能會持續一段時間。

★現在完成式 (has / have + PP)

凡是表示從過去某時間點一直持續到現在的事情或狀態的句子，一律用現在完成式；以 has / have + PP 表示。

◎ I' **ve lived** with Eric / for more than five years.   （99 年國中第二次基測）
  S   V
我已經和艾瑞克住在一起 / 超過五年

※ 1. 主詞 I 搭配動詞 have lived，即意為「我已經住了～」。

2. I've 是 I have 的縮寫。現在完成式 have lived 暗示這件事已經發生了五年，並且可能會延續下去。

◎ The internet / **has become** / the main source / for national and international
　　　S　　　　　V

news for people. （98 年大學指考）

網際網路 / 已經成為 / 主要來源 / 人們吸收國家和國際新聞

※ 1. 主詞 The internet 搭配動詞 has become，即意為「網際網路已經成為～」。

2. 現在完成式 has become 暗示網際網路的重要性已經從過去的某時間點持續到現在，而且將來還可能會持續下去。

◎ The Paralympic Games / **have** always **been held** / in the same year as the
　　　　　S　　　　　　　　V

Olympic Games. （98 年大學指考）

殘障奧運 / 總是被舉辦 / 跟奧運同一年

※ 1. 主詞 The Paralympic Games 搭配動詞 have been held，即意為「殘障奧運總是被舉辦～」。

2. 現在完成式 have...been held 暗示殘障奧運從以前到現在都跟奧運同一年舉辦，而且將來還可能會持續下去。

Grammar for
Global English
時態

6

重點整理

◎現在式（**V, V-s, V-es** 或 **V-ies**）：描述事實或狀態；第三人稱動詞要加 **-s, -es** 或 **-ies**。

ex) The Paralympics are... / When people feel...

◎過去式（**V-ed** 或不規則變化）：描述過去的事件或狀態；動詞分規則變化及不規則變化。

ex) The pineapple...was not... / The mirror slipped...

◎未來式（**will / shall + V** 或 **am / is / are + going to + V**）：描述未來發生的事件或狀態。

ex) You will need... / The new design will roll out...

◎現在進行式 **(am / is / are + Ving)**：強調當下正在發生的行為或狀態。

ex) Tension is running high... / English-teaching robots are helping...

◎現在完成式 **(has / have + PP)**：強調事情或狀態由過去持續到現在，並暗示可能延續到未來。

ex) The internet has become... / The Paralympics Games have...been held...

◎在同一個句子中，可能因為情境的不同而參雜一個以上的時態。

ex) "The new design will...," Facebook said.

練習

第 1 題到第 4 題，請依照括號內的提示，將句子改成適當的時態。第 5 題到第 6 題，請用適當的時態將句子合併成一句。

範例：Frank struck a deeply skeptical tone about the value of going public. (since Facebook grew popular)

Since Facebook grew popular, Frank has struck a deeply skeptical tone about the value of going public.

或 Frank has struck a deeply skeptical tone about the value of going public since Facebook grew popular.

1. Inventors always look for ways to make our lives easier, greener and a whole lot more fun. （強調 inventors 總是不停尋找靈感）

   _____

2. Do you dream of becoming a superhero? (ever)

   _____

3. The Hardworking Robot is the perfect office helper. (will)

   _____

4. Some foreign high-speed train producers teach China how to make a bullet train. (years ago)

   _____

5. { The chemistry of the world's oceans is changing at a rate not seen for 65 million years.
   A new United Nations study releases. (last Thursday)

   _____

6. { The new profile page enables users to see all the things in common with a friend. (will)
   Facebook CEO acclaims.

   _____

Grammar for Global English
時態

6

請依照括號內的提示，用適當的時態將下列的字組重新組合成一個句子。

範例：When / mammals take over / dinosaurs die out (about 65 millions ago)
(mammals: 哺乳類；take over: 稱霸)

When dinosaurs died out *about 65 millions years ago*, mammals took over.

1. does not think / Sally Ride / her dream would come true (as a kid)

_____

2. is / to travel into space / Sally Ride / the first American woman (描述一事實)
(space: 外太空)

_____

3. breaks / Shanghai-Beijing train / world speed record (已經)

_____

4. the information I choose to share / Does this impact / on the internet? (will)

_____

5. the release of iPad 3 / All the buyers / look forward to (正引頸盼望)

_____

6. the arrest of their leader / A Wikileaks spokesman says / is an attack on media freedom. (last week)

_____

7. 連接詞

這一章要談的是「連接詞」這個概念。連接詞的作用就像是扣環一樣,將句子一個一個串聯起來,以加強句子間的關係。

連接詞有兩種:對等連接詞和連接副詞。

對等連接詞(and / or / because / so...)是真正的連接詞,作用在將兩個句子連結起來,以形成一個「合句」(一個包含了兩個子句的長句),強調兩個句子之間的邏輯關係;連接副詞(however / therefore / nevertheless / on the other hand...)是具有連接詞功能的副詞,通常用來轉折語氣,以強調上下文的關係,但並不是真的將兩個句子連結成一個合句。至於詳細的用法,請看接下來的解說。

對等連接詞（and, or, because, so, etc）：

◎ Mr. Hutman was very happy and made Henry a new cook of the restaurant. （99 年國中第一次基測）

◎ The scientist believes that dinosaurs died out when a giant asteroid or comet crashed into Earth.（*Time for Kids*）

（asteroid：小行星；comet：彗星；crash：撞擊）

◎ In the elections of Taiwan, most publics vote for either KMT or DPP.

（KMT：國民黨；DPP：民進黨）

◎ In the future, neither teachers nor students should come to class for teaching and learning.

◎ Tiny mammals can survive mass distinction because / for they can live underground.（*Time for Kids*）

（mammals：哺乳類動物；mass distinction：大滅絕）

◎ Nobody answers the call so Matilda leaves a message on the answering machine.（answering machine：電話答錄機）

◎ Ken's brothers like to watch tennis, but / yet Ken doesn't.

（99 年國中第二次學測）

連接副詞（however, therefore, etc.）：

◎ Marsha thought her friends would do something special to celebrate her birthday; however, they just gave her a little card.

（改寫自 99 年國中第一次基測）

◎ There's something wrong between Gina and Greg. Therefore, they haven't talked to each other for one month. （99 年國中第二次學測）

◎ Now Time River is going to be filled in to make more land to build on. People are happy that they will have more living space. On the other hand, they feel sorry that they must say good-bye to their old friend.

（99 年國中第二次學測）

◎ Sandra doesn't like to go shopping. Nonetheless / Nevertheless, she goes for her grandfather's birthday present.

★ 對等連接詞

　　對等連接詞用來連接兩個性質相同、重要性相等，而且邏輯關係密切的單句，以形成一個效果比較強烈的「合句」。不一樣的對等連接詞會有不一樣的效果。

☆ And

And 用來連接兩個性質相同的字詞或單句，以強調彼此的關連。

◎ Mr. Hutman / was very happy // **and** // made Henry a new cook of the restaurant.
　　　S　　　　　V　　　　　　　　　　　　V　　　　　（99 年國中第一次基測）

哈特曼先生 / 非常高興 //　並且 //（哈特曼先生）任命亨利為餐廳的新廚師

※ 因為主詞 Mr. Hutman 貫穿整個句子，因此我們直接用 and 連結兩個動詞，使兩個動詞的關係看起來更密切。

◎ In society, / the former player / does not look upon himself as a lone wolf /
　　　　　　　　　　S　　　　　　　V

who has the right to remain isolated from the society // **and** // go his own way.
　S　　V　　　　　　　　　　　　　　　　　　　　　　　　　　　V

（99 年大學學測）

在社會中 / 退休的足球員 / 並不將自己當作一匹孤獨的狼 /（孤狼）有權在社會中保持孤立 //　並且 //（孤狼有權）過自己的生活

※ 1. 主要結構：In society, the former player...as a lone wolf.
　　 次要結構：who has the right to remain...and go on his own way.
　 2. 因為主詞 a lone wolf 貫穿次要結構，因此我們直接用 and 連結兩個動詞，使兩句話的關係變得更密切。
　 3. 再將次要結構用 who 與主要結構結合，形成較為簡短俐落的長句。

Grammar for Global English
連接詞

7

☆ Or / Either...or... / Neither...nor...

Or, either...or 和 neither...nor 都是提供選擇。or 暗示了多重選項的可替代性，either...or... 則只能二選一，neither...nor... 則是指明兩者皆「不」。

◎ The scientist believes that / dinosaurs died out / when a giant asteroid or
　　　　　S　　　V　　　　　　　　　　　　　　　　　　　　　N
comet / crashed into Earth.　　　　　　　　　　　　　　　（*Time for Kids*）
　N

科學家相信 / 恐龍滅絕 / 當一個巨大的小行星或是彗星 / 撞擊地球

※ 根據文意，科學家相信小行星或是彗星衝撞地球是造成恐龍滅絕的主因。用連接詞 or，
　表示其中一項選項。

◎ Studies show that / asking children to do house missions, / such as taking
　　S　　　V　　　　　　　　　　　　　　　　　　　　　　　　　　　　N
out the trash or doing the dishes, / helps them grow into responsible adults.
　　　　　　　　　N　　　　　　　　　　　　　　　　　　　　　（99 年大學學測）

研究顯示 / 要求孩童做家事 / 例如倒垃圾或洗碗 / 幫助他們長成具責任感的大人

※ 1. 根據文意，做家事可以幫助培養孩童的責任感。用連接詞 or，表示僅作為舉例用，兩
　　　個選項沒有太大差別。
　 2. 如果想多舉點例子，亦可將本句改成 such as taking out the trash, doing the dishes,
　　　making the laundry,..., or fix meals。無論共有多少選項，連接詞 or 暗示著所有選項
　　　的平等性，兩者都是可以的。

◎ In the elections of Taiwan, / most publics vote for / either KMT or DPP.
　　　　　　　　　　　　　　　　S　　　V　　　　　　　N　　　N

在臺灣的選舉中 / 大部分選民投給 / 要嘛國民黨 / 要嘛民進黨

※ 1. 根據文意，臺灣大部分選民投票給國民黨或是民進黨。連接詞 either...or... 暗示兩個
　　　選項互相排斥，只能選擇其一。

2. 注意 either...or... 連接的 KMT 及 DPP 詞性相同，皆為名詞。

3. 為幫助理解，此處 either...or... 的翻譯「要嘛～要嘛～」為一般口語的用法，較為正式
的說法仍為「～或者～」。

◎ Teachers / **either** combine volunteer work with classroom lessons **or** make
      S   V   V

service work a requirement. （98 年大學指考）

教師們 / 要嘛在班上推行自願服務 / 要嘛規定同學參與服務活動

※ 1. 根據文意，教師們要推行自願服務或是規定同學參與服務活動。連接詞 either...or... 暗
示兩個選項互相排斥，只能選擇其一。

2. 注意 either...or... 連接的 combine 及 make 詞性相同，皆為動詞。

◎ In the future, / **neither** teachers **nor** students / should come to class / for
                           S   V

teaching and learning.

在未來 / 不論是老師或是學生 / （都不用）到教室 / 教學和上課

※ 1. 根據文意，老師和學生們未來都不必到教室上課。連接詞 neither...nor... 暗示兩者皆
不。

2. 注意 neither...nor... 連接的 teachers 和 students 詞性相同，皆為名詞。

3. 後方的連接詞 and 連接 teaching 和 learning，意指這兩件事的重要性相同，並且在
本句有相同的立場（兩件事都不會在教室發生了）。

◎ While **neither** North Korea **nor** South Korea / is willing to reconcile, // the
                           S   V   S

tension / arouses the worries / for a coming war.
          V

當北韓和南韓 / （都沒有）意願和解 // 這樣的緊張氣氛 / 引起
擔憂 / 可能引發的戰爭

**Grammar for
Global English**
連接詞
ㄱ

※1. 根據文意，因為南、北韓無和解意願，造成開戰的隱憂。連接詞 neither...nor... 暗示南、北韓雙方的否定狀態（拒絕和解）。

　2. 注意 neither...nor... 連接的 North Korea 和 South Korea 詞性相同，皆為名詞。

☆ For / Because / So

For, because 和 so 都表現因果關係。for 和 because 強調「因為～」，兩者意義相同，so 則是強調「所以～」。但在英文中，**For / Because 和 So** 兩者不可以同時使用。

◎ Tiny mammals / can survive mass distinction // **because** // they / can live
　　　S　　　　　V　　　　　　　　　　　　　　　　　S　　　V

underground.　　　　　　　　　　　　　　　　　　　　　　　　（*Time for Kids*）

小型哺乳動物 / 能夠在大滅絕中存活 // 因為 // 牠們（小型哺乳動物）/ 能夠在地底下生存

※ 1. 結果：Tiny mammals can survive mass distinction.

　　　原因：Tiny mammals can live underground.

　2. 兩個句子間有因果關係，前者為果，後者為因，故以 because 連結，強調二者的因果關係。連接詞 because 尤其強調原因的重要性。

　3. 當 for 用來表示原因時，意思與 because 接近。除了不能放句首以外，for 的用法也與 because 接近。故本句亦可代換為：

　　　Tiny mammals can survive mass distinction for they can live underground.

　4. 本句亦可用 so 代換，即成為：Tiny mammals can live underground **so** they can survive mass distinction. →強調結果的重要性。

　5. 注意 because / for / so 連接的都是兩個完整子句。

◎ Cases have shown that / the bought goods / will be hidden or destroyed, //
　　　S　　V　　　　　　　S　　　　　　　　V　　　　　V

because // the person concerned / feels ashamed of their addiction / and /
　　　　　　　　S　　　　　　　　　V

tries to conceal it.　　　　　　　　　　　　　　　　　　　（98 年大學指考）
　　V

94

案例已顯示 / 被購入的商品 / 將會被藏起來或是被破壞 // 因為 // 當事人（購物狂）/ 為他們的購物慾感到羞恥 / 並且 / 試圖隱藏（購物慾）

※ 1. 主要結構：Cases have shown that...

次要結構：

原因 1：the person concerned feels ashamed of their addiction

原因 2：the person concerned tries to conceal it

結果：the bought goods will be hidden or destroyed

2. 原主詞 The person concerned 貫穿原因 1 與原因 2，因此以連接詞 and 將兩句話合成一句，暗示 feels ashamed of 和 tries to conceal 兩個動作之間彼此相關。

3. 再以 because 連接原因與結果，強調因果關係。連接詞 because 尤其強調原因的重要性。

4. 同上個例子，because 亦可用 for 代換。若用連接詞 so 強調結果，則句子應改為 The person concerned feels ashamed of their addiction and tries to conceal it **so** the bought goods will be hidden or destroyed.

◎ Nobody answers the call // **so** // Matilda leaves a message on the answering
     S   V   S   V
machine.

沒有人接電話 // 因此 // 瑪蒂達在電話答錄機上留了言

※ 1. 原因：Nobody answers the call.

結果：Metilda leaves a message on the answering machine.

2. 兩個句子間有因果關係，故以 so 連結，強調兩者的因果關係。連接詞 so 尤其強調結果的重要性。

3. 若要強調原因，則可以用 because 或 for 來連結句子，變成：

Matilda leaves a message on the answering machine **because** / **for** nobody answers the call.

4. 注意連接詞 so 連接的是兩個子句。

Grammar for
Global English
連接詞
7

◎ Peter stayed up late last night, // **so** // he drank a lot of coffee this morning /
　　S　　　V　　　　　　　　　　　　　　S　　V

to keep himself awake in class.　　　　　　　　　　　　　　　（99 年大學學測）

彼得昨晚熬夜 // 因此 // 他今早喝了很多咖啡 / 在課堂上維持清醒

※ 1. 原因：Peter stayed up late last night.

　　結果：Peter drank a lot of coffee this morning to keep himself awake in class.

　 2. 觀察發現，兩個句子主詞相同，且彼此有因果關係，故省略主詞並以 so 連結，強調
　　　兩者的因果關係。連接詞 so 尤其強調結果的重要性。

　 3. 若要強調原因，則可以用 because 或 for 來連結句子，變成：

　　　Peter drank a lot of coffee this morning to keep himself awake in class **because** / **for** he
　　　stayed up late last night.

　 4. 注意連接詞 so 連接的是兩個子句。

☆ **Yet / But**

Yet 與 but 皆呈現對比的效果，有「但是」的意味。但是 yet 常用於口語中，較不
正式。

◎ Ken's brothers like to watch tennis, // **but** // Ken doesn't.
　　S　　　　　V　　　　　　　　　　　　　　S　　V

（99 年國中第二次學測）

肯的兄弟們都喜歡看網球 // 但是 // 肯並不喜歡

※ 1. 前句：Ken's brothers like to watch tennis.

　　後句：Ken doesn't (like to watch tennis).

　 2. 觀察發現，兩個句子呈現對比作用，因此用連接詞 but 連接兩個句子，強調對比效果。

　 3. 因為兩句的動詞相同，因此以 but 連結後，後半句的動詞可以省略，並且兩句的順序
　　　並不影響語意，亦可寫成：Ken doesn't like to watch tennis, **but** Ken's brothers do.

◎ Many people <u>like to drink</u> bottled water // because // <u>they</u> <u>feel</u> that / <u>tap water</u>
　　　　S　　　　　V　　　　　　　　　　　　　　　　　　　S　　V　　　　　　S

<u>may not be</u> safe, // **but** // <u>is</u> <u>bottled water</u> really any better?
　　　V　　　　　　　　　　　　V　　　　S　　　　　　　　　　（99 年大學學測）

很多人喜歡喝瓶裝水 // 因為 // 他們覺得 / 自來水可能不安全 // 但是 // 瓶裝水真的
有比較好嗎？

※ 1. 結果：Many people like to drink bottled water.

　　原因：They feel that tap water may not be safe.

　　質疑：Is bottled water really any better?

2. 觀察發現，前兩句之間有因果關係，因此用 because 連接，強調原因，合成長句：
　Many people like to drink bottled water **because** they feel that tap water may not be
　safe.

3. 然而這個結果卻受到質疑，因此用連接詞 but，強調對比作用：瓶裝 水真的有比較好
　嗎？

 重 點 整 理

◎ 連接詞的作用在於連接兩個性質相同、重要性相近，且有密切邏輯關係的
　句子，使之合併成一個合句。

◎ **And** 暗示兩個連接的字詞或句子彼此相關。

◎ **Or / either...or... / neither...nor...** 都提供了選擇。**or** 暗指每個選擇重要性相
　等，選項間彼此可互相代換，且可能有多重選項；**either...or...** 強調選項的
　互斥性，只能二選一；**neither...nor...** 則否定兩個選項，強調「兩者皆不」。

◎ **For / because / so** 皆表示因果關係。**for** 和 **because** 強調原因，**so** 強調結果，
　三者可視情況互相代換。

◎ **Yet / but** 強調對比作用，只是 **yet** 較為口語。

**Grammar for
Global English**
連接詞

7

★連接副詞

連接副詞指的是具有連接詞功能的副詞，常用於語氣上的轉折，以銜接上下文語意，不像連接詞是用於合併句子。使用時通常會在連接副詞之前加上 and 或分號（;）連接兩句話。

☆ However

However 表示語氣的轉折，暗指前後文互斥，後句駁斥前句，有「然而」的意味。

◎ Marsha thought / her friends would do something special to celebrate her
　　S　　　V　　　　S　　　　V

birthday // ; **however,** // they just gave her a little card.
　　　　　　　　　　　　S　　　V　　　　（改寫自 99 年國中第一次基測）

瑪莎以為 / 她的朋友們會做一些特別的事慶祝她的生日 // 然而 // 他們只給了她一張小卡片

※ 1. 推想：Marsha thought her friends would do something special to celebrate her birthday.

事實：Marsha's friends just gave her a little card.

2. 句中推想與事實有強烈的落差，因此用連接副詞 however 將兩個句子合併，以強調瑪莎落空的期待。

3. 分號（;）的作用相等於 and，用於連接兩個句子。

4. 本句亦可用連接詞 but, yet 代換 however，只是必須將分號（;）去掉。

◎ There are no standard rules for writing textese. // **However,** / the common
　　S　V　　　　　　　　　　　　　　　　　　　　　　　　　　　　S

practice is / to use single letters, pictures, or numbers / to represent whole
　　　　V

words.　　　　　　　　　　　　　　　　　　　　　　　（99 年大學指考）

寫簡訊並沒有任何標準規則 // 然而 / 一般實際使用情形就是 / 用單一字詞、圖片，或是數字 / 表示完整的字詞

※ 1. 推想：There are no standard rules for writing textese.

　　 事實：The common practice is to use single letters, pictures, or numbers to represent whole words.

　 2. 觀察發現，推想與事實有強烈的落差，因此用連接副詞 however 將兩個句子合併，以強調一般使用情形與「寫簡訊沒有準則」這件事的落差。

　 3. 本句亦可用連接詞 but, yet 代換 however，變成：There are no standard rules for writing textese **but** / **yet** the common practice is to use single letters, pictures, or numbers to represent whole words.

☆ Therefore

連接副詞 therefore 表「因此」，暗示兩個句子間有因果關係，通常為前句（原因）造成後句的結果。

◎ There's something wrong between Gina and Greg. // **Therefore**, / they
　 S　 V　　　　　　　　　　　　　　　　　　　　　　　　　　　　　　　　 S
　 haven't talked to each other for one month.　　　（99 年國中第二次基測）
　　　　　 V

吉娜和葛雷之間發生了一些問題。 // 因此 / 他們有一個月沒有跟對方說話

※ 1. 結果：There's something wrong between Gina and Greg.

　　 原因：They haven't talked to each other for one month.

　 2. 句中有因果關聯，因為吵了架，而後不說話。因此用連接副詞 Therefore，強調兩句的因果關係。

　 3. 連接副詞 therefore 亦可以用對等連接詞 because / for / so 代換，變成：
Gina and Greg haven't talked to each other for one month **because** / **for** there's something wrong between them. 或是：
There's something wrong between Gina and Greg **so** they haven't talked to each other for one month.

Grammar for Global English
連接詞

7

◎ Both competitors <u>know</u> their own drawbacks and limitations very well // ;
　　　　　　S　　　　V

　therefore, / <u>they</u> jointly <u>decide to have</u> one last race.　　　　（98 年大學學測）
　　　　　　　S　　　　　　V

兩邊的選手都相當清楚他們自己的弱點和極限 // 因此 / 他們協議只比最後一場賽

※ 1. 原因：Both competitors know their own drawbacks and limitations very well.
　　 結果：Both competitors jointly decide to have one last race.
　 2. 兩句之間有因果關連，因為兩邊選手都已經達到極限，所以協議只多比一場賽。
　　 因此用連接副詞 therefore，強調兩句的因果關係。

☆ **On the other hand**

On the other hand 表示「在另一方面」，代表用不同的角度去看同一件事情的新
觀點。

◎ Now Time River <u>is going to be filled in</u> / to make more land to build on. //
　　　　　S　　　　　V

　<u>People</u> <u>are</u> happy that / they will have more living space. // **On the other**
　　S　　V

　hand, / <u>they</u> <u>feel</u> sorry that / they must say good-bye to their old friend.
　　　　　　S　　V　　　　　　　　　　　　　　　　　（99 年國中第二次基測）

Time River 將會被填平 / 為了創造更多可建地 // 人們很高興 / 他們將擁有更多的
生活空間 // 在另一方面 / 人們也感到遺憾 / 他們必須和老朋友說再見

※ 1. 情境：Now Time River is going to be filled in to make more land to build on.
　　 結果 1：People are happy that they will have more living space.
　　 結果 2：People feel sorry that they must say good-bye to their old friend.
　 2. 在這個特殊情境（河水要被填平）之下，產生兩種不同的結果：人們的期待和不捨兩
　　 種矛盾的情緒。因此用 On the other hand 將兩種結果連接起來，以強調相同情境之
　　 下兩種不一樣的觀點。

◎ The scientists trained the cockroaches to prefer the peppermint smell / by
　　S　　　V

rewarding the insects / with a taste of sugar water / when they approached a
　　　　　　　　　　　　　　　　　　　　　　　　　　　　　S　　　V

peppermint smell. // When these insects moved toward a vanilla smell, /
　　　　　　　　　　　　　S　　　　V

on the other hand, / they were punished / with a taste of salt.
　　　　　　　　　　S　　　V　　　　　　　　　　　　（99 年大學指考）

科學家們訓練蟑螂偏好薄荷的味道 / 藉由獎賞那些昆蟲 / 可以嘗糖水 / 當牠們接
近薄荷的味道時 // 當這些昆蟲接近香草的味道時 / 在另一方面 / 牠們就會被處
罰 / 要嘗鹽水

※ 1. 情境 1：

The scientists trained the cockroaches to prefer the peppermint smell by rewarding
the insects with a taste of sugar water when they approached a peppermint smell.

情境 2：

When these insects moved toward a vanilla smell, on the other hand, they were
punished with a taste of salt.

2. 情境 1 和 2 都是在談論科學家如何訓練蟑螂的行為，並且情境 1 和 2 各自提供不一樣
的方法，以達到相同的訓練效果。因此用連接副詞 on the other hand 作連接，強調
不一樣的立場。

☆ Nevertheless / Nonetheless

Nevertheless 和 nonetheless 的意思和用法完全相同，用來表示「讓步」。

◎ Sandra doesn't like to go shopping. // **Nonetheless,** / she goes / for her
　　S　　　V　　　　　　　　　　　　　　　　　　　　　S　　V

grandfather's birthday present.　　　　　　　（99 年國中第二次基測）

珊卓拉並不喜歡逛街 // 可是 / 她去逛街 / 為了她爺爺的生日禮物

※ 1. 事實：Sandra doesn't like to go shopping.

特例：Sandra goes shopping for her grandfather's birthday present.

2. 事實指出珊卓拉並不喜歡逛街，但是在某特殊情境之下（為了爺爺的生日禮物）珊卓拉願意去逛街。為了強調珊卓拉的讓步，因而使用 Nonetheless 作為兩句的連結。

3. Nonetheless 亦可以改用 Nevertheless，語氣、意義完全不變。

◎ Due to the tension between North Korea and South Korea, / our plan to
                                                                    S

Korea was cancelled. // **Nevertheless,** / still we could have Japan / as the
            V   S   V

substitution.

因為南韓和北韓之間的緊張局勢 / 我們去韓國的計畫被取消 // 可是 / 我們還是可以去日本 / 作為替代

※ 1. 限制：Due to the tension between North Korea and South Korea, our plan to Korea was cancelled.

退讓：Still we could have Japan as the substitution.

2. 限制指出我們取消去韓國的計畫，但是卻仍有替代方案可以出國旅行。因此使用連接副詞 Nevertheless 來作連結。

3. Nevertheless 和 Nonetheless 兩者可互換。

 重 點 整 理

◎ 連接副詞指的是具有連接詞功能的副詞,通常用作語氣的轉折,以凸顯上
下文的關係。

◎ 連接副詞通常可大寫當作句首,以「A子句. 連接副詞, B子句」的形式出現,
例如:There's something wrong between Gina and Greg. Therefore, they
haven't talked to each other for one month.

◎ 連接副詞亦可用來連接兩個子句,以「A子句; 連接副詞, B子句」的形式
出現,例如:Marsha thought her friends would do something special to
celebrate her birthday; however, they just gave her a little card.

◎ 分號(;)的作用如同對等連接詞 and,功能是用來連接兩個子句。因此,
當連接副詞被用來連接兩個子句時,因為它並不是真正的連接詞,就需要
分號(;)來連結句子。

◎ However 通常強調前後文互相駁斥的情境,表示「然而」。

◎ Therefore 表因果關係,暗示前句(原因)造成後句的結果。

◎ 在以另一個新角度看待同一件事情時,我們用 On the other hand。

◎ Nevertheless 和 Nonetheless 表示讓步,暗示在某種條件之下,有特例發
生。

練習

　　請從下列方格中選擇適當的對等連接詞或連接副詞,填入各句的空格中,每個只
能使用一次。

---

nonetheless / because / but / or / therefore

however / so / on the other hand / and

---

1. I cannot understand why Steven bought so many watches

_____ never wears any.（99 年國中第一次基測）

2. Elsa hates going shopping. _____ , she went last night when her grandpa asked her to buy some medicine for him. （99 年國中第一次基測）

3. I let the meat cook too long, _____ it was burned black.

（99 年國中第一次基測）

4. I could not resist the sweet smell from the bakery, so I walked in _____ bought a fresh loaf of bread. （99 年大學學測）

5. _____ fresh onions have a higher water content, they are typically sweeter and milder tasting than storage onions. （99 年大學學測）

6. There isn't a brand _____ a trend that these young people are not aware of. （99 年大學學測）

7. In the United States, parents and educators have come to regard the prom as an important lesson in social skills. _____ , proms have been held every year in high schools for students to learn proper social behavior.

（prom: 畢業舞會）（99 年大學學測）

8. The French government plans to promote the program with an advertising campaign aimed at young readers and their parents. _____ , when asked how to attract young readers to the printed press, the government said the primary channel for the ads would be the Internet. （99 年大學指考）

9. Fresh onions are available in yellow, red and white throughout their season, March through August. Storage onions, _____ , are available August through April. （99 年大學學測）

請選擇適當的連接詞或連接副詞填入空格內，每個只能使用一次。

> so / however / therefore / for / but
> neither...nor... / on the other hand / nevertheless

1. Steven has several meetings to attend every day; _____ , he has to work on a very tight schedule.

2. It is not easy for old people to scratch their backs, _____ they need help when their backs itch.

3. She never really wanted to be popular, _____ she did want to have someone to share secrets and laughs with.

4. The government is doing its best to preserve the cultures of the tribal people _____ fear that they may soon die out.

5. If you touch your finger to a hot stove, you know it's going to hurt. _____ , if you convince yourself beforehand that the pain won't be so bad, you might not suffer as much.

6. Today, the Somali people remain split among Ethiopia, Kenya, Somalia, and Djibouti. _____ , almost every African nation is home to more than one ethnic group.

7. _____ Valentine's Day _____ Christmas is a traditional holiday in Taiwan, but people celebrate them.

8. Everyone runs the risk of accidents, and no one can be sure of avoiding chronic disease. _____ , poor diet, stress, a bad working environment, and carelessness can promote good health.

Grammar for Global English
連接詞

7

105

8. 被動式

一、在英文中，「被動式」是很特別的用法。相較於在一般動詞用法中的主詞具有行
　　為能力，被動式用法中的主詞往往不具有行為能力，或只具有有限的行為能力。
　　換句話說，在一般動詞用法中，主詞做出了動作；在被動用法中，主詞卻是承受
　　了某個動作。只要稍加理解被動用法的這一點特色，其實就掌握了被動式的意義。

二、被動式除了呈現被動的狀態以外，還有另一種特殊的情態用法。在英文中以「人」
　　為主詞時，常常會用被動式來表達主動的情緒、情態，例如 "I am excited / I was
　　exhausted..."，在本課中會另作介紹。

三、本課為了說明方便，會出現「一般動詞用法」與「被動用法」等說法，但這只是「主
　　動」與「被動」的差異而已。讀者並不需要特別記憶這些名詞，只要抓住被動的
　　意義即可。

四、至於被動式的用法，一律都是主詞 (S) + Be 動詞 (Be V) + 過去分詞 (PP)，亦可在過
　　去分詞之後加上 by + N，補充說明主詞是以什麼樣的方式承受某種動作。

五、最後要特別強調，在一般認知中，主動和被動是可以互換的，但這其實是錯誤的
　　認知。被動式的使用往往配合了三種特殊情境：

　　1. 強調被施受的主詞或是動作

　　2. 施受的主詞不確定

　　3. 為了上下文的轉折，使語氣更順暢

　　因此，主動和被動的使用應該是由上下文來判斷情境，而一般來說是不能互換。

句型範例

◎ I let the meat cook too long, so it was burned black.（99 年國中第二次基測）

◎ He was bothered by a small irritation every Sunday as he sang in the church choir.（98 年大學學測）

◎ When I heard my baby girl say her first word, my heart was filled with joy.

（97 年國中第二次基測）

◎ The manager was exhausted by keeping apologizing for his poor decision.

文法解析

★被動式 (S + Be V + PP) + (by + N)

當主詞因為無行為能力，或是只具有有限的行為能力而承受某種動作時，就應使用被動式 (S + Be V + PP)。by + N 可作為補充，說明主詞是被什麼事情、以什麼方式承受動作。

◎ I / let the meat cook too long, // so // it / **was burned** / black.

  S   V   S   V   （99 年國中第二次基測）

我 / 讓肉煮得太久 // 所以 // 肉 / 被燒得 / 焦黑

※ 1. 在前半句中，主詞 I 具有行為能力，並且做出「煮肉」這個動作，因此是一般動詞用法（主動）。

   2. 在後半句中，因為主詞 it 不具有行為能力，只能承受「煮」這個動作，因此用被動式呈現「被燒焦」的狀態。

   3. 更正確的說法是，為了強調「肉被燒焦」，我們才使用被動式。

◎ He **was bothered** / by a small irritation / every Sunday / as he sang in the

  S   V

  church choir.

（98 年國中第二次基測）

他被干擾 / 被一個小小的激怒 / 每個星期天 / 當他在教會唱詩班唱歌的時候

※ 1. 主詞 He 搭配動詞 was bothered，表示主詞承受 "a small irritation" 這件事的干擾，
因此用被動式表達。

2. by a small irritation 則是作為補充，說明主詞是被什麼事干擾。

3. 更正確的說法是，為了強調「他被干擾」，並且因為施受的主詞不確定（是什麼事產
生干擾並不重要），於是使用被動式。

◎ <u>Ms. Wang</u> / <u>found that</u> // <u>her key</u> / <u>was</u> on the table / and / **was covered** / by a
     S   V   S   V   V

book.
（97 年國中第二次基測）

王小姐 / 發現 // 她的鑰匙 / 在桌上 / 並且 /（她的鑰匙）被蓋住 / 用一本書

※ 1. 在主要結構 Ms. Wang found that... 中，主詞 Ms. Wang 具有行為能力，並且做出「發現」
這件事，因此是一般動詞用法（主動）。

2. 在次要結構 her key was...by a book 中，連接詞 and 連接了兩個子句（her key was on
the table // her key was covered by a book）。

3. 在子句 her key was on the table 中，Be 動詞 was 呈現鑰匙的「狀態」是「放在桌上」，
與動詞的主動、被動無關。

4. 在子句 her key was covered by a book 中，因為主詞 the key 不具有行為能力，只能承
受「蓋住」這個動作，因此用被動式呈現「被蓋住」的狀態。

5. by a book 則是用來補充，說明鑰匙是被書本蓋住。

6. 更正確的說法是，為了強調「鑰匙被蓋住」，於是使用被動式。

◎ When / <u>I heard</u> / my baby girl / say her first word, / <u>my heart</u> / **was filled with**
        S V   S   V

joy.
（99 年國中第一次基測）

當 / 我聽見 / 我的寶貝女兒 / 說出她第一個字 / 我的心 / 被喜悅盈滿

※ 1. 在前半句中，主詞 I 具有行為能力，只能做出「聽」這個動作，因此是
一般動詞用法（主動）。

2. 在後半句中，主詞 my heart 不具有行為能力，並且承受「充滿」這個
動詞，因此以被動用法呈現「被盈滿」這個動作。

Grammar for
Global English
被動式

8

109

3. 因為 be filled with + N 是慣用片語，所以不再另外用 by + N 來補充說明主詞是被什麼樣的心情盈滿。

4. 更正確的說法是，為了強調「心被喜悅盈滿」這個狀態，於是使用被動式。

◎ These panels / **are covered with** glass / and / **are painted** black inside / to
     S   V   V

absorb as much heat as possible.　　　　　　　　　　　　　（98 年大學指考）

這些面板 / 被玻璃覆蓋 / 而且 / 從裡面被漆成黑色 / 以達到吸收熱能的最大效果

※1. 主詞 These panels 不具有行為能力，只能承受「覆蓋」與「漆上」這兩個動詞，因此以被動用法呈現「被覆蓋」與「被漆上」這兩個動作。

2. be covered with + N 為固定用法，表示「用……覆蓋」，不用 by + N。

3. 更正確的說法是，為了強調「面板被覆蓋」以及「面板被漆上」這個狀態，並且因為施受的主詞不確定（是誰把面板漆成黑色的並不重要），於是使用被動式。

★被動式的情態用法

以人為主詞時，被動式也可用來形容主詞，表達主詞的各種情態。

◎ The manager / **is exhausted** / by keeping apologizing / for his poor decisions.
        S   V

那位經理 / 感到筋疲力盡 / 因為持續道歉 / 為了他的錯誤決定

※ 1. 片語 by keeping apologizing 指出主詞 The manager 是為了什麼事感到筋疲力盡。

2. 然而，主詞 The manager 是具有行為能力的。主詞 The manager 對「持續道歉」一事做出反應，是主動的行為，因此事實上雖然是被動式，卻是主動用法。

3. 或者我們也可以說，為了強調經理「被搞得筋疲力盡」這個狀態，於是使用被動式。

4. 但是讀者不必刻意細分被動式與主動用法的不同，只須謹記這種特殊用法即可（be exhausted 表示某人很累）。

◎ **I am surprised** that // the young Taiwanese pianist / performed remarkably
  S   V   S   V

well / and / won the first prize / in the music contest.
          V   （97 年國中第二次基測）

我很驚訝 // 那個年輕的台灣鋼琴家 / 演奏得極好 / 並且 / 贏得第一名 / 在那場音樂比賽中

※ 1. 因為 that 子句（鋼琴家得獎一事）使主詞 I 感到驚喜，因此以被動式來表達主詞受到刺激的情態。

    2. 或者也可以說，為強調主詞「被驚喜」這個狀態，於是使用被動式（be surprised）。

    3. 然而，主詞 I 是具有行為能力的。主詞 I 對年輕鋼琴家得獎的事做出反應，是主動的行為，因此事實上雖然是被動式，卻是主動用法。

有時候為了使上下文的語意轉折更為順暢，以同一名詞作各句主詞，必要時我們也會使用被動式。

◎ Siena is an old city / in the north of Italy. / It began with a group of people living on its hills / over 2,900 years ago. / Around the year 1100, / Siena became an important business center in Italy. / In 1472, / the first bank of the world / **was built** in this city / and has been doing business ever since. / Also, / many old buildings / **are seen** at the Piazza del Campo, / the most important meeting place of the city.

（98 年國中第一次基測）

錫耶納是座古老的城市 / 在義大利北方 / 最早有一群人住在山坡上 / 超過 2900 年以前 / 大約西元 1100 年 / 錫耶納成為義大利重要的商業中心 / 西元 1472 年 / 世界第一家銀行 / 被建在這座城市裡 / 從此開始營業至今 / 另外 / 許多古老的建築 / 也能在康波廣場被看見 / 義大利最重要的聚會地點

※ 在本文中，可明白得知錫耶納是本文重點，因此每一句話皆以錫耶納作主詞（Siena / It），以維持一致性，並加強讀者的記憶。為了維持這樣的一致性，遇到需要介紹其他名詞的時候（the first bank of the world / many old buildings），我們就改用被動式，以維持「錫耶納」在本文中的主導地位（in this city / of the city）。如此一來，即便有其他名詞的干擾，「錫耶納」仍主導了整篇文章的意義，語意也順暢許多。

Grammar for
Global English
被動式

8

重點整理

◎ 被動式暗示主詞承受了某種動作。

◎ 被動式的使用情境有三：

  1. 強調被施受的主詞或是動作

  2. 施受的主詞不確定

  3. 為了上下文的轉折，使語氣更順暢

◎ 被動式的基本文型為 **am / are / is + PP**，若要補充說明是以什麼樣的方式承受動作，可視情況使用 **by + N** 進行補充。

◎ 以「人」為主詞時，某些被動式形式的動詞亦可用來表示主動含義。

  ex) He is exhausted... / I am surprised...

練習

請依情境判斷動詞為主動、被動，並以適當的型態填入句子。

範例： I ＿put＿ the fish in the ice box to keep it fresh. (put)（99年國中第一次基測）

1. I ＿＿＿＿＿＿ that Steven bought so many watches but never wears any. (surprise)

2. The oldest café in Paris ＿＿＿＿＿＿ in 1686 by Francesco Procopio dei Coltelli, the man who turned France into a coffee-drinking society. (open)

（改寫自97年大學指考）

3. Before Sandra goes to Iran, she ＿＿＿＿＿＿ that the place was dangerous due to the war. (warn: 警告)

4. Students ＿＿＿＿＿＿ to revise or rewrite their compositions based on the teacher's comments. (ask)　　　　（98年大學學測）

5. Some small schools in rural areas _____ cooperative programs to share their teaching and library resources to overcome budget shortages. (set up)

（97 年大學指考）

6. The new stadium _____ at a convenient location, close to an MRT station and within walking distance to a popular shopping center. (build: 建造)

（97 年大學指考）

GL⦿BAL 作業

請依照提示將句子以被動方式表達。

範例： The resulting product _____ the Post-it, one of 3M' s most successful office products. (call)

The resulting product was called the Post-it, one of 3M' s most successful office products.

1. My pink notebook _____ my schedules.（fill with: 填滿 ）

_____

2. My mom _____ everything I told her, especially those happened in school. (interest in)

_____

3. Jack _____ the rare privilege of using the president' s office, which made others quite jealous. (give)

（97 年大學學測）

_____

Grammar for
Global English
被動式

8

113

4. Linda _____ and does not know in which part she should believe, for the two sides give totally opposite explanations. (confuse: 困惑)

_____

5. By the end of the 18th century, all of Paris _____ coffee and the city supported some 700 cafés. (intoxicate with: 陶醉在～)

（97 年大學指考）

_____

6. At first, the use of plastic for toy manufacture _____ by retailers and consumers of the time. (regard: 認可) (否定) （97 年大學指考）

_____

9. 比較級

如同中文一樣，英文也有「比較」的觀念，對應的文法就是「比較級」。

比較級的概念相當簡單，可分為「自我的比較」、「自我與他人的比較」以及「自我與多者的比較」。若再加上副詞的應用，則可衍伸出各式各樣的變化。

但是，所有的比較級都不脫以下幾種用法：

(A) am, are, is：

1. A + am / are / is + Adj-er + than B → A 比 B 還～

2. A + am / are / is + as Adj as B → A 和 B 一樣～

3. A + am / are / is + the most / the best / Adj-est（N）→ A 是最～的

(B) 其它動詞

1. A + V + Adv-er / more adv + than B → A 比 B 還～

2. A + V + as Adv as + B → A 和 B 一樣～

3. A + V + the most / the best / Adv-est → A 最～

◎ **She is wiser than before.**（99 年國中第二次基測）

◎ **Most Japanese live longer than their Asian neighbors.**

◎ **Thinking is more interesting than knowing, but less interesting than looking.**

◎ **Are things as simple as black and white?**

◎ **I did not want to follow any rules, and I was as angry as the burning sun in the summer day.**（99 年國中第二次基測）

◎ **He is the cutest thing I've ever seen.**（99 年國中第二次基測）

文法解析

★自我的比較

☆ **A + am / are / is + Adj-er + than + B**

　 A + V + Adv-er + than + B

　　自身與自身的比較通常會牽扯到「時間」這個因素。隨著時間更迭變化，自己也產生變化，才會有比較的可能。

◎ She / **is wiser than** / before.　　　　　　　　（99 年國中第二次基測）
　 A　　　　　　　　　 B

她 / 更有智慧 /（比）以前（的她）

※ 在本句，before 指的是「以前的她」（she was before），因此可看出本句的比較對象 A 與 B 都是同一個人，只是一個是現在的她，一個是過去的她。

◎ After the training, / Adam / **runs faster than** / he did / and / becomes the
　　　　　　　　　　　　　 A　　　　　　　　　 B

vanguard of his team.

訓練過後 / 亞當 / 跑得更快 /（比）他以前跑步 / 並且 / 成為他隊上的前鋒

※ 在本句，he did 指的是亞當以前的跑步速度，因此可看出本句的比較對象 A 與 B 都是亞當的表現，只是一個是現在的表現，一個是過去的表現。

★ 自我與他人的比較

☆ **A + am / are / is + Adj-er + than + B**
A + V + Adv-er + than + B

只要在兩個不同的對象（包含人、事、物）之間有共同點，就可以針對共同點進行比較。

◎ **Are** / you **smarter than** / a fifth grader?
　　　　　A　　　　　　　　　B

你 / 比～更聰明 / 一個小學五年級的學生嗎？

※ 針對共同點（智力），拿 A（你）與 B（小五生）互相比較。

◎ Most Japanese / **live longer than** / their Asian neighbors.
　　　　A　　　　　　　　　　　B

大部分的日本人 / 活得更久 /（比）他們的亞洲鄰國人民

※ 針對共同點（平均年齡），拿 A（大多數的日本人）與 B（亞洲鄰國人）互相比較。

◎ With the help of the computer, / we / **can work more efficiently than** / the
　　　　　　　　　　　　　　　　A　　　　　　　　　　　　　　　　B

earlier generations.

由於電腦的協助 / 我們 / 可以工作更有效率 /（比）前幾代的人

※ 針對共同點（工作效率），拿 A（我們）與 B（過去幾代的人）互相比較。

Grammar for Global English
比較級

9

◎ Thinking / **is more interesting than** / knowing, / but / **less interesting than**
　　　A　　　　　　　　　　　　　　　　　　　B

looking.
　C

思考 / 更為有趣 / （比起）了解 / 但是 / 更不有趣 / （比起）觀看

※ 1. 針對共同點（有不有趣），先拿 A（思考）與 B（了解）進行比較，再拿 A（思考）與 C（觀
　　　看）進行比較。

　2. 連接詞 but 分隔了 B 與 C，因此是 A 分別與 B、C 作比較，B 與 C 之間並沒有直接進
　　　行的比較。

　3. 副詞 more / less 改變了比較的方式（更有趣 / 更不有趣），讓比較級更有變化了。

☆ **A + am / are / is + as Adj as + B**

　　A + V + as Adv as + B

比較級也能用作比喻。as...as... 就是「如同～一樣」，可用作比較，亦可
用作譬喻。

◎ Are / things / **as simple as** / black or white?
　　　　　A　　　　　　　　　　B

事情 / 如～一樣簡單 / 黑或白嗎？

※ 針對共同點（簡不簡單），拿 A（事情）與 B（黑白兩色）作比較；因此在這裡，
　　as...as... 是用作比較。

◎ The music **is** not / **as exciting as** / it should be / during exciting moments.
　　　　A　　　　　　　　　　　　B

音樂不 / 如～一樣刺激 / 它應有的 / 在刺激的時刻

※ 1. as exciting as... 即意「如同～一樣刺激」。

　2. A 與 B 都是音樂本身，因此在這裡，as...as... 是用作比較（自我比較）。

118

◎ I / did not want to follow / any rules, / and / I **was** / **as angry as** / the burning

                                            A   B

sun in the summer day.   （99 年國中第二次基測）

我 / 不想要遵守 / 任何規則 / 而且 / 我 / 如～一樣生氣 / 夏日天空中的炎熱太陽

※ 1. as angry as... 即意「如同～一樣生氣」。

  2. A（人）與 B（太陽）並沒有比較基準；拿「生氣」這個共同點作比較，其實是將太陽擬人化，將太陽的顏色比擬為人生氣臉紅的樣子；因此在這裡，as...as... 是用作譬喻。

★ 自我與多者的比較：表示（主詞）是最好的（文法稱最高級）

A + am / are / is / V + the best (+ N)

A + am / are / is + V + the most + Adj / Adv

A + am / are / is / V + the Adj-est / Adv-est

比較對象有兩個以上時，我們往往會注意到「最～」的那個，這時候就會依形容詞或副詞的不同用法，以上列三種方式呈現 A 的特殊性。

◎ He / **is** / **the cutest** thing / I' ve ever seen.   （99 年國中第二次基測）

   A   B

他 / 是 / 最可愛的東西 / 我曾看過的

※ 1. 因為 B（我曾看過的東西）是多數，因此拿 A（他）來與 B 作比較時，就是自我與多者的比較。

  2. 因為形容詞 cute 是短音節的單字，因此最高級直接變化為 Adj-est 即可。

◎ Family / **is** / **the most beautiful** thing / in the world.

   A   B （Princess Diana 黛安娜王妃）

家庭 / 是 / 最美的事物 / 世界上

※ 1. 因為 B（世界上的事物）是多數，因此拿 A（家庭）來與 B 作比較時，就是自我與多者的比較。

  2. 形容詞 beautiful 是長音節的單字，因此最高級直接加上 the most 即可。

◎ You know the world is going crazy / when / **the best** rapper / is a <u>white guy</u>, /

the best golfer/ is a <u>black guy...</u>　　　　　　　　（Chris Rock 克里斯・洛克）

你知道這世界瘋了 / 當 / 最好的饒舌歌手 / 是個白人 / 最好的高爾夫球手 / 是個
黑人……

※1. 在這段話中，a white guy 與 a black guy 分別被點出是「所有」饒舌歌手及高爾夫球
　　手中最傑出的，因此是自身與多者的比較。

2. 因為比較的對象太多，所以直接用 the best 強調 a white guy 和 a black guy 的特殊性
　即可。

 重 點 整 理

◎ 先抓出句子中的主詞及動詞就對了！

◎ 比較分三種：自我的比較、自身與他者、自身與多者！

◎ 自我的比較、自身與他者的比較，皆適合下列的句型：

A + am / are / is + Adj-er + than + B

A + V + Adv-er + than + B

ex) is wiser than, live longer than...

◎ 如果是自我與多者的比較，則是下列的句型：

● **A + am / are / is / V + the best (+ N)**

　ex) the best rapper, the best golfer...

● **A + am / are / is / V + the most + Adj / Adv**

　ex) the most beautiful thing...

● **A + am / are / is / V + the Adj-est / Adv-est**

　ex) the cutest thing...

◎ 副詞的變化會影響句子的意義，比方說：

more interesting than / less interesting than...

◎ **as + Adj / Adv + as** 可用作比較，也可用作譬喻！

ex) as exciting as it should be / as angry as the burning sun...

練習

請依照句子的情境，變換適當的比較。

範例：Steven is as _____ as other students in class. (smart)
　　　Steven is as _smart_ as other students in class.

1. This summer vacation is _____ one I have ever had. (good)

2. After some practice, Ann can play that song as _____ as her teacher does. （fluently: 流暢地）

3. Fast food is _____ food among teenagers. (popular)

4. The _____ thing is not to stop question. (important)
（Einstein 愛因斯坦）

5. It is _____ to have fought and lost, than never to have fought at all. (good)
（Arthur Hugh Clough 克拉夫）

Grammar for
Global English
比較級

9

121

 作業

請用 _____ 中的字，依照句子的情境，寫出適當的比較形式。

範例：It's <u>good</u> to fight for good than to fail at the ill.　（Tennyson 丁尼生）
It's **better** to fight for good than to fail at the ill.

1. The <u>important</u> thing in life is to have a great aim, and the determination to attain it.　（Goethe 歌德）

_____

2. How <u>sharp</u> than a serpent's tooth it is to have a thankless child!
（《李爾王》by Shakespeare 莎士比亞）

_____

3. Living without an aim is <u>aimless</u> sailing without a compass.
（aimless: 漫無目的的）　（Alexandre Dumas 大仲馬）

_____

4. Unbidden guests are often <u>welcome</u> when they are gone.
（unbidden: 不請自來的）　（《亨利六世》by Shakespeare 莎士比亞）

_____

5. Victory belongs to <u>preserving</u>.（preserving: 堅毅的）　（Napoleon 拿破崙）

_____

10. 強調

　　在英文中，遇到需要強調某個名詞或某個動作的時候，除了在語氣上加強之外，也可以在文法上作強調的處理。強調的用法很簡單，只有下列三種：

1. It + be + 強調部分 + that ～
2. S + do / does / did + 原形 V
3. 倒裝：Adv + V + S

　　在口語中，又以前兩種最為常見。較不常見的倒裝句已經在第三章「十大句法」中說明過，這裡就不再特別介紹。

◎ It is her beautiful smile that catches my eyes.

◎ It is the ability to do the job that matters, not where you come from or what you are.

◎ Steve does have several meetings to attend every day.
（改寫自 99 年國中第二次學測）

◎ Typhoon Morakot did claim more than six hundred lives in early August of 2008.（改寫自 98 年大學指考）

文法解析

★ It + be + 強調部分 + that ～

有時候為了強調某個名詞或片語，我們會用 It be...that... 的句子將要強調的部分獨立出來，以便立即吸引讀者或聽者的注意。

◎ It is / **her beautiful smile** / that catches my eyes.

正是 / 她迷人的微笑 / 吸引了我的目光

※ 一般而言，我們可以省略 it，直接以 Her beautiful smile catches my eyes. 敘述這一件事。但是 It + be...that... 的句型能夠將 her beautiful smile 獨立出來，達到強調效果。

◎ It is / **the ability to do the job** / that matters, / not where you come from / or what you are.

正是 / 做這份工作的能力 / 才是關鍵 / 而不是你來自哪裡 / 或是你的職業

※ 一般而言，我們可以省略虛主詞，直接以 The ability to do the job matters, not where you come from or what you are. 來陳述這一件事。但是 It + be...that... 的句型能夠將 the ability to do the job 獨立出來，達到強調效果。

★ do / does / did + 原形 V

在肯定句中，有時候為了強調某個動作，我們會使用 do / does / did + 原形 V 來進行強調。

◎ Steve **does have** / several meetings to attend / every day.

（改寫自 99 年第二次學測）

史提夫真的有 / 數個會議要開 / 每一天

※ 一般來說為了方便，肯定句中的助動詞往往會被省略。但是為了強調，我們就會搬出 do / does / did，來吸引讀者或聽者注意後方的動詞。

◎ Typhoon Morakot **did claim** / more than six hundred lives / in early August of 2008.

（改寫自 98 年大學指考）

莫拉克颱風的確奪走 / 超過六百條生命 / 在 2008 年八月初

※ 同上題，did 原本可以省略，但為了強調，就故意提出，以吸引讀者或聽者注意後方的動詞。

 重 點 整 理

◎ **It** + **be** + 強調部分 (N) + **that** ～的句型通常是用來強調名詞。
◎ 助動詞（**do / does / did**）+ 原形 **V** 則是用來強調動詞。

Grammar for
Global English
強調

10

請依照括號中的提示，填入適當的強調用法。

範例：_____ that Alison quitted her job and moved to a small village. (this reason)

It is for this reason that Alison quitted her job and moved to a small village.

1. _____ that attracted the audience's interest.
   (the young man's talent)

2. We _____ that there will be no war in the world and that all people live in peace and harmony with each other. (hope)

   （改寫自 98 年大學學測）

3. _____ that gives Taiwanese songs a new life.
   (Wang Tsai-Hua's ong "Bobee")

4. _____ that hindered Ninna's learning while others were in great progress. (deafness) （hinder: 阻礙）

5. This information _____ a very reliable source, so you don't have to worry about being cheated. (come from)　　（改寫自 98 年大學學測）

6. Mary is suffering from a stomachache and _____ eat food which is easy to digest. (need to)　　（改寫自 97 年大學學測）

作業

請依照括號內的提示，將原句改寫為強調句。

範例：The Paralympics are for athletes with a disability.

(athletes with a disability)

It is athletes with a disability that Paralympics are for.

1. Rapid advancement in motor engineering makes it technically possible to build a flying car in the near future.

(rapid advancement in motor engineering) （98 年大學學測）

_____

2. Since our classroom is not air-conditioned, we have to tolerate the heat during the hot summer days. (have to tolerate) （97 年大學學測）

_____

3. Susan believed that the fragrance of flowers refreshed her mind. (refresh) （97 年大學學測）

_____

4. This math class is very demanding; I have to spend at least two hours every day doing the assignments. (for this demanding math class) （97 年大學指考）

_____

5. My brother enjoys having cold drinks, so he always puts his Coke in the refrigerator. (enjoy) （98 年國中第一次基測）

_____

Grammar for
Global English
強調
11

127

6. Jim grew up with many animals at home and knows well how to take care of pets. (know)

（98 年第一次基測）

_____

應用篇

聽力

　　對非母語人士來說，英文「聽、說、讀、寫」四大能力中，聽力算是較為困難的一部分，主要是因為在聽的時後，需要立即將聲音轉換成訊息，一旦卡在某個單字上，大腦一時無法將聲音轉換成自己了解的語意，就會無法掌握訊息。但是聽力訓練其實是有訣竅的，這訣竅不外乎以下三點：

1. 單字的語意

2. 語法結構中的語意重點

3. 語調

　　「單字的語意」就是將聽見的聲音對應到腦子中的英文單字，然後掌握語意；「語法結構中的語意重點」指的是抓出一句話裡面影響語意的關鍵字，並且忽略相對之下比較不重要的單字；「語調」指的是抑揚頓挫，因為聲調不僅會影響語意，有時候也

會影響讀者對關鍵字的掌握,當然個人口音也會有影響。

　　了解單字、掌握結構重點、熟悉語調,是練習聽力最重要的三大面向。首先,我們要掌握單字的語意,增進對英文單字的熟悉度。很多人聽到英文單字的第一時間會先想到中文意思,這種方式跟一般人背單字的習慣一樣,是不對的。學單字的正確步驟應該是:一、熟悉聲音,二、了解語意。

　　平常掌握單字時第一個要記的不是字母的拼法,而是字母的聲音。想要記住一個單字,一定要大聲唸出來,再將聲音與語意連在一起。比方說,今天學了一個新單字give,就要大聲唸出 give 這個單字,並重複五次,將這聲音記憶下來;接著利用這個單字造一個句子,例如:I give Mom a bunch of flowers on Mother's Day. 這樣才能同時將聲音與字意一起記下來。必要時也可以將自己的聲音錄下來反覆聆聽,進一步加深記憶。如此一來,聽見別人說 give 這個單字的時候,我們就可以很自然且迅速地將 give 的聲音與「給予」這個字意連在一起,再也不用面臨抓破頭都想不出來的窘境了。

　　聽力訓練的第二步,就是透過句型結構去抓出關鍵字。關鍵字是一句話中最重要的內容,可以幫助我們快速掌握重點、了解句意。和英文閱讀一樣,我們已經知道「主詞＋動詞」是英文文法最基本的結構,因此練習聽力時必須多多注意主詞和動詞。主詞一般來說都是名詞(人、事、物,或是 I, we, he, she, you, they 等),動詞則大多跟在主詞後面,表示「動作」,於是名詞、動詞可說是句子中的 strong words(強字:有內容、含意的字詞),其餘則是 weak words(弱字,例如助動詞或介系詞等)。讓我們來看看以下這個例子:

The builder in Germany says / that a Maglev train / can go / as fast as 300 miles per hour.
　　　　　　　　　　　　　　　　　　　　　　　　　　　　(全民英檢中級聽力預試)

那位德國的建造師說 / 磁懸浮列車 / 能夠跑 / 時速三百哩這麼快

　➡ 主詞 The builder 搭配動詞 says,後接 that 子句,整個句構即為十大句法六:SB says, "...",主要含意即為「那位建造師說(磁懸浮列車時速可達三百哩那麼快)」。主要結構中的 The builder(S), Germany(N)、says(V),和次要結構中的 a Maglev train(S), go(V) , 300 miles(N) , hour(N) 都是本句的 strong words;其餘的 in, that, as, per 等則是 weak words。只要掌握了 strong words,就能夠掌握八成的句意,就算沒聽清楚 weak words,也可以在腦海裡自行補足意思,不會影響理解。

　　另外,聽新聞報導時,有意義的字詞多會特別強調,唸得比較清晰,而 weak words 就會輕讀帶過,輕重不同的語調就是這樣形成的。

聽力訓練的第三步，就是熟練常見的英文表達方式與句型結構。請看以下的例子：

China Makes Arrests in Tainted Milk Scandal

Chinese authorities have **arrested** four people in its latest crackdown on melamine-tainted dairy products. Official media **reported** Wednesday that three dairy plant managers and one milk powder dealer *have been arrested* in northwestern Shanxi province. The state-run Xinhua news agency **says** three of the people were officials with Lekang Dairy Company, which *was named* in a previous toxic milk scandal. Xinhua **says** the suspects *were charged with* manufacturing and selling food that does not meet hygiene standards. The government Monday **launched** a 10-day emergency inspection of dairy products, following reports that tainted milk products *were found* in several provinces. Melamine-laced milk has killed at least six infants and sickened some 300,000 other children in China since the substance was discovered in a wide range of Chinese dairy products in late 2008.

（本文取自美國之音 VOA，網址：http://www.ept-xp.com/?ID=2204030203）

tainted：汙染的	inspection：檢查
melamine-tainted：受三聚氰氨汙染的	The state-run Xinhua news agency：官方新華社
toxic milk scandal：毒奶粉事件	hygiene standards：衛生標準

➡ 標題 China Makes Arrests in Tainted Milk Scandal 清楚指出本篇新聞的主角是中國政府，主題是毒奶粉事件。在接下來的新聞內容中，前五句的主詞（底線部分），都是與政府有關的單位、發言人等，他們做出了各種行動（粗體字）。這樣的方式能夠使文章的主詞維持一致性，加強讀者或聽者的理解。而其他有關毒奶粉的人、事等，則通通都以被動的型態出現（斜體字），此舉再度加強政府這個角色的重要性，讓讀者或聽者覺得毒奶粉事件已在政府的掌握之中。最後一句依照新聞寫作的習慣，以毒奶粉事件的最新情況作為總結。本篇言簡意賅，算是相當典型的英文新聞範例。

Grammar for Global English
聽力

★英文特殊表達方式

順帶補充，英文有些特殊表達與中文不同，例如方向，中文慣採東方、西方定位，先講東西再講南北，如東南、西北等；英文主要是用南北定位，先南北再東西，所以英文是講 north-west（西北）或 south-east（東南），聽英文的時候要習慣用英文思考，否則根本無法聽懂整句話。

特殊的英文表達要多加練習，否則聽力永遠無法進步，尤其數字是聽力中最難的一環，因此要習慣以聲音思考，不斷練習數字的說法，並說出聲音，對聽力的精進將會更有幫助，例如四百五十八萬的說法，中文是以千、萬定位，英文則是用千、百萬定位：

four million five hundred and eighty thousand

4 , 580, 000

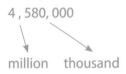

million   thousand

最後，我們要談的是訓練聽力的方法。訓練聽力的方法其實很簡單，只要反覆練習並持之以恆。大家可以利用平常聽到的英文（如新聞或英語雜誌，這些都有英文稿外加英文錄音）將關鍵字用立可白塗掉或留白，接著聽英文錄音，輔以正確的文法觀念（例如 take 的過去式要改成 took），再把正確的英文字填入空格中即可。接著一再播放錄音，跟著複誦，讓聲音透過耳朵，在腦中產生印象。把聲音轉換成語意的另一個方式，就是先從簡單的句子開始，「挖」出動詞、名詞，然後複誦一遍。這個方法不只訓練聽力，同時也訓練口語。比方說，p.133 文中有一句可挖空如下：

Xinhua says _____ _____ were charged with _____ and

_____ that does not meet _____ _____.

★複誦是訓練聽力的最重要方法

聽力訓練最重要的關鍵是「複誦」，因為複誦不僅可以訓練聽力，同時也是開始

說話的第一步。聽外國人說話時可以在心中複誦一遍，因為語言就是模仿學習（偷別人的話），先聽人家怎麼說，再學別人那樣說。

最後，我們再強調一次訓練聽力的正確方法。首先，透過聲音理解、記憶單字，並且實際使用；接著透過句構抓出關鍵字，以快速理解句意。此外，我們也建議讀者多熟悉一些特定場景的相關單字，例如開會的慣用字（suggest, recommend, propose, agree 等），這些慣用字都可以幫助我們快速抓住語意，進而理解句子。

聽力訓練的進階練習是「聽實境英文」，建議大家可上網下載 VOA、BBC 或電影精彩片段的文稿，將 strong words 塗掉，然後開始練習填字及複誦。

練習與作業

現在請上 VOA 的網站 http://www.voanews.com/learningenglish/home/education/Websites-Show-Young-People-How-to-Save--129416083.html 聆聽聲音檔，完成以下已經挖空的文稿：

Websites Show Young People How to Save

Young people are perhaps better-known for _____ money than

_____ it. But some new _____ websites are _____ to change

that. These websites _____ young people the information and tools they

need to _____ _____ their money. The websites also let the users

_____ their _____ experiences with other young people.

Grammar for Global English
聽力

_____-year-old Alix Scott has been working at a store this summer.

She is saving money to _____ for college next year.

ALIX SCOTT : "I have to save for all my college money because my

_____, they can't _____ to co-sign on _____. So, I have to

_____ on my own savings."

But _____ of putting her money in a local bank, Miz Scott _____

using SmartyPig, a web-based banking service.

建議大家可以試著分析每一句話的句法結構，先找出主詞和動詞，接著聆聽聲音檔，把空白的字填回去，再將全篇複誦一遍。

無論如何請大家切記，想要精進聽力，一定要反覆練習才能見效。只要確實做到以上的方法，保證不出數月，你的聽力一定大躍進。

口語訓練

★尋找一個好夥伴

口語訓練最重要的就是開口！如何開口講英文？可以先從日常生活的英文開始，找個朋友和你一起練習，增加對話的機會。不過要找到與自己程度相當，可以每天練習的朋友還滿困難的，因此各位不妨多多與「自己」練習，從「自言自語」與「自問自答」開始。

★如何開口

所有英文句子都由「主詞＋動詞」構成，尤其動詞更決定了句子的組成。剛開始練習時，可以從平時的生活習慣開始，每天練習對自己說話，而且一定要確實發出聲音、說出口。從日常生活開始讓英文確實貼近自己的生活，例如：

I like to take High Speed Rail.

（我喜歡搭高鐵。）

I take Bus 236 to NCCU. It takes me almost an hour from Taipei Main Station to my school.

（我搭 236 公車到政治大學。從臺北車站到我的學校大概要花一個小時。）

★口說英文的第一步就是描述自己一天的生活

☆主詞＋動詞 （我 I＋動詞）

此處的動詞大都是生活類的動詞，例如 have dinner / watch television / chat / have some snack / take shower / go to bed 等。如果想形容晚上的家庭生活，就可以說：

I always have dinner with my family. After dinner we often watch television together and have some chat. Having some snack is necessary during our talk. When our chat is finished, I always take a nice shower before I go to bed.

每天重複的生活習慣可以幫助我們熟悉常說的話，偶爾有些變化的生活習慣則是可以幫助我們創造新的練習內容。請記得一定要唸出聲音，遇到不懂的單字可以上網查網路字典、善用 Google，或是到相關的英文網站查特殊單字，例如可到悠遊卡股份有限公司的官方網站查詢「加值悠遊卡」的說法（deposit...in my Easy Card）。

請記得一定要開口說一遍，這句話才會變成自己的。光是閱讀不出聲，對口語是沒有幫助的。

★持續練習

訓練自己一看到人或物，就造一個英文句子，例如好想認識眼前的正妹、有個帥哥跟我搭訕、那位辣媽踩著 18 公分的高跟鞋、那個小朋友一直吵著吃冰淇淋，真的好任性、有群人在捷運上大聲說話，超沒公德心等等，應用自己所學的英文句法造句，並盡可能地變化句法並延長句子，例如：

There is a child. → There is a child wearing a red jacket. → The child who wears a red jacket wants to eat ice cream. → The child who wears a red jacket and wants to eat ice cream is so annoying.

　　如果遇到不會說的單字務必記錄下來，勤查字典後收錄進自己特有的單字庫。久而久之，以後再遇到相同的狀況就可以使用已學到的單字了。

☆名詞與動詞的使用

　　如果遇到不會的名詞（主詞或是受詞），建議各位一定要隨手記下，日後再查字典、上網搜尋相關詞庫，或是查閱各種專用字典。在此向各位推薦圖解字典《English Duden》，網路上有免費版本，可以協助大家找到各種物品的名詞說法（如各項汽車零件、廚房用品、辦公室用品等等）。

　　如果遇到不會說的動詞或不會表達的內容，建議各位依照日常生活的習慣，先找出常用的 50 個動詞，隨身攜帶，隨時查用。除了國中學過的通用動詞，如 do, take, make, have, go, run, walk, put, sit, watch, am, are, is, look, let, give, bring, tell 之外，請多加使用一些有意義的動詞（如下所示），應付日常口語保證沒問題：

accept 接受	adjust 調整	admire 崇拜	afford 足以	appear 出現
brush 刷	call 打電話	change 改變	check 檢查	choose 選擇
climb 爬	communicate 溝通	confirm 確認	continue 繼續	control 控制
decide 決定	deliver 傳送	develop 發展	drink 喝	dress 穿著
expect 期待	express 表達	identify 辨認	increase 增加	influence 影響
involve 參與	manage 管理	mention 提及	mistake 錯誤	oppose 反對
pass 通過	pick 挑選	place 放置	protect 保護	prove 證明

Grammar for Global English
口語練習

provide 提供	realize 實現	receive 接收	recognize 辨認	reject 拒絕
remind 提醒	represent 代表	ride 騎	suppose 假設	support 支持
suggest 建議	warn 警告	wake 叫醒	wish 希望	wear 穿著

☆使用同義字字典

　　想要認識更多類似的動詞或不一樣的動詞，可以利用同義字典，以上列動詞為基礎，進而衍生出更多實用動詞。如果想要熟悉這些動詞的用法，可以用造句的方式來實際應用，就可以幫助記憶與理解。

　　因此，每學到一個新單字（尤其是動詞），就一定要應用在每天的「自言自語」、甚至「自問自答」的練習中，這樣單字就不會忘記！也可以活用 What, When, Who, Where, Why 和 How 等疑問詞來造句，以生活中實際發生的情節來想像食衣住行育樂等相關情境，例如：

有關飲食的問題：

Q : What kind of food do you like?

A : I like Japanese food. It's much healthier.

　　（問：你喜歡哪種食物？）

　　（答：我喜歡日本料理。健康多了。）

有關娛樂的問題：

Q : How is your weekend?

A : Fantastic! I dated with my boyfriend and it's really gorgeous.

　　（問：你的週末過得如何？）

　　（答：超讚的！我跟男朋友去約會，真的很棒。）

有關衣著的問題：

Q : Why do you always wear T-shirt?

A : Because it's really comfortable and convenient.

　　（問：妳為什麼總是穿 T 恤？）

　　（答：因為這樣很舒適又方便。）

☆現在式與過去式的練習

像是三餐吃什麼、從事什麼社交娛樂活動等，都可以用英文想像，再以口語表達出來。建議大家先練習現在式，等一個月之後比較熟練，再練習過去式，描述昨天、前幾天等過去發生的事，以不同的場景來敘述。

這樣的練習對準備英檢中級口說能力測驗的「回答問題」很有幫助，以下為全民英檢中級口說預試的試題（參閱全民英檢網站，網址 http://GEPT.org.tw）：

GEPT 中級預試　口說能力測驗

第二部分：回答問題

共 5 題。題目不印在試卷上，經由耳機播出，每題播出兩次，兩次之間約有 1~2 秒的間隔。聽完兩次之後請立即回答，每題回答時間 15 秒，請在作答時間內盡量的表達。（以下摘錄 3 題）

Question no. 1 : What are you doing right now?

　　　　　　　　（你現在正在做什麼？）

Question no. 2 : How old were you when you went to junior high school?

　　　　　　　　（你幾歲開始讀國中？）

Question no. 3 : Do you feel more relaxed in the morning, the afternoon,

　　　　　　　　or the evening? Why?

　　　　　　　　（你覺得早上、下午、晚上哪個時段比較放鬆？為什麼？）

※ 可參考解答 p237 之口說能力測驗範例

★其他練習

接著還可以學習說英文笑話，試著將自己覺得好笑的事情用英文說一遍，這對拓展社交生活頗有幫助。此外，請大家務必熟悉中國食物的英文名稱，因為跟老外交際應酬時，最好的話題之一就是將食物主題融入文化之間來討論。而數字和方向的英文表達方式難度頗高，自己的電話號碼最好平常就練得很熟，可以不用思考就脫口而出（請見「應用篇：聽力」）。

Grammar for Global English
口語練習

此外，非英語母語人士在口語中最容易混淆時態及人稱代名詞。在時態上，過去式比較常用，因此要多加注意動詞的變化（尤其是 was 和 were，或不規則變化的動詞；如 -ed, 結尾的動詞在口語中常會因連音而模糊帶過，所以建議說話時可以點出時間，例如 yesterday 或 last week）。

人稱的性別，如 she、he 兩個代名詞，說話時不小心混淆的話，常常會讓外國人搞不清楚，最好的練習方式就是多練習用 she，以矯正大家一般不分男女都用 he 的錯誤習慣。

★ 結論

總之，英文口語練習不講究複雜的句法，一般多使用主詞＋動詞的結構，不會使用複雜的分詞構句，也不太使用假設法；就連形容詞子句都可以拆成另一句話來說，因此簡單句是最好也最實用的口語句型。

GLOBAL　練習與作業

其實練習英文口語並不難，只要起了個頭，日常生活中便處處都是靈感。現在請你依照下面的提示，說出你從早上起來到出門的所有動作，一一練習造句：

範例：

· 你今天幾點醒來？幾點起床？I wake up...but get up...

· 你今天吃了什麼當早餐？你喜歡嗎？I have...for breakfast, and I...

· 今天穿了什麼衣服？I put on...

· 你今天預備做什麼活動？I plan to...

· 你今天準備怎麼出門？I take...

· 要出門了，心情如何呢？I feel...

這樣的句子可以無限延伸，重點在於讓你習慣開口說英文。等你越來越能自然隨口說出現在式句型之後，我們不妨拿上個週末所發生的事當作例子，一起來練習過去式的說法。

比如說：

・上個週末有什麼有趣的活動嗎？ Last weekend I had...

・你去了哪裡？做了什麼？跟誰一起？ I went to...for...with...

・這場活動是為了慶祝什麼嗎？ We did this to celebrate...

・你的打扮如何？ I wore...

・有什麼人 / 事 / 物讓你印象深刻嗎？為什麼？ ...impressed me because...

・那場活動讓你心情如何？ I was really... / I felt...

　　同樣的，這樣的練習可以無限擴大，並且建議大家能夠盡量加進一些補充片語或者是連接詞。練習的次數越多，就越熟練現在式和過去式的用法。只要這兩個用法熟練之後，口說英文對你就不再陌生，功力自然大幅增進。

※ 可參考解答 p237 ～ p238 之範例

Grammar for Global English
口語練習

應用篇

閱讀

　　閱讀一篇英文文章，最重要的是理解其中的語意，最困難的是遇到不懂的單字與複雜的句型。有時即使每個單字都懂，也可能因為不懂句型而無法理解語意，這是因為英文的邏輯思考和書寫習慣與中文稍有不同。

　　想要理解英文，不論是口語溝通或是閱讀，一般來說都需要三種知識：

1. 單字
2. 文法與字的排序位置
3. 上下文的關係

★別讓不熟的單字阻礙你的閱讀

　　很多人認為單字是閱讀的障礙，因此在閱讀時就會花很多時間先把不懂的單字找

出來，如此一來閱讀效率不彰，成就感也跟著降低。其實，如果不懂的字並非關鍵字的話，我們大可直接將那個字省略，運用想像力去聯想可能的意思，這樣反而有助於理解文章，也能提升成就感。所以千萬不要一看到陌生單字就舉白旗投降，記得要先理解句型的文法結構，利用主詞＋動詞、主要結構與從屬結構的關係，將句子拆解為小單元，就能掌握全句的主要語意。

以下以 99 年國中第二次基測的閱讀測驗為例：

Dear Grandma, /

I've been in ~~Bluelake~~ / for two months now. / It's a beautiful small city. / Schools here begin / at the end of August. / I like my school / and I'm having a great time / teaching ~~Art History~~ here. /

I'm now living / in an apartment / with a friend. / From the window of my bedroom, / I can see a beautiful green hill / with flowers and trees. / Many people go there / to have a picnic / or to fly kites. / I enjoy taking a walk there / every day after work / and watching the people. /

I miss you very much, / Grandma, / and I hope you can come / and visit me here / some day. /

Love, Jude

親愛的奶奶 /

我已經來藍湖 / 兩個月了 / 這是個漂亮的小鎮 / 這裡的學期開始 / 在八月底 / 我喜歡我的學校 / 而且我過得很開心 / 在這裡教藝術史 /

我現在正住在 / 一間公寓 / 和一個朋友 / 從我臥室裡的窗戶向外看 / 我可以看到美麗的綠色山丘 / 有花和樹 / 很多人去那裡 / 野餐 / 或放風箏 / 我很愛在那邊散步 / 每天下班之後 / 和觀察路人 /

我很想念妳 / 奶奶 / 而且我希望妳可以來 / 這裡拜訪我 / 有一天 /
愛妳的裘德

首先將句子拆解成小單元，並將比較難、不確定的單字予以刪除（上例中的單字僅供參考，請按照自己的程度挑選單字），接著請從文章的上下文解讀整體語意，必要時可以適度發揮想像力。

第一段以完成式開頭，指出裘德在新地方居住了一段時間；接著二、三句以標準的「主詞＋動詞」結構介紹環境；第四句則是以連接詞 and 告知裘德的近況。第二段以現在進行式開始介紹她的住處，第二句應用十大句法五：Phrase, S＋V；第三、四句

則是以連接詞 or / and 連接兩個動詞。第三段則是運用兩個 and，第一個 and 連接兩個子句、第二個 and 則是連接動詞 come 和 visit，使句子變得更長，也更生動。

在這篇範例中，我們可以明顯發現，就算刪除文章中一些非關鍵的單字，也不會影響理解，而且那些被刪除的地方，其實是可以用想像力輕鬆填補上去的。這樣的閱讀技巧一樣可以應用在較為困難的文章上，以下為 99 年大學學測的閱讀測驗：

The word "prom" was first used in the 1890s, / referring to formal dances / in which the guests of a party / would display their fashions and dancing skills / during the evening's ~~grand~~ march. / In the United States, / parents and ~~educators~~ have come to regard the prom / as an important lesson in social skills. / Therefore, / proms have been held every year in high schools / for students to learn proper social behavior.

「Prom」這個字在 1890 年代第一次被使用 / 指的是正式的舞會 / 舞會中的客人 / 會展示他們的穿著及舞蹈技巧 / 在那晚的盛大遊行 / 在美國 / 父母和師長已經認為正式舞會 / 是一個重要的社交技巧課程 / 因此 / 正式舞會每年都在高中舉行 / 為了讓學生學習適當的社交行為

第一句的句型較為複雜，以 S＋V, Ving＋關係子句的型態提供了許多關於 prom 這個字的訊息。因為 prom 這個字不斷在文章中重複出現，我們很容易就可以發現它是這一段文章中的關鍵字。第二句和第三句的句型都是十大句法五：Phrase, S＋V 的形式，介紹更多關於 prom 的訊息。因此，就算不懂 prom 這個字，我們還是可以從上下文推敲出大概的意思。

同樣的技巧一樣可以運用在更難的文章上，以 99 年指考閱讀測驗為例：

Günter Grass was the winner of the 1999 Nobel Prize in Literature. / His talents are revealed in a variety of ~~disciplines~~: / He is not only a novelist, poet and ~~playwright~~, / but also a renowned painter and ~~sculptor~~. / As he himself ~~stresses~~, / his creations are closely related to his unique personal history. / His father was a German / who joined the ~~Nazi party~~ in World War II, / while his mother was ~~Polish~~. / As a result, / he constantly suffered ~~contradictory~~ feelings: / as a ~~Pole~~ who had been victimized, / and as someone guilty of harming the ~~Poles~~. / The ~~torment~~ in his heart led him to denounce the ~~Nazis~~ / and his ~~political activism~~ has continued throughout his career. / His commitment to the peace movement / and the environmental movement / as well as his ~~unfailing~~ quest for justice / has won him praise as "the conscience of the nation."

鈞特 · 葛拉斯是 1999 年諾貝爾文學獎的得主 / 他的才能顯現在不同的領域中：/ 他不但是小說家、詩人以及劇作家 / 他還是有名的畫家和雕刻家 / 一如他自述 / 他的創作和他個人獨特的成長過程緊密相關 / 他父親是德國人 / 在第二次世界大戰加入納粹黨 / 然而他母親是波蘭人 / 因此 / 兩種矛盾的感覺不斷折磨他：/ 受（納粹）迫害的波蘭人 / 傷害波蘭人帶來的罪惡感 / 他內心的糾結使他譴責納粹主義 / 而且他對政治的積極（行為）和他的文學生涯緊密相關 / 他對和平運動的承諾 / 和環境運動 / 以及他對正義永恆的追求 / 讓他贏得「國家之良知」的美譽

★排除「阻礙」之後，好好運用想像力與理解力

從以上三個例子我們可以發現，透過拆字及刪除部分不懂的單字，整句話的語意就大致浮現出來了。以最後一個例子為例，即使我們不曉得 Günter Grass, Nazi party, Polish, Pole 這幾個專有名詞，我們仍舊可以依文章內容推敲出第一個單字是人名，Nazi party 和 Polish / Pole 有相當的敵對關係，而 Polish 和 Pole 則是有高度相關性的單字。

因為這篇文章較難，在這個段落中我們就會看到更多的句型變化。第一個「主詞＋動詞」簡單句先帶出本篇的主角 Günter Grass（鈞特．葛拉斯），第二句則是以 His talents 當作主詞，以被動的型態向讀者介紹葛拉斯的才華。值得注意的是，這裡的抽象主詞 His talents 帶出了中文和英文的不同之處。英文文章很常使用抽象的事情當作名詞，以表現這件事的重要性，相當於中文的擬人法，因此讀者要多運用想像力來理解。第三句 not only...but also... 的句型很巧妙的將葛拉斯的各種身分連接起來，使讀者一目了然。第四句為十大句法八：Adv clause, Main clause；第五句則是用連接詞 while 呈現葛拉斯父母衝突的身分。第六句 Phrase, S + V 與 ...and... 的句型同樣巧妙地將身分的衝突共置於葛拉斯身上，與第七句恰成對比。最後一句中，連接詞 ...and...as well as... 的連用更是將所有的影響通通連結在一起，讓文章有個豐富有力的結尾。

★拆解句子結構

當句子太長或太複雜時，一定要耐著性子嘗試拆解句子。一旦判斷出句子的主要結構及次要結構，我們就可以更進一步將句子拆成小單元，將長句切成好理解的短句，就可以消化句意。再以第三句為例：

His talents are revealed in a variety of disciplines : / He is **not only** a novelist, poet and playwright, / **but also** a renowned painter and sculptor.

首先，我們可以在標點符號的地方作一個分解，然後再在慣用語 not only...but also... 作另一個分解，同時刪去不懂的單字，即可以將落落長的句子分解成簡單好理解的短句，這個句子就一點都不難了。

★上下文的關係是掌握語意的重要關鍵

除了了解單字與語言規則之外，透過上下文語意去理解句意也是很重要的閱讀技巧。例如上文中的 discipline 常作「規範」解釋，但是從後方 not only...but also... 我們可以發現這個句子呈現一連串不同的身分，因此稍加思考後就可以從 discipline 聯想到「領域」這個意思。如此一來我們對 discipline 這個單字就又多了一層認識，文章閱讀起來也更加生動。

★了解英文文章的寫作風格

有時候即便認識單字，也掌握了文法，卻還是不能理解句意的時候，其實是因為不習慣英文寫作方式的關係。請見以下範例：

When I was a child, / I could not wait to see the world. / I grew / like the spring flowers / in the garden.

當我還是孩子的時候 / 我等不及要看看這個世界 / 我成長 / 像春天的花朵 / 花園裡

When I was a teenager, / I could not wait to leave home. / I did not want to follow any rules, / and I was as angry as / the burning sun / in the summer sky.

當我還是青少年的時候 / 我等不及要離開家 / 我不想要遵守任何規則 / 而且我和……一樣生氣 / 像炎熱的太陽 / 夏日天空中

But then, / I learned to think carefully / before doing anything. / Both good and bad things / in the past / became parts of my life, / like autumn harvests for a farmer.

但是之後 / 我學會謹慎思考 / 在做任何事之前 / 好事和壞事都 / 在過去的 / 變成我生命的一部分 / 像秋天的收成之於農夫

Now I am old. / My body is weak, / but my mind has become strong and clear / because of those experiences in my younger days. / I am like a winter leaf, / ready to take a good rest.

現在我老了 / 我的身體虛弱 / 但是我的心智變得堅決和清明 / 因為我年輕歲月的那些經驗 / 我像冬天的葉子 / 準備要好好休息

These are the four **seasons** of my life.

這些是我生命中的四季

Elizabeth Owen

July 10, 2010

（99 年國中第二次基測）

　　這篇是國中基測常考的書信測驗，顯示出一個中、英文寫作風格大不同之處，也就是一開始就沒有開宗明義說出想要表達的重點，而是先描繪出細節，用四段文字、不同的時態（過去與現在），將人生的童年、青少年、成年、老年時期以春夏秋冬來比喻，直到最後一句才導出重點：這些是我人生的四季。

　　像這種以細節或特殊意象撰寫文章的方式，常會讓不熟悉英文寫作方法的非英語母語人士摸不著頭緒，有時還會抓不到重點。遇到這類狀況就已經不只是單字和文法的問題，而必須去探究語意表達和寫作風格。上述的寫作風格常常出現英文的報章雜誌和散文中，也很容易在各類考試中出現。

有了以上的基本概念以後，我們來練習一篇閱讀。這篇愛因斯坦的散文不但文采優美、寓意也深刻，相當適合用作閱讀練習。請各位運用本篇的重點提示，按照以下的步驟來閱讀：

1. 仿照第一段先練習拆解句子，找出每一句的主要子句及其他補充片語。
2. 理解每句的語意後，試著連結前後句，找出段落重點，可用筆畫出段落中最重要的那句話，或者在段落旁邊寫出本段重點
3. 最後綜合前後段的理解，找出文章的主旨，並試著替這篇文章下個英文標題。

好的英文文章通常相當有邏輯，不但每段都會有重點，段跟段之間也會有強烈的邏輯關聯。只要反覆練習，提升閱讀能力並不是問題：

Strange / **is** / our situation here / upon earth. / **Each of us** / **comes** for a
　　S　　　V　　　　　　　　　　　　　　　　　　　S　　　　V

short visit, / not knowing why, / yet sometimes <u>seeming to divine a purpose.</u>

（段落重點：Each of us / comes / ...seeming to divine a purpose →每個人 / 來到世上 / 似乎是為了某個神聖的目的）

From the standpoint of daily life, however, there is one this we do know that man is here for the sake of other men — above all for those upon whose smile and well-being our own happiness depends, and also for the countless unknown souls with whose fate we are connected by a bond of sympathy. Many times a day I realize how much my own outer and inner life is built upon the labors of my fellow men, both living and dead, and how earnestly I must exert myself in order to give in return as much as I have received. My peace of mind is often troubled by the depressing sense that I have borrowed too heavily from the work of other men.

To ponder interminably over the reason for one's own existence or the meaning of life in general seems to me, from an

Grammar for Global English
閱讀

objective point of view, to be sheer folly. And yet everyone holds certain ideals by which he guides his aspiration and his judgment. The ideals which have always shone before me and filled me with the joy of living are goodness, beauty, and truth. To make a goal of comfort and happiness has never appealed to me; a system of ethics built on this basis would be sufficient only for a herd of cattle.

— Albert Einstein

GLOBAL ENGLISH

應用篇

寫作

任何英文寫作會面臨到的困境大概可歸納為以下四種：

1. 詞彙不足、句型單調
2. 句子與段落轉折不順暢、思考過於跳躍
3. 內容貧乏沒有深度
4. 中英文思考混亂

★建立句型的概念

但是與考試不同的是，一般職場或日常生活使用的英文對於文章結構的要求並沒有那麼嚴謹，反而是語意的表達比較重要，而語意表達的重點在於「主詞」與「動詞」。想要加強英文寫作能力，從句法開始就對了！建立句型的概念即為寫好英文作文的首

要之務。誠如本書一再強調的，任何英文句子一定是由「主詞＋動詞」構成的，而整句的結構為何，則由動詞來決定，因此動詞可以說是英文句子的靈魂。

★名詞與動詞

寫作最大的問題是不會用單字，或者字彙量不足，如果再加上沒有句法觀念，就很難寫出好文章。因此，首先要建立英文的句法觀念（請參考第三章：「十大句法」），有了精準的句法觀念再運用自己所知且適切的單字去寫主詞、動詞，就可以完成一個英文句子。因此，認識名詞與動詞的正確使用方法極為重要。

英文的主詞有三種：人、物，以及抽象的名詞與概念。其中最常用的大概是以人為主的主詞了，例如 I, you, he, she, we, they 等，大多用於書寫 email，而使用最為頻繁的就是 I 跟 you，請見下例：

I'm so glad to receive your invitation for Linda's birthday.

此句以 I'm so glad 為主要結構，to 後面銜接讓人開心的事。因為是為了「收到邀請」這件事情感到開心，並且前面已經有 am，所以用 to + V 來表示收到邀請這件事。在英文中，每個句子都只能有一個動詞，因此如果有第二個動作概念，第二個動詞就要使用 Ving, Ved, 或 to + V 來表示。

除了用你、我、他當主詞以外，英文也常常以特定的人物當主詞，例如 My guitar tutor, That pretty girl 等。使用的名詞愈精確，句子就愈生動活潑，請看以下範例：

Dress → white dress → laced white dress → laced white dress in wedding-style

名詞愈精確，意義就愈明顯。在以上的例子中，廣義的 dress 意義太模糊，很難使人產生明確的印象，但隨著細節的增加，讀者或聽者就可以根據更多線索，在腦海中勾勒出一件有蕾絲花邊的白色結婚禮服，如此一來句子不但更為生動活潑，也可以讓人留下深刻的印象。

除了人、物之外，抽象概念也可以當主詞。非母語人士常會忽略主詞的變化，但其實只要改變主詞，動詞也會跟著活潑起來，例如以下範例：

Honesty is the best policy. （英文諺語）

誠實為上策。

→ Honesty 當主詞

First love is a little foolishness and a lot of curiosity.

（George Bernard Shaw 劇作家蕭伯納）

初戀只不過是一點點愚蠢加上很多好奇。

→ First Love 當主詞

除了主詞之外，動詞也應力求精確；好的作者通常都會在這兩者特別下功夫。既然動詞是句子的靈魂，寫作時就應該要力求精確，多多使用精確動詞，減少使用弱動詞（比較不精確的動詞，例如 do, let, make, take, have 等），才能激發讀者更多想像力，並留下印象。請看以下兩個例子：

弱動詞：Days in army ~~make~~ a man better.

精確動詞：Days in army **refine** a man.

弱動詞：That speech ~~makes~~ him think more.

精確動詞：That speech **enlightens** him.

此外，選擇不同的精確動詞，就會產生不同的意義，給予人不同的印象。例如要表達「他對著……笑」，至少會有以下數種不同的表達方式：

He smiles at...	他對著……微笑
He grins at...	他對著……咧著嘴笑
He giggles at...	他對著……咯咯笑
He laughs at...	他對著……大笑
He taunts at...	他對著……嘲笑

Grammar for Global English
寫作

★轉折與時態

適當的連接與轉折可以幫助整合思考，避免文章邏輯的跳躍；接著輔以句型觀念，練習以英文思考，將想法轉譯並整理成文字，就能夠寫出順暢的文章。最後別忘了運用正確的字詞與文法，配合時態（現在、過去、未來即完成式等）變換動詞（如在過去式中，動詞要加 -d, -ed, -ied 等）。以下整理出較為常見的連接詞與轉折詞，建議大家可多多運用：

◎ **Though / Although / However / Nevertheless / Nonetheless** →表語氣轉折

◎ **Hence / Therefore** →表因果關係

◎ **In a word / In brief / To sum up** →表總結

註：有關進階寫作，可參考聯經出版公司出版之《一生必學的英文寫作》

GLOBAL　　練習與作業

提升作文能力的方法別無其他，就是勤練而已。今天開始就以一天中所發生最讓你印象深刻的事情為主題，寫下一篇日記吧！以下有一篇範例，請依照段落提示，試著一步步填滿空格，學習如何用簡單卻富有變化的文法完成段落。最後的結尾則留給大家，請發揮你的想像力，幫文章寫下屬於你的結局。請注意由於今天的事情都已經發生過了，因此在日記中，請不要忘記使用過去式來描述今天所發生的一切。

範例：　　　　　　　　　**難忘的一幕**

我每天都搭公車上學，還有回家也一樣。公車上總是擠滿了和我一樣的學生。每個人都在車上大聲聊天。公車又吵又擠，我常常都心情不好。不過今天有點不一樣。

I go to school by bus every day, and go home by bus as well. The bus is always filled with＿＿＿. Everyone ＿＿＿ aloud. The bus is ＿＿＿＿＿; I'm always ＿＿＿. But today ＿＿＿＿＿.

在回家的途中有個男生上了車，頂著閃耀的金髮。他的外表引起了我的好奇心。公車司機跟他說話時，他只搖搖頭並且微笑。好像聽不懂一樣。一直到他走到我附近，我才發現原來他是個外國人。

_____ a boy _____, _____. His looks aroused my curiosity. When the bus driver _____, he merely _____ _____. It seemed he _____. Until he walked near me, I _____ he _____.

其他人都投以好奇的眼光，但隨即就移開視線。那個男生站在人群裡，默默接受著大家的好奇眼光。突然公車一個急速轉彎。那男孩失去平衡，眼看就要跌倒……

Other students _____, and soon _____. That boy _____, silently accepting people's curiosity. Suddenly _____. _____ ...

翻譯

　　我們常常告訴英語學習者：要用英文來思考！也就是直接以英文的單字或句法來思考，不要先用中文的語意來想，而後再翻譯成英文。但是對於非英語母語使用者來說，這種英文思考的過程需要一段過渡時期。首先，一般人會習慣透過母語思考，再轉換成英語語法；也就是說話者心中先有一些想法，再將這些想法以英文句法來表達，等到這種轉換的機制非常熟練與快速，就接近用英文思考的境界了。

　　大學考試的翻譯考題就是這種轉換機制的檢驗，其目的並非考翻譯（用字遣詞或修辭能力），而是測驗學生如何將中文語意轉換成英文句法，並針對中文與英文表達中不同的字序（word order）及一些常用的表達方式，要求學生確實掌握，以奠定寫作的基礎。

　　為了計分方便，大考的翻譯試題多以兩段式結構為主。首先是看應考者對句型的

應用，也就是英文字序是否排列正確，這樣就可以得到一半的分數；接著再看用字遣詞是否正確傳達語意，最後一步則是檢查拼字、標點符號等。因此，掌握正確的句型是很重要的關鍵。本章將從基本的中英文句法轉換談起，並應用講述過的十大句法及相關文法觀念，建立大家翻譯寫作的信心。

★中翻英解題四步驟

一般人在處理中翻英時，往往會落入逐字翻譯的陷阱，以中文句法表達英文，而完全忽略應有的英文句構。切記，中翻英的時候，首重了解句子的結構，確立正確的字序。

英文句構與中文句法不同，因此如果想要輕鬆解決中翻英的題目，除了找出適當的字詞之外，還可以依循以下四個步驟進行中翻英：

1. 找出主詞和動詞
2. 將句子的主要結構寫出來，其次納入次要結構
3. 找出句子的一些關鍵字詞，並放入適當的位置
4. 加入其他字詞，最後檢查標點符號、主動詞一致性、名詞單複數、冠詞及拼字

請見 99 年大學學測的翻譯考試範例：

在過去，腳踏車主要是作為一種交通工具。
　　　　　　S　　　　V

接著我們以剛剛的四個步驟為準，一步一步來翻譯：

首先，此句的主要結構語意是「腳踏車是（一種交通工具）」。
1. 找出主詞和動詞：
　　腳踏車 (the bicycle) ＋是 (was) （用過去式）
2. 句子主要結構：主詞＋動詞＋主詞補語
　　腳踏車 (the bicycle) ＋是 (was) ＋交通工具 (tool for transportation)
3. 找出句子的關鍵字：
　　交通工具：tool for transportation
　　→ The bicycle was a tool for transportation.

4. 加入其他字詞，並檢查冠詞、名詞單複數、標點符號、拼字等：

  → The bicycle was a kind of tool mainly for transportation in the past.

另外，也請大家注意中英文字序的轉換：

在過去，腳踏車主要是作為一種交通工具。

The bicycle was a kind of tool mainly for transportation in the past.

（英文中一些表示狀況的字詞，如 in the past，通常會放在句子最後面或最前面。）

讓我們再看第二個例子，一樣是 99 年大學學測翻譯考題：

然而，騎腳踏車現在已經成為一種熱門的休閒活動。
　　　　　S　　　　　　　V

接著我們以剛剛的四個步驟為準，一步一步來翻譯：

首先，此句的主要結構語意是「騎腳踏車（這件事）已經成為（一種熱門的休閒活動）」。

  1. 找出主詞和動詞：

  騎腳踏車（Riding a bicycle）＋成為 (become)

  2. 句子主要結構：主詞＋動詞＋主詞補語

  騎腳踏車（Riding a bicycle）＋成為 (become) ＋ 休閒活動 (entertainment)

  3. 找出句子的關鍵字：

  休閒活動：entertainment

  → Riding a bicycle becomes an entertainment.

  4. 加入其他字詞，並檢查時態、標點符號、冠詞、拼字等：

  → However, riding a bicycle has become a popular entertainment.

  （使用完成式，表示已經的意思）

另外，也請大家注意中英文字序的轉換：

Grammar for Global English
翻譯

然而，騎腳踏車現在已經成為一種熱門的休閒活動。

However, riding a bicycle has become a popular entertainment now.

在本題中，中英文字序恰好能夠互相呼應，但讀者們千萬要切記英文的字序與中文有所不同，應仔細檢查。

> 補充說明：此處 bicycle 在英文中是所謂的可數名詞，單獨使用要加 "a" 或 "the"，也可以使用 bicycles，表示腳踏車。這與中文不同，中文的名詞大部分都可以單獨使用。

中文轉換成英文句法時，跟分析長句結構一樣，最重要的是先找出主詞與動詞、主要結構與次要結構，然後找出適當的字詞與動詞用法，再加上其他關鍵字或是修飾語。英文是種衍生的語法結構，先有基本結構（S＋V），其餘的字詞就堆疊上去即可。

有時中英文字序恰好能夠互相呼應，但讀者們千萬要切記大部份時候英文的字序會與中文有所不同，應仔細檢查。

以下為 97 年指考的翻譯考題，大家可以小試身手：

專家 警告我們不應該再將食物價格低廉視為理所當然。
S　　V

首先，此句的主要結構語意是「專家警告（我們不應該再將食物價格低廉視為理所當然）」。

(a) 找出主詞和動詞：

→專家（Experts）＋ 警告 (warn)

(b) 句子主要結構：主詞 ＋ 動詞 ＋ that 子句

→專家（Experts）＋ 警告 (warn) ＋ that 子句

(c) 找出句子的關鍵字：

食物價格低廉：low price of food

→ Experts warn that...low price of food...

(d) 視……為理所當然：

→ take...for granted

(e) 加入其他字詞，並檢查時態、標點：

→ Experts <u>warn</u> that we shouldn't take the low price of food for granted.
      S   V

另外，也請大家注意中英文字序的轉換：

專家 警告我們不應該再將食物價格低廉視為理所當然。

Experts warn that we shouldn't take the low price of food for granted.

因為是使用很直接的翻譯，所以在這裡中英文字序沒有太大的不同。但同樣的中文亦可以翻成以下的句子：

專家 警告我們不應該再將食物價格低廉視為理所當然。

We have been **warned** by **experts** that we shouldn't take the low price of food for granted.

在這樣的句型架構中，by experts 用來補充說明「是誰」發出警告。試著改變字序，你就會發現句子的重點變得不一樣了。

★大考最常出現的句型

掌握中文語意轉換成英文句法，是突破大考中翻英試題最有效的方法。所以判斷主詞與動詞結構非常重要，也就是說英文寫作最重要的工作就是先找出主詞與動詞。此外，英文的句法也是關鍵，尤其大考常考兩段式結構，所以十大句法中具備兩段結構的句法，就是大考最常出現的句型，整理如下：

1. S + (...) + V

2. Ving(Ved)(To-V)..., S + V

3. S + V...(to-V), Ving(Ved)

Grammar for Global English
翻譯

4. With / Without + N (+ Ving or Ved), S + V 或 S + V, with / without + N (+ Ving or Ved)

5. Phrase, S + V 或 S + V, Phrase

6. 從屬結構 + S + V

7. S + Adj 子句 (which, that, who...)+ V

Ex) 近二十年來我國的出生率快速下滑。　　　　　　　　（99 年大學指考）
　　　　S　　　　　V

句型結構：主詞（片語）+ 動詞 + Phrase →句型 5

→ The birthrate of our nation has rapidly decreased in these two decades.
　　　　　　S　　　　　　V　　　　　　　　　　Time Phrase

Ex) 這可能導致我們未來人力資源的嚴重不足。　　　　　　（99 年大學指考）
　　S　　V

句型結構：主詞 + 動詞 + Phrase →句型 5

→ This could lead to a serious shortage of human resources in our future.
　　S　　V　　　　　　　　　　　　　　　　　Time Phrase

一般來說，兩段式翻譯要注意三大要點：

一、複句結構（或是 Ving, Ved, To V 結構）

二、主詞字彙、動詞選擇

三、字序（word order）

Ex) 玉山 是東亞第一高峰，以生態多樣聞名。　　　　　　（98 年大學指考）
　　S　V

句型結構：主詞 + (...) + 動詞→句型 1

→ Yu-shan, famous for ecological variety, is the highest mountain in East Asian.
　　S　　　　　　　　　　　　　　V

Ex) 大家在網路上投票給它，要讓它成為世界七大奇觀之一。　（98 年大學指考）
　　　S　　　　　　V

句型結構：主詞＋動詞＋從屬結構（to＋V）→句型 6

→ People vote to Yu-shan on the internet to make it become one of the Seven
　　S　　V　　　　　　　　　　　　　　to＋V

　　Wonders of the World.

　　此外，時態的變化也因中文的時間表達有不同的方式，表示已經、曾經等語意時，須用現在完成式（has / have＋PP），如前面的出生率，在二十年來，用 has decreased；表示過去發生的事情（如 three years ago 等）則用過去式，而使用現在式表示現在狀態。

　　在翻譯的過程中，主詞常常是關鍵，一些與社會時事有關的名詞常會成為考題，如高速鐵路（high speed rail）、糧食危機（food crisis）、教改（educational reform）、全球暖化（global warming）、新流感（H1N1 Flu）、海嘯（tsunami）、土石流（mudslide or landslide）等，建議多注意報章雜誌中出現的一些議題。

★熟悉常用動詞的用法

　　經常使用的動詞，如 warn（警告）、encourage（鼓勵）、allow（允許）、confirm（確定）、prove（證明）、believe（相信）、focus on（集中於）、pay attention to（注意）、apply for（申請）等，對於這些動詞，必須盡量知道它的用法，可以每個動詞造兩個句子、每句十個字以上，對於了解這些動詞來說相當有幫助。

　　大考英文的翻譯寫作，最重要的是將想法化成英文句法，努力以「英文」來思考，發展自己的一些看法；如能進一步活用所學的動詞與名詞，就可以輕鬆面對寫作。詳細的寫作課程可以參考《一生必學的英文寫作》（陳超明教授與溫宥基老師合著，聯經出版）。

Grammar for Global English
翻譯

★實用網站

☆ VOA Special English 美國之音學習版
http://www.voanews.com/specialenglish

　　VOA（美國之音廣播電台）的網路圖文、音檔並茂，標榜以「非英語系國家的人」都能理解的英語播報世界新聞，不但播報速度較慢，也不會使用冗長的複合子句，以及不常用的俚俗語。特別推薦 VOA 網頁上「Our Word Book」所列出的 1500 個英文單字，只要記住這些單字，就能聽懂約 95% 的新聞內容。

☆ BBC Learning English
http://www.bbc.co.uk/worldservice/learningenglish/

　　BBC（英語國家廣播公司）所架設的這個網站，內容隨時更新、完全免費，蒐羅全球時事、科技、藝術人文等文章，亦有文法與片語的介紹。

☆紐約時報精選周報
http://city.udn.com/593

　　《聯合報》與《紐約時報》合作的「紐約時報精選周報」可以讓你更了解世界趨勢、擁有科技及藝術知識，部份英文文章也會附上中文翻譯，訓練閱讀之餘，亦可增加時事字彙庫。

☆台灣光華雜誌
http://www.taiwan-panorama.com/ch/

　　可以檢索許多中英文章，許多你想知道的英文時事單字都可以在這網站找到用法和例句。

練習與作業

　　了解翻譯的步驟之後，我們不妨來練習幾句。以下有五句電影經典名言，請發揮你的想像力翻譯，再比對看看外國人是怎麼翻譯的，你就能領略翻譯的有趣之處：

1. 生活就像一盒巧克力，你永遠不知道你會吃到什麼口味。（《阿甘正傳》）
   （A 就像 B：A＋be V＋like＋B）

   _____

2. 這世界上一定存在著許多良善值得我們去奮鬥。（《魔戒二‧雙城奇謀》）
   （良善：good；奮鬥：fight for）

   _____

3. 洋蔥有層次，妖怪也有層次，我們都有層次！　　　　　（《史端克》）
   （洋蔥：onion；妖怪：ogre；層次：layer）

   _____

4. 能力越大，責任越大。　　　　　　　　　　　　　　　（《蜘蛛人》）
   （責任：responsibility）

   _____

5. 跟朋友親近，跟敵人要更親近。　　　　　　　　　　　（《教父 II》）
   （敵人：enemy）

   _____

Grammar for Global English
翻譯

考試篇

★文法是補助工具，而非主要考試重點

很多人認為英語考試，除了考單字以外，就是測試考生的文法觀念，其實這是完全錯誤的想法。當然我們要累積足夠的單字，才能有基本語意的了解，但是文法絕對不是英語檢定考試的重點。如果仔細研究多益考試，可能會發現部分題目本身的文法其實有誤。有些題目看起來是要測試文法或用法，**但其實著重的仍是語意的理解，不了解語意，只靠僵硬的文法規則，可能還是無法獲得高分。**

本章針對多益所出現的一些題目進行分析，強調文法句型只是幫助了解，並非考試的重點。熟悉某些文法規則，有利句子的拆解與語意的掌握。即使是考文法試題，也是影響語意的文法試題。而且不管是單字或是閱讀測驗，所有選項答案的文法大多是正確的，只是錯誤的選項在用法或是語意表達方面與題目不符。

所以，在多益要拿高分，其實最重要的還是要多閱讀、多熟悉實用的語法，知道句子的結構，然後掌握一些常用的動詞用法或是語氣的轉折，就很容易選出答案。我並不想傳授所謂的解題技巧，而是想提出如何透過文法的基本觀念去理解文意。再次強調，英檢考試的文法觀念都在本書所談的範圍之中，只要活用本書所提的文法與語法觀念，就可以提昇自己的英文實力。

語意的理解過程：（與前述閱讀的技巧一樣）

1. 找出主詞與動詞
2. 將句子拆解成具語意觀念的小單元
3. 熟悉各種不同情境的動詞或是名詞表達方式

在以上三種英文理解過程中，重視的有兩點：

◎與情境相關的單字學習
◎透過句法分析或是拆解後，理解文意

請見以下範例：（TOEIC 官方範例試題）

The new economy has created great business opportunities as well as great turmoil. Not since the Industrial Revolution have the stakes of dealing with change been so high. Most traditional organizations have accepted, in theory at least, that

TOEIC 多益

★解題非重點，提升英文能力才是重點

　　為了國際職場競爭，很多人必須擁有英文能力證明，其中尤以多益（TOEIC）檢定考試最受青睞。很多補習班或是語言中心開設多益檢定考試的進修班，而市面上也充斥準備考試的書籍。大抵而言，這類進修課程或書籍都強調兩點：一是單字的增強，二是解題的技巧。看似可以提升成績，卻忽略了考試的本質：測驗英文的實用能力；也就是說，如果你的英文能力沒有實質提升（閱讀理解為重點），就算背很多單字或是不斷熟悉解題技巧，也無法有明顯的進步。

they must make major changes. Even large new companies recognize that they need to manage the changes associated with rapid entrepreneurial growth. Despite some individual successes, however, this remains difficult, and few companies manage the process as well as they would like. Most companies have begun by installing new technology, downsizing, restructuring, or trying to change corporate culture, and most have had low success rates. About 70 percent of all change initiatives fail.

The reason for most of these failures is that in their rush to change their organizations, managers become mesmerized by all the different, and sometimes conflicting, advice they receive about why companies should change, what they should try to accomplish, and how they should do it. The result is that they lose focus and fail to consider what would work best for their own company. To improve the odds of success, it is imperative that executives understand the nature and process of corporate change much better.

Most companies use a mix of both hard and soft change strategies. Hard change results in drastic layoffs, downsizing, and restructuring. Soft change is based on internal organizational changes and the gradual development of a new corporate culture through individual and organization learning. Both strategies may be successful, but it is difficult to combine them effectively. Companies that are able to do this can reap significant payoffs in productivity and profitability.

（引自多益官方網站—— http://toeic.com.tw/pdf/newtoeicsampletest.pdf）

此篇文章談論工業革命所帶來的經濟轉變，以及不同的轉變方式。

閱讀文章時，熟悉某些單字固然重要，但絕非關鍵；關鍵的反而是語意之間的連接。看到長篇文章，首先針對每一句話找到主詞與動詞，然後再將長句依照句法結構拆成具語意的小單元。以第三段為例：

The reason for most of these failures is / that in their rush to change their organizations, / **managers become mesmerized** / by all the different, / and sometimes conflicting, / advice they receive / about why companies should change, / what they should try to accomplish, / and how they should do it. / **The result is** / that **they lose focus** / **and fail to consider** / what would work best for their own company. / To improve the odds

Grammar for
Global English
TOEIC 多益

of success, / **it is** imperative / that **executives understand** / the nature and process / of corporate change much better.

此段的主詞＋動詞結構很簡單，都很容易找到（粗體字部分）。文法上則是大量使用了主、次結構和連接詞（and）。如此拆解分析完後，其實選擇題第 1 的答案就出來了：

題目 1

According to the article, why do so many attempts to change fail?

(A) Soft change and hard change are different.

(B) Executives are interested only in profits.

(C) The best methods are often not clear.

(D) Employees usually resist change.

這個問題比較屬於事實的題目，因此閱讀內容後（經理人常常被來自四面八方、互相牴觸的意見混淆，以至於看不清該怎麼做），就知道答案為 (C)（最好的解決方法常常都不清楚）。

讓我們再看一題：

題目 2

What is soft change based on?

(A) Changes in the corporate culture

(B) Reductions in company size

(C) Relocating businesses

(D) Rinancial markets

此題測驗在考文意的理解。請先閱讀第四段：

Most companies use a mix / of both hard and soft change strategies. / **Hard change results in / drastic layoffs, / downsizing, / and restructuring. / Soft change is based on / internal organizational changes / and the gradual development / of a new corporate culture / through individual and organization learning.** / Both strategies may be successful, / but it is difficult to combine them effectively. / Companies that are able to do this / can reap significant payoffs / in productivity / and profitability.

　　本段開頭即指出有兩種改變的方式，一為 hard change，一為 soft change。文中粗體字即為兩種改變的不同策略。很顯然的，將句子適度拆解後，答案便浮現了：(A) Changes in the corporate culture

　　多益考題主要是測試理解力，因此除了對單字的認識外，出現的文章大多在釐清一些與我們息息相關的問題，有時也會有這種知識性的文章。這類與生活息息相關並且靈活的文章，最常被用來測驗考生的英文理解力！

★文法試題

　　除了閱讀測驗，其實情境題或單字題也只要運用基本的語法與文法就可以解決。例如以下此多益的考題，似乎完全是考文法，但是它的文法是跟著語意的，如果不知道整句話的意義，就會很容易答錯：

_____ in the late 1800's, many of the coastline's lighthouses remain standing today, having withstood the forces of nature for decades.

(A) Built　　　　　　　(B) Building

(C) To build　　　　　(D) Having built

1. 此句的主詞為 many of the coastline's lighthouses，動詞為 remain。
2. 此句型為本書十大句法二：Ving (Ved) (To V)..., S+V。
3. 燈塔是被建造的，所以用被動 built，時間是 1800's，表示過去被建造，所以答案是 (A)。

　　即使是文法題，也不需要很複雜的文法知識，只要掌握英文中一句話只有一個動詞，出現第二個動作，就要使用 to V, Ved 或 Ving，再加上基本的時態觀念（如現在、過去、完成等），就可以找出答案（請見十大句法二）。

Grammar for Global English
TOEIC 多益

從以上例子可知,不管是閱讀測驗或文法試題(我個人偏好稱之為「用法試題」),其實只要掌握句法、時態、比較等本書所提示的一些基本文法觀念,就可以了解語意、找出答案,實在沒有必要苦讀厚重的文法書。

★語意才是考試重點

最後,再提醒讀者,文法不是考試的重點,語意才是。唯有了解句子的整體涵義,才能找出正確的答案。為了挑戰應試者的英文閱讀與分析能力,題目大都設有陷阱(文章的涵義都與一般傳統看法不同),以測試應試者是否真正理解!英檢考試的文章富有知識性與邏輯性,建議多閱讀如《國家地理雜誌》(*National Geographic*)、《科學人》(*Scientific American*)、《紐約時報》(*The New York Times*)等,掌握人文、科學新知或社會文化現象的新趨勢,知名報章雜誌都是很好的閱讀內容,也是考試的好題材。

練習與作業

請閱讀以下短文,請選出最適合的答案,使整篇文章完整。

Ms. Monica Eisenman
555 King Street
Auckland
New Zealand

Dear Ms. Eisenman:

I am __(1)__ to confirm our offer of part-time employment at Western Enterprise.

In your role as research assistant, you will report to Dr. Emma Walton, who will keep you informed of your specific duties and projects. Because you will be working with confidential information, you will be expected to __(2)__ the enclosed employee code-of-ethics agreement.

As we discussed, you will be paid twice a month __(3)__ the company's normal payroll schedule. As an hourly employee working fewer than twenty hours per week, you will not be __(4)__ to receive paid holidays, paid time off for illness or vacation, or other employee benefits.

Your employment status will be reviewed in six months.

If you have any questions, please feel free to contact me. Otherwise, please sign and return one copy of this letter. You may keep the second copy for your files. We look forward to working with you.

Sincerely,

Christopher Webster

Christopher Webster

Human Resources

Enclosures

題 1

(A) pleased   (B) pleasing   (C) pleasant   (D) pleasure

題 2

(A) follow   (B) advise   (C) imagine   (D) require

題 3

(A) accords   (B) according   (C) according to   (D) accordance with

題 4

(A) tolerable   (B) liberal   (C) eligible   (D) expressed

※ 以上題目出自 *New TOEIC–Official Test Preparation Guide*

Grammar for Global English
TOEIC 多益

考試篇

全民英檢中級

　　還記得前幾年全民英檢（GEPT）打出了一個口號，說考英檢是「全民運動」，標榜大家都應該透過英檢檢視自己的英文能力。英檢的分級制度對應了目前臺灣的英語教育程度，雖然方便，但大家不應受限於分級制度。

　　全民英檢中級對應的是高中程度的英文，大約與學測的程度相同，所以大家也不用太感驚慌，一樣掌握基本的文法結構即可。只是英檢的題目較學測多，方向也比較偏生活化。建議大家平常可以多閱讀來提升速度，並增加接觸實用英文的機會。本書從活用的文法觀點出發，介紹大家如何增進聽、說、讀、寫的能力，只要按照書上的方法練習，全民英檢中級也不是難事。

★文法要點

☆ 時態

After the police arrive, they will begin to interview the people who **were** in the jewelry store at the time of the robbery.

☆ 被動式

This proposal for a new high speed train **will be rejected** because the cost is too high.

☆ 主詞＋動詞 (S＋V)

Aluminum has many desirable qualities which make it a commercially very useful metal.

☆ 從屬結構 (S＋V, Adj clause)

...she was thirty minutes late for work, **which** made her boss very angry.

★範例說明

After the police arrive, they will begin to interview the people who _____ in the jewelry store at the time of the robbery.

(A) have been   (B) will be

(C) were   (D) are

1. 我們可先將句子拆解如下：

    After the police arrive, / they will begin to interview the people / who _____ in the jewelry store at the time of the robbery.

    警察抵達後 / 他們將會開始調查那些人 /（那些）在搶劫發生時（剛好）_____ 珠寶店裡的人

2. 拆解過之後，發現這句話的句構為「次要結構（副詞字句）＋主要結構＋次要結構（形容詞字句）」，得知此題的考試重點為從屬結構，是十大句法八：Adv clause, Main clause＋V 與十大句法九：S, Adj clause, V 的綜合與變化。

3. 觀察四個選項可知本題的考試重點為時態變化。配合 people 這個複數名詞與時態（搶案已經發生），即可選出 were（在……）這個過去式選項。

This proposal for a new high speed train _____ because the cost is too high.

(A) rejected

(B) has rejected

(C) had been rejected

(D) will be rejected

1. 我們可先將句子拆解如下：

This proposal for a new high speed train _____ / because the cost is too high.

這項建造新高鐵的提案 _____ / 因為成本太高

2. 拆解過後，發現這句話的句構為「S＋V＋連接詞＋S＋V」，得知前後句有邏輯關係。因此空格應選被動式，以表示提案被否決。

3. 觀察四個選項可知本題的考試重點為時態變化與被動式，配合句子的時態呈現在語意 the cost is too high，可選出 (D) will be rejected（未來式，將被拒絕）這個答案。

_____ many desirable qualities which make it a commercially very useful metal.

(A) Aluminum has

(B) That aluminum has

(C) Aluminum having

(D) Aluminum to have

1. 我們可先將句子拆解如下：

Grammar for Global English
全民英檢中級

_____ many desirable qualities / which make it a commercially very useful metal.

_____ 許多有用的特質 /（那些特質）讓鋁成為極具商業用途的金屬

2. 拆解過後，發現這句話的句法為「S + V + Adj clause」。

3. 觀察選項發現這一題在考主詞與動詞的基本概念。本句缺少一個動詞，因此選擇 (A) Aluminum has（鋁含有）即可。

Susan had a terrible day. First she __(1)__ up by a strange phone call at four o' clock this morning. When she was about to __(2)__ the receiver, the phone stopped ringing. Then she got up at late and __(3)__ the company bus, so she was thirty minutes late for work, __(4)__ made her boss very angry. What was __(5)__ , when she got home this afternoon, she couldn' t open the door because she had left her keys at her office.

題 (1)

(A) woke   (B) was woken

(C) wakes   (D) is awake

1. 題 1 的句子可以拆解如下：

First she __(1)__ up by a strange phone call / at four o' clock this morning.

首先她被一個陌生的來電 __(1)__ / 今早四點鐘

2. 觀察選項發現本題在考主動與被動的概念，因此只要配合時態，即可選出 (B) was woken（被吵醒）這個答案。

題 (4)

(A) that   (B) this

(C) what   (D) which

1. 題 4 的句子可以拆解如下：

Then she got up at late / and __(3)__ the company bus, / so she was thirty minutes late for work, / __(4)__ made her boss very angry.

然後她晚起 / 而且 <u>(3)</u> 公司巴士 / 所以她上班遲到了三十分鐘 / <u>(4)</u> 使得她的老闆非常生氣

2. 拆解過後，發現這句話的句法為「S + V + 連接詞 (so) + S + V」，得知前後句有關邏輯關係，而且後 so 之後的子句又包含從屬結構「S + V + 形容詞子句」。

3. 這題在考關係詞的概念，根據關係代名詞的特性（that 之前不可以有逗號），即使不看題 (3)，我們仍然能夠選出 (D) which 這個答案。

誠如在上一章「 多益篇」解說有關語意的理解與閱讀技巧，全民英檢考試的閱讀測驗也可用同樣的方式來閱讀。

語意的理解過程：（與前述閱讀的技巧一樣）

1. 找出主詞與動詞
2. 將句子拆解成具語意觀念的小單元
3. 熟悉各種不同情境的動詞或是名詞表達方式

在以上三種英文理解過程中，重視的有兩點：

◎與情境相關的單字學習
◎透過句法分析或是拆解後，理解文意

以下挑戰一篇較長的文章範例：（全民英檢中高級新型閱讀測驗）

Biofuel industries are expanding in Europe, Asia, and the U.S. Globally, biofuels are most commonly used to power vehicles. They have become popular among car drivers nowadays because they are less expensive than gasoline and other fossil fuels, particularly as worldwide demand for oil increases. Nevertheless, doubts have been raised as to whether biofuel production does more good than harm.

One of the claimed advantages of biofuels is that they are kinder to the environment than fuels made from petroleum, whereas in fact, biofuels increase the amount of carbon dioxide in the air even further when they are burned. According to biofuel proponents, this is more than offset by the crops raised for biofuel production, for these absorb carbon dioxide and release oxygen as they grow. Recent research, however, shows that the energy used to cultivate and process these crops also causes pollution. **So in reality, biofuels offer no overall benefit for the environment.**

Other advocates support the production of biofuels because they enhance energy security. Countries like the U.S. claim that domestic biofuel production can protect the integrity of their energy sources by reducing their current dependence on fuel imports. **But even if official goals are met, biofuels will supply only 5% of the transportation fuel requirements in the U.S. by 2012.**

This will have a negligible effect on America's reliance on imported oil. The U.S. government believes that the use of food-based biofuels should increase because of national energy security and high gas prices. **On the contrary, some international food scientists have recommended forbidding the use of these biofuels, which would reduce corn prices by 20%.** Since 2005, grain prices have increased by up to 80% worldwide. One major factor contributing to the dramatic rise is that the grain needed to feed people has been diverted to biofuel production. **This has led to a global food crisis.**

Clearly, the alleged benefits of today's biofuels are illusory. However, scientists are developing second-generation biofuels made from algae and waste wood. These new biofuels may indeed help the environment without reducing the grain supply. But until they are ready, **biofuel production must be halted in order to relieve pressure on grain prices and help the world's poor.**

（引自語言測驗中心網頁 http://www.lttc.ntu.edu.tw/geptnews/questions.htm）

此篇文章談論生質燃料的發展，並論及此燃料的一些好處與缺失等。

閱讀文章時，熟悉某些單字固然重要，但絕非關鍵；關鍵的反而是語意之間的連接。看到長篇文章，首先針對每一句話找到主詞與動詞，然後再將長句依照句法結構拆成具語意的小單元。以第一段為例：

Biofuel industries are expanding / in Europe, / Asia, / and the U.S. Globally,/ biofuels are most commonly used / to power vehicles. **They have become** popular / among car drivers / nowadays / because **they are** less expensive / than gasoline and other fossil fuels, / particularly as worldwide demand for oil / increases. Nevertheless, / **doubts have been raised** / as to / whether biofuel production does more good / than harm.

此句的主要都是「主詞＋動詞」結構，很容易就可找到（粗體字部分）。文法上只有兩個重點：一是時態（第一句為現在進行式，其他句為完成式 have / has＋PP），另一個重點是比較（less expensive than...）。如此拆解分析完後，選擇題第二題的答案就出來了：

題目：According to this article, why do drivers prefer biofuels to gasoline?
    (A) They are more fuel-efficient.
    (B) They are more affordable.
    (C) They are better for the engine.
    (D) They are more powerful.

這個問題在詢問事實，因此閱讀內容後（駕駛喜歡生質燃料，因為它們比較便宜 less expensive than gasoline and other fossil fuels），可知答案為 (B) They are more affordable.（比較負擔得起）。

題目：What does the author mainly argue in this article?
    (A) Biofuel production should be discouraged.
    (B) Corn biofuels should be promoted more.
    (C) Biofuel manufacturers should be rewarded.
    (D) Higher biofuel goals should be set.

此題測驗應試著對整篇文章的理解，詢問「作者的主要主張為何？」儘管前面提到生質燃料的好處，但是中間也提及一些生質燃料的問題，請先閱讀文中的粗體字，如 ：On the contrary, / some international food scientists / have recommended / forbidding the use of these biofuels, / which would reduce corn prices / by 20%. 再閱讀最後一句話：But until they are ready, / biofuel production / must be halted / in order to / relieve pressure on / grain prices / and help the world's poor. 此句主要結構為生質燃料的生產應該要停止（halted）。

全文一方面陳述燃料的好處，一方面提出反對意見，最後建議停止生產，因此第一題的答案為 (A) Biofuel production should be discouraged.（不應該鼓勵生產生質燃料）。

英檢考題主要是測試理解力，因此除了對單字的認識外，出現的文章大多在釐清一些與我們息息相關的問題，有時也會反駁一些舊有的看法（如上文，大家長久以來認為生質燃料很環保，應該多用，但是作者認為問題很多！）這種類型的文章最常用來挑戰應試者的英文理解能力。

以下為一篇克漏字填空，請按照本篇的說明，先拆解句子，再根據選項判斷考題重點，選出正確答案。

（引自全民英檢中級閱讀能力測驗預試 Form RTI-A）

Because the beautiful lake country of central Canada has few roads but thousands of lakes and streams, __(1)__ is best explored by canoe. All the lakes are connected to __(2)__ by trails, called portages, and most lakes have one or two camping areas to choose from. Visitors can start their __(3)__ on one lake, paddle their canoe __(4)__ lake. In this way, they can __(5)__ from lake to lake while they enjoy the fresh air, clean water and quiet surroundings of this beautiful area.

題 1

(A) there   (B) it   (C) which   (D) that

題 2

(A) another   (B) the other   (C) each other   (D) other

題 3

(A) journey   (B) flight   (C) hike   (D) course

題 4

(A) beside   (B) within   (C) across   (D) toward

題 5

(A) drive   (B) begin   (C) ride   (D) travel

指考

　　大學入學指定考科測驗可以說是目前最困難的升學測驗。一般考生都認為指考的考試範圍太過龐大，不知該如何準備，於是只能拚命練習坊間的參考書與測驗卷，用亂槍打鳥的方式，增進自己的英文能力。

　　但是，指考的內容是可以掌握的。指考之所以困難，是因為它跳脫課本，考了日常生活所應用的英文，並且增加翻譯與寫作這項考題。

　　如同本書一再強調的，常使用的英文文法其實沒那麼多。幾乎所有的句子都是「S＋V＋O」的基本句型、加上主、次結構的概念，頂多加上前面所介紹的十大句法，應付指考的文法測驗，便已綽綽有餘。

　　指考真正難的地方是測驗學生是否能夠靈活運用英文。相較於基測、學測考的是學生的「英文知識」，指考考的是學生的「基本英文能力」。知識並不等同於能力。你能夠背誦許多文法細節和單字，卻不能夠靈活使用，那就是讀死書而已。但如果你能夠隨心所欲的使用英文寫出一篇日記或是作文而沒有阻礙（尤其是不用翻工具書），

那才叫做有英文「能力」。如果你能夠打開英文網站卻不感到排斥，或是閱讀英文小說、新聞而不感困難，那就是你真正接受英文了。這也就是為什麼指考的作文占了 20% 的配分。只有將英文內化，才能夠真正運用英文。分辨誰只有英文知識、誰才有英文能力，這才是指考測驗的真正目的。

★文法要點

☆ 動詞語意

In fact, the Earth **receives** 20,000 times more energy from the sun than we currently use.

☆ 介系詞用法

For instance, many satellites in space are equipped with large panels whose solar cells transform sunlight directly **into** electric power.

☆ 形容詞語意

To begin with, it is a clean fuel. In contrast, fossil fuels, such as oil or coal, release **harmful** substances into the air when they are burned.

☆ 連接詞語意

What's more, fossil fuels will run out, but solar energy will continue to reach the Earth long after the last coal has been mined and the last oil well has run dry.

★ 範例說明

The sun is an extraordinarily powerful source of energy. In fact, the Earth (1) 20,000 times more energy from the sun than we currently use. If we used more of this source of heat and light, it (2) all the power needed throughout the world.

We can harness energy from the sun, or solar energy, in many ways. For instance, many satellites in space are equipped with large panels whose solar cells transform sunlight directly (3) electric power. These panels are covered with glass and are painted black inside to absorb as much heat as possible.

Solar energy has a lot to offer. To begin with, it is a clean fuel. In contrast, fossil fuels, such as oil or coal, release (4) substances into the air when they are burned. (5) , fossil fuels will run out, but solar energy will continue to reach the Earth long after the last coal has been mined and the last oil well has run dry.

題 1
(A) repeats   (B) receives   (C) rejects   (D) reduces

1. 首先我們可將句子拆解如下：

   The sun is an extraordinarily powerful source of energy. / In fact, / the Earth (1) 20,000 times more energy from the sun / than we currently use.

   太陽是一個驚人的能量來源 / 事實上 / 地球從太陽 (1) 多了兩萬倍的能量 / 比我們目前使用的能量

2. 根據選項判斷本題在考動詞語意；又根據上文得知太陽提供了驚人的能量，因此選擇 (B) receives，以表示地球從太陽接收能源。

題 2
(A) supplies   (B) has supplied   (C) was supplying   (D) could supply

1. 首先我們可將句子拆解如下：

   If we used more of this source of heat and light, / it (2) all the power needed / throughout the world.

   如果我們使用更多這樣的熱能和光能 / 它就 (2) 所有的能源需求 / 整個世界

Grammar for Global English
指考

191

2. 根據題目中的 if 判斷本題在考假設「If S + were / Ved, S + 助動詞 + V」，因此選
   (D) could supply。(假設法請參考附錄二的說明)

題 3

(A) into   (B) from   (C) with   (D) off

1. 首先我們可將句子拆解如下：

   For instance, / many satellites in space / are equipped with large panels / whose
   solar cells transform sunlight directly / (3) electric power.
   例如 / 許多太空中的衛星 / 都裝設大型面板 /（這些面板的）太陽能電池能夠直
   接轉換太陽能 / (3) 電能

2. 根據選項判斷本題在考介系詞用法。配合動詞 transform 的片語用法「transform
   A into B」（將 A 轉變成 B），因此可選出 (A) into 這個答案。

題 4

(A) diligent   (B) harmful   (C) usable   (D) changeable

1. 首先我們可將句子拆解如下：

   To begin with, / it is a clean fuel. / In contrast, / fossil fuels, / such as oil or coal, /
   release (4) substances into the air / when they are burned.
   首先 / 它是乾淨的燃料 / 相反的 / 礦物燃料 / 例如石油或碳 / 釋放 (4) 物質到空
   氣中 / 當它們燃燒的時候

2. 根據選項判斷本題在考形容詞語意，再根據句中的轉折 In contrast，可知應選
   與 clean 對比的詞彙，因此 (B) harmful 為最適合的答案。

題 5

(A) Otherwise   (B) Therefore   (C) What's more   (D) In comparison

1. 首先我們可將句子拆解如下：

   (5) , / fossil fuels will run out, / but solar energy will continue to reach the Earth
   / long after the last coal has been mined / and the last oil well has run dry.

(5)　／礦物燃料會有用完的一天／但是太陽能將會持續傳遞到地球／一直到最後一個煤礦被挖出／以及最後一個油井被採光

2. 根據選項判斷本題在考連接詞語意，再根據上下文，可得知此句接續上文，持續談論太陽能的優點，因此可知最符合的答案為 (C) What's more（而且，再者）。

練習與作業

　　以下為一篇克漏字測驗，請按照本篇的說明，先拆解句子，再根據選項判斷考題重點，並選出正確答案。

Signs asking visitors to keep their hands off the art are everywhere in the Louvre Museum, Paris. But one special sculpture gallery invites art lovers to allow their hands to ＿(1)＿ the works. The Louvre's Tactile Gallery, targeted at the blind and visually ＿(2)＿, is the only space in the museum where visitors can touch the sculptures, with no guards or alarms to stop them. Its latest exhibit is a ＿(3)＿ of sculpted lions, snakes, horses and eagles. The 15 animals exhibited are reproductions of famous works found elsewhere in the Louvre. Called "Animals, Symbols of Power," the exhibit ＿(4)＿ animals that were used by kings and emperors throughout history to symbolize the greatness of their reigns. The exhibit, opened in December 2008, ＿(5)＿ scheduled to run for about three years. During guided tours on the weekends, children can explore the art with blindfolds on.

題 1

(A) fix up
(B) run over
(C) take away
(D) knock off

Grammar for Global English
指考

193

題 2

(A) impair   (B) impairs   (C) impaired   (D) impairing

題 3

(A) collection   (B) cooperation   (C) completion   (D) contribution

題 4

(A) examines   (B) protects   (C) represents   (D) features

題 5

(A) is   (B) being   (C) has   (D) having

考試篇

學測

　　如同國中基測，高中升大學的學科能力測驗也不困難，只是考試的範圍多了「語意理解」一項。一般來說，在溝通時最常使用的文法在國中英語教育裡就已經全部教授完畢，高中只是重新複習，並且學習如何綜合不同的文法結構，將句子拉長而已。

　　只是一旦將句子拉長，語意的理解就相對困難。但是，其實只要掌握住主結構、次結構的分別，就能夠輕鬆拆解句子、理解語意。如果國中英文底子不好，也不用擔心。同樣只要掌握基本句型「S＋V＋O」，並且仔細學習主、次結構的用法，高中文法一樣不成問題。相較之下，若是已經掌握了文法結構的變化，則是建議大家多多閱讀課外讀物，例如英文小說或是新聞英文，以增加單字量。

★文法要點

☆ 名詞語意

Due to **inflation**, prices for daily necessities have gone up and we have to pay more for the same items now.

☆ 副詞語意

John has been scolded by his boss for over ten minutes now. **Apparently**, she is not happy about his being late again.

☆ 介系詞語意

Fresh onions are available **in** yellow, red and white throughout their season, March through August.

☆ 形容詞語意

More often than that, those in their early twenties are the more **informed** consumers.

☆ 動詞片語語意

Interestingly, both of them **ended up** buying the same pair of jeans.

★範例說明

Due to _____, prices for daily necessities have gone up and we have to pay more for the same items now.

(A) inflation　　　(B) solution　　　(C) objection　　　(D) condition

1. 首先我們可將句子拆解如下：

   Due to _____ , / prices for daily necessities have gone up / and we have to pay more for the same items now.

   因為 _____ / 生活必需品價格上漲 / 而我們現在必須花更多錢去買一樣的物品

2. 觀察四個選項可知本題的考試重點為 inflation / solution / objection / condition 四個名詞的語意。配合文意即可選出 (A) inflation（通貨膨脹）這個答案。

John has been scolded by his boss for over ten minutes now. _____ , she is not happy about his being late again.

(A) Expressively 　　(B) Apparently 　　(C) Immediately 　　(D) Originally

1. 我們可先將句子拆解如下：

   John has been scolded by his boss for over ten minutes now. / _____ , / she is not happy about his being late again.

   約翰現在已經被他老闆罵超過十分鐘了 / _____ / 她對約翰又遲到這件事感到不悅

2. 觀察發現四個選項得知本題考試重點為 expressively / apparently / immediately / originally 這四個副詞的語意。配合文意即可選出 (B) Apparently（顯然地）這個答案。

More often than that, those in their early twenties are the more _____ consumers. There isn't a brand or a trend that these young people are not aware of.

(A) informed 　　(B) informative 　　(C) informal 　　(D) informational

1. 我們可先將句子拆解如下：

   More often than that, / those in their early twenties / are the more _____ consumers.

   更重要的是 / 那些二十出頭的年輕人 / 是比較 _____ 顧客

Grammar for Global English
學測

2. 觀察四個選項可知本題的考試重點為形容詞的語意。配合下一句文意即可知應選 (A) informed（訊息豐富）這個答案。

Onions can be divided into two categories: fresh onions and storage onions. Fresh onions are available _____ yellow, red and white throughout their season, March through August.

(A) from   (B) for   (C) in   (D) of

1. 我們可先將句子拆解如下：

Onions can be divided into two categories: / fresh onions and storage onions. / Fresh onions are available / _____ yellow, red and white / throughout their season, / March through August.

洋蔥可分為兩種 / 新鮮洋蔥和貯藏洋蔥 / 新鮮洋蔥是可取得的 / _____ 黃色、紅色和白色 / 在洋蔥盛產季裡 / 從三月到八月

2. 觀察四個選項可知本題的考試重點為 from / for / in / of 四個介系詞的語意。配合文意可知需選 (C) in ＋顏色，表示洋蔥有……的顏色。

以下有一篇克漏字填空,請按照本篇的說明,先拆解句子,再根據選項判斷考題重點,並選出正確答案。

Many people like to drink bottled water because they feel that tap water may not be safe, but is bottled water really any better?

Bottled water is mostly sold in plastic bottles and that's why it is potentially health __(1)__ . Processing the plastic can lead to the release of harmful chemical substances into the water contained in the bottles. The chemicals can be absorbed into the body and __(2)__ physical discomfort, such as stomach cramps and diarrhea.

Health risks can also result from inappropriate storage of bottled water. Bacteria can multiply if the water is kept on the shelves for too long or if it is exposed to heat or direct sunlight. __(3)__ the information on storage and shipment is not always readily available to consumers, bottled water may not be a better alternative to tap water.

Besides these __(4)__ issues, bottled water has other disadvantages. It contributes to global warming. An estimated 2.5 million tons of carbon dioxide were generated in 2006 by the production of plastic for bottled water. In addition, bottled water produces an incredible amount of solid __(5)__ . According to one research, 90% of the bottles used are not recycled and lie for ages in landfills.

題 1
(A) frightening   (B) threatening   (C) appealing   (D) promoting

題 2
(A) cause   (B) causing   (C) caused   (D) to cause

Grammar for Global English
學測

題 3

(A) Although   (B) Despite   (C) Since   (D) So

題 4

(A) display   (B) production   (C) shipment   (D) safety

題 5

(A) waste   (B) resource   (C) ground   (D) profit

統測

　　四技二專的統測難度，大約接近大學學測。如同前面一再強調的，只要掌握基本的「S＋V＋O」結構、十大句法，以及主次結構的概念就綽綽有餘了。

　　和學測相同，統測也測驗學生的語意理解能力，與日常生活的英文使用能力。同樣建議大家要跳脫課本，不要讀死書。盡量多接觸日常生活中真正有在使用的英文，你才能夠將課本所教的死文法變靈活運用。多看看大家怎麼說、怎麼寫、怎麼用，自然而然英文就會被內化成為你腦中的一份子。

Mother : You look tired. Why don't you go to bed earlier today?
Jimmy : I can't. I have an English test tomorrow.
Mother : Don't worry. You'll be fine.
Jimmy : I haven't finished reviewing yet. I don't want to take any chances.

☆ 名詞語意

According to some religious leaders, people who come to pray should wear clothing that shows respect and **admiration** for their religion.

☆ 形容詞用法

On the other hand, there are many religious leaders who don't care about such **material** issues.

☆ 關係代名詞用法

They believe that religion, **which** is a spiritual matter, isn't concerned with clothing.

☆ 介系詞用法

Most people think that the issue actually goes **beyond** clothing.

★範例說明

Mother : You look tired. Why don't you go to bed earlier today?
Jimmy : I can't. I have an English test tomorrow.
Mother : _____
Jimmy : I haven't finished reviewing yet. I don't want to take any chances.

(A) Don't worry. You'll be fine.

(B) You should study earlier.

(C) How about a cup of coffee?

(D) Is that the only test tomorrow?

1. 首先，我們先理解文意：

   媽媽：你看起來很累。今天怎麼不早點睡呢？

   吉米：不行啊。我明天要考英文。

   媽媽：＿＿＿＿＿＿＿＿＿＿＿＿＿＿＿＿

   吉米：我還沒複習完。我可不想心存僥倖。

2. 根據選項判斷本題在考文意理解。由吉米的最後一個回應「還沒複習完、不想心存僥倖」，即可得知吉米婉拒了媽媽的某種好意，因此 (A) 是最好的答案。

Opinions are strongly divided about the type of clothing which is appropriate for worship. According to some religious leaders, people who come to pray should wear clothing that shows respect and __(1)__ for their religion. They shouldn't be wearing clothes that are for jogging, shopping, or attending a ball game. On the other hand, there are many religious leaders who don't care about such __(2)__ issues. They believe that religion, __(3)__ is a spiritual matter, isn't concerned with clothing. They welcome everyone who attends religious services. Most people think that the issue actually goes __(4)__ clothing. More formal clothing usually accompanies an atmosphere which is more traditional and __(5)__. Informal clothing, however, is more acceptable in religious services that are more contemporary and informal.

題 1

(A) limitation   (B) admiration   (C) restriction   (D) comparison

1. 首先我們可以把句子拆解如下：

   According to some religious leaders, / people who come to pray should wear clothing / that shows respect and __(1)__ / for their religion.

Grammar for Global English 統測

203

根據一些宗教領導者 / 前來祈禱的人們的穿著應該 / 表現尊敬和 __(1)__ / 對他們的宗教

2. 根據選項可判斷本題在考名詞語意，再根據連接詞 and 即可得知本題應選擇與 respect（尊敬）有關的正面詞彙，因此選 (B) admiration（讚賞）。

題 **2**

(A) healthy   (B) diligent   (C) sincere   (D) material

1. 首先我們可以把句子拆解如下：

On the other hand, / there are many religious leaders / who don't care about such __(2)__ issues.

在另一方面 / 也有許多宗教領導者 / 並不在意這些 __(2)__ 問題

2. 本題在考形容詞用法，根據文意可判斷這裡談論的 issue 應該是衣著問題，由下句的 spiritual matter（心靈層面的事情）判斷，應選擇與 spiritual 成對比的形容詞，故選擇 (D) material（物質的）。

題 **3**

(A) who   (B) what   (C) which   (D) why

1. 首先我們可以把句子拆解如下：

They believe that religion, / __(3)__ is a spiritual matter, / isn't concerned with clothing.

他們相信宗教信仰 / __(3)__ 是心靈層面的事情 / 跟服裝無關

2. 判斷句構為「S + V + that 子句 (S + Adj clause + V)」。

3. 本題在考關係詞（which）的用法，根據句構與 religion，即可選出 which 來修飾說明前面的 religion。

題 **4**

(A) beyond   (B) along   (C) against   (D) between

1. 首先我們可以把句子拆解如下：

   Most people think / that the issue actually goes __(4)__ clothing.

   大部分的人認為 / 事實上這個議題其實 __(4)__ 服裝（層面）了

2. 根據選項可知本題在考搭配動詞 go 的介系詞用法，再根據下文（正式服裝和非正式服裝適合穿著場合的不同），即可得知服裝與一個人對宗教的虔敬程度事實上並沒有任何相關，也就是此議題已經 go beyond（超越，超出）服裝層面了，因此選 (A)。

題 **5**

(A) playful   (B) naughty   (C) serious   (D) casual

1. 首先我們可以把句子拆解如下：

   More formal clothing usually accompanies an atmosphere / which is more traditional and __(5)__ .

   較正式的服裝通常伴隨著一種氛圍 /（這種氛圍）較為傳統且 __(5)__

2. 根據選項判斷本題在考形容詞語意，再根據連接詞 and 得知本題應選擇與 traditional 有關的詞彙，因此 (C) serious（嚴肅的）是最佳答案。

Grammar for Global English
統測

練習與作業

以下為一篇克漏字測驗，請按照本篇的說明，先拆解句子，再根據選項判斷考題重點，並選出正確答案。

The tiger may be more ancient and distinct than we thought. Tigers are less closely related to lions, leopards and jaguars __(1)__ these other big cats are to each other, according to a new study. The genetic analysis also reveals that the tiger began evolving 3.2 million years ago, and its closest living __(2)__ is the equally endangered snow leopard. __(3)__ the popularity and endangered status of tigers, much remains to be discovered about them, including how they evolved. It has long been known that the five species of big cat—the tiger, lion, leopard, jaguar and snow leopard—and the two species of clouded leopard are more closely related to each other than to other smaller cats. But it has been difficult to pin __(4)__ the exact relationships between them. So to find out more, scientists __(5)__ an analysis of the DNA of all these species.

題 1

(A) than   (B) while   (C) before   (D) since

題 2

(A) demand   (B) battery   (C) method   (D) relative

題 3

(A) Both   (B) Despite   (C) Without   (D) From

題 4

(A) to   (B) on   (C) down   (D) under

題 5

(A) conducted   (B) mistreated   (C) ridiculed   (D) neglected

基測

國中基本能力測驗，顧名思義就是測驗最基本的英語能力。過去幾十年來，英語教學多注重在文法的細節以及單字的背誦，造成考生認為英文文法眾多、繁雜，且單字永遠背不完。但其實並不然。

最基本的英語能力，其實就是能夠使用單字的用法、基本的文法規則，以及一些基本詞性（如：動詞／助動詞／介系詞等）。這些東西都不難，只要有英文句型最基本的「S + V + O」概念，再掌握課本中的基本單字，國中基測輕而易舉就能拿高分。雖然未來將不再舉辦基測考試，但其試題仍可作為我們練習之用。

★文法要點

☆ 助動詞用法

Ken's brothers like to watch tennis, but Ken **doesn't**.

☆ 介系詞用法

There's something wrong **between** Gina and Greg.

☆ 動詞用法

The little boy jumped up and down happily when he saw a bee **flying** into the house.

☆ 關係代名詞用法

My father told me last night **that** we're going to the Food Festival this weekend.

☆ 比較

This restaurant sells the best steak in Taipei; you can't find **more delicious** steak in the city.

☆ 時間副詞用法

I'm really sorry, but the kitchen is very busy. You'll have it **soon**.

★範例說明

Ken's brothers like to watch tennis, but Ken _____ . He is crazy about baseball.

(A) is   (B) isn't   (C) does   (D) doesn't

1. 我們可以把句子拆解如下：

   Ken's brothers like to watch tennis, / but Ken _____ . / He is crazy about
   baseball.

   肯的哥哥很喜歡看網球 / 但是肯_____ / 他為棒球瘋狂

2. 判斷句構為「S＋V＋連接詞＋S＋V」，得知前後文有邏輯關係。

3. 根據選項可知本題在考助動詞用法。依照文意，發現 but 前後文的意思不同，
   因此空格內應為否定用法；再配合動詞 watch，即可選出答案 (D) doesn't。

There's something wrong _____ Gina and Greg. They haven't talked to each
other for over one month.

(A) beside   (B) between   (C) during   (D) under

1. 我們可以把句子拆解如下：

   There's something wrong / _____ Gina and Greg. / They haven't talked to
   each other / for over one month.

   有一些誤會 / _____ 吉娜和葛瑞 / 他們已經沒有跟對方說話 / 超過一個月了

2. 根據選項判斷本題在考介系詞（between）用法，因此 (B) between（在……之
   間）為最佳答案。

The little boy jumped up and down happily when he saw a bee _____ into
the house.

(A) flown   (B) to fly   (C) flying   (D) has flown

Grammar for
Global English
基測

1. 我們可以把句子拆解如下：

   The little boy jumped up and down happily / when he saw a bee
   / _____ into the house.

   那個小男孩開心地跳上跳下 / 當他看見一隻蜜蜂 / _____ 那棟房子

2. 判斷句構為「S＋V＋連結詞＋S＋V」。

3. 根據選項判斷本題在考動詞（see）的用法。配合 see 的動詞用法 (see ＋受詞＋
   V／Ving)，可知 (C) flying 為正確答案。

My father told me last night _____ we're going to the Food Festival this
weekend. My brother and I felt very excited.

(A) whether   (B) where   (C) what   (D) that

1. 我們可以把句子拆解如下：
   My father told me last night / _____ we're going to the Food Festival this
   weekend. / My brother and I felt very excited.
   我爸爸昨晚告訴我 / _____ 我們週末要去參加美食節 / 我哥和我感到非常興奮

2. 判斷句構為「S＋V＋關係代名詞＋名詞子句」。

3. 根據選項可知本題在考 whether／where／what／that 四個關係代名詞的用法，
   因此可根據關係代名詞 that 的特性（that ＋名詞子句）選出答案 (D)。

This restaurant sells the best steak in Taipei; you can't find _____ steak in the city.

(A) delicious   (B) more delicious
(C) the most delicious   (D) deliciously

1. 我們可以把句子拆解如下：
   This restaurant sells the best steak in Taipei; / you can't find ____ steak / in the
   city.
   這家餐廳販賣臺北最好吃的牛排 / 你沒辦法找到 _____ 牛排 / 在這個城市裡

2. 根據選項可知本題在考比較的用法。因為前文已經說這家餐廳的牛排是「最」好吃的，所以我們就選 (B) more delicious，表示沒有辦法再找到比這「更好的」牛排了。

Anita : I saw Nora in the teacher' s office this morning.

        Do you know _____ she was there?

Brian : She cheated on tests.

(A) how   (B) if   (C) when   (D) why

1. 我們可以把句子拆解如下：

    Anita : I saw Nora in the teacher' s office this morning.

        Do you know _____ she was there?

    Brian : She cheated on tests.

    艾妮塔：今早我看見諾拉在教師辦公室裡 / 你知道 _____ 她在那裡嗎

    布萊恩：她考試作弊

2. 根據選項，判斷本題在考 how / if / when / why 四個疑問詞的用法。再根據文意，即可知 (D) why 為正確答案。

Bobby : Where' s the food I ordered? I' ve waited for thirty minutes!

Waiter : I' m really sorry, but the kitchen is very busy. You' ll have it _____ .

(A) already   (B) early   (C) once   (D) soon

1. 我們可以把句子拆解如下：

    Bobby : Where' s the food I ordered? / I' ve waited for thirty minutes!

    Waiter : I' m really sorry, / but the kitchen is very busy.

        / You' ll have it _____ .

    鮑比：我點的食物呢 / 我已經等三十分鐘了

    服務生：真的非常抱歉 / 但是廚房非常忙碌

         / 你 _____ 就會有你點的菜了

Grammar for Global English
基測

2. 根據選項判斷本題在考 already / early / once / soon 四個時間副詞的用法，
   再依文意判斷可知答案為 (D) soon（很快）。

 練習與作業

　　以下有一篇克漏字測驗、一篇閱讀測驗，請按照本篇的說明，先拆解句
子、再根據選項判斷考題重點，並選出正確答案。

〈克漏字測驗〉

　　A small town has a good chance of (1) that can bring in a lot of money,
if it has something special to be proud of. One example is Gukeng town of
Yunllin, Taiwan. Gukeng has long been famous for growing good coffee, but
the town didn't start to make much money from it until some years ago. As
more and more people have visited Gukeng for its coffee, the coffee farmers
have begun to open their farms to the public. At these farms, people can
have the fun of finding out where coffee comes from. (2) , coffee shops are
opened all over Gukeng, and people can take a rest and taste delicious coffee
on the sidewalks in or after a day's visit. The new businesses make a better life
possible for those who (3) the town. They don't have to leave the town to
find jobs in other places.

題 1

(A) growing the best tea   (B) starting a new business
(C) selling old farming lands   (D) opening a shopping center

題 2

(A) First   (B) Also   (C) However   (D) For example

題 3

(A) live in   (B) hear about   (C) take a trip to   (D) are interested in

〈閱讀測驗〉

Read Cindy's diary and answer the questions.

Nov. 13, 1990

    Today I got a letter from Jenny, my new friend in America. I wrote her last week, and it was my first time to write a letter in English. I was worried that she wouldn't get my letter. But **she did**, and she wrote back a nice long letter. She told me a lot about her family, school life, and the things she likes to do on holidays. I found we both love watching basketball games and think of Michael Jordan as the greatest player ever.

    I can't wait to get a letter from Jenny again. It's so much fun to share things with a foreign friend. In my next letter, I will tell her some interesting things about my school.

題 4

What does **she did** mean?

(A) Jenny got the letter.

(B) Jenny wrote in English.

(C) Jenny wrote back a nice long letter.

(D) Jenny told Cindy about her family and school life.

題 5

Which is said about Cindy?

(A) She is a sports fan.

(B) She will visit Jenny.

(C) She wants to teach Jenny to speak Chinese.

(D) She often writes to foreign friends in English.

Grammar for Global English
基測

附錄一

五大句型

　　「英文文法那麼多,該怎麼辦?」這往往是英文學習者最感頭痛的問題。但英文文法再多,其實也不脫五種最基本的句型。這些句型雖然基本,但同時也是最重要的句型,因為比較複雜的文法往往是從這些句型演變出來的。因此,只要理解這五種句型,便可以運用自如。

1. 主詞 + 動詞（S + V）
2. 主詞 + 動詞 + 受詞（S + V + O）
3. 主詞 + 動詞 + 修飾主詞的字詞（S + V + C）
4. 主詞 + 動詞 + 受詞 + 受詞（S + V + O1 + O2）
5. 主詞 + 動詞 + 受詞 + 修飾主詞的字詞（S + V + O + C）

　　從前面五大句型來看,「動詞」就是影響這些句型的主要關鍵。在此,其實不用在意這些動詞是所謂「及物」或「不及物」動詞,只要知道不同的動詞產生不同的句法即可。

◎ **She / runs.**

◎ **I / like / roses.**

◎ **The weather / is / nice and cool today.**

◎ **Please hand/ it / to me.** （98 年國中第二次基測）

◎ **I / have / a math test / at four o'clock.** （98 年國中第二次基測）

★主詞 + 動詞（S + V）

「主詞 + 動詞」是最為基本的句型，也是每個完整的句子都必備的基本元素。但在這種句型中，動詞可以獨立發生，自行有所動作。

◎ She / runs.
   S   V
  她 / 跑步

◎ Nothing / happens.
    S   V
  沒有任何事 / 發生

★主詞 + 動詞 + 修飾主詞的字詞（S + V + O）

除了上面的動詞之外，有一種動詞不能夠獨立發生，而是需要一個受詞（名詞）來承受這個動作。

◎ I / like / roses.
 S V O
  我 / 喜歡 / 玫瑰

※ 如果這個句子只寫成 I like，讀者或聽者就無法得知說話的人喜歡什麼東西；因此受詞 roses 是必要的存在。少了這個受詞，I like 這個句子就不完整了。

◎ The cat / drinks / some milk.
　　　 S　　　 V　　　　O

那隻貓 / 喝 / 一些牛奶

※ 同理，如果這個句子只寫成 The cat drinks，讀者或聽者就無法得知那隻貓喝了什麼東西；
　 因此受詞 some milk 是必要的存在，沒有這個受詞的話，句子就不完整了。

★主詞 + 動詞 + 修飾主詞的字詞（S + V + C）

所謂「修飾字詞」就是拿來當作說明的用語，在此句型中是拿來對主詞作補充說
明，或修飾補充一些讀者或聽者可能不知道的、關於主詞的資訊，使語意完整。

◎ The weather / is / nice and cool / today.　　　　（98 年國中第二次基測）
　　　 S　　　 V　　　 C

天氣 / 是 / 很好而且涼爽 / 今天

※ 如果這個句子只寫成 The weather is，讀者或聽者就不會知道今天的天氣到底如何。後
　 方的 nice and cool 指出今天是涼爽的好天氣，這才說明了主詞 The weather 是處於什麼
　 樣的狀態。

◎ The tall man over there / is / our new English teacher, / isn't he?
　　　　　 S　　　　　　　 V　　　 C

那邊那個高高的男子 / 是 / 我們的新英文老師 / 不是嗎

※ 同理，如果這個句子只寫成 The tall man over there is，讀者或聽者就不會懂這句話到底
　 要說什麼。後方必須再寫出 our new English teacher，才能讓人理解原來 The tall man
　 是我們新英文老師。

★主詞 + 動詞 + 受詞 + 受詞（S + V + O1 + O2）

「授予動詞」的用法較為特殊。因為牽涉到兩個對象及一個物品，
因此會出現兩個受詞的情況。

Grammar for Global English
附錄一
五大句型

◎ Please <u>hand/</u> <u>it</u> / <u>to me.</u>   （98 年國中第二次基測）
        V   O₁   O₂

請傳遞 / 那個 / 給我

※ 因為 hand（傳遞）這個動作牽扯到兩個人和一個物品，所以會出現「A 把某物傳給 B」
　 這樣的情形，那某物和 B 就是「傳遞」這個動作的兩個受詞了。

◎ <u>The woman</u> you met in the library yesterday / <u>will give</u> / <u>our school</u> / <u>a lot of</u>
        S   V   O₁   O₂
<u>books.</u>   （98 年國中第二次基測）

你昨天在圖書館遇到的那個女人 / 將會給 / 我們學校 / 很多書

※ 同理，因為 give（給予）這個動作牽涉到兩個人和一個物品，所以會出現「A 給 B 某物」
　 這樣的情形，而 B 和某物就是「給予」這個動作的兩個受詞。

★主詞 ＋動詞＋受詞＋修飾主詞的字詞（S ＋ V ＋ O ＋ C）

除了主詞之外，修飾主詞的字詞也能拿來替受詞作補充說明，使語意完整。

◎ <u>We</u> / <u>call</u> / <u>the new pet</u> / <u>Cathy.</u>
    S   V   O   C

我們 / 叫 / 新的寵物 / Cathy

※ 這個句子如果只說 We call the new pet 意思不完整，加上 Cathy 來修飾 pet 意思才完整。

◎ <u>The fireworks</u> / <u>made</u> / <u>the shows</u> / <u>more interesting.</u>
      S   V   O   C

煙火 / 讓 / 表演 / 更有趣

※ 後面加上 more interesting 來修飾 the shows，才會是 make ＋ N ＋ Adj（使……是……的
　 意思）。

假設法

「假設法」一直是學英文的過程中最讓人感到挫折的環節之一，一來用法特殊，二來文法較為繁複。中文多以「如果」、「假如」、「假設」來提示某種設想的情境，但英文卻會用時態變化或某些助動詞來提示。少了「如果」、「假如」、「假設」這些提詞，英文的假設法好像就變難了。

但是事實卻相反，我們恰好可以利用英文的時態變化，來抓住假設法的精髓。假設的表達方式有三種：與現在事實不同、與過去事實不同，與未來事實不同的假設，其文法變化如下：

◎與現在事實不同的假設：were 或 Ved

◎與過去事實不同的假設：had + PP 或 助動詞 + have + PP

◎與未來事實不同的假設：were to + V

看懂了嗎？其實只要將時態往「過去」多推一個時間點，就是假設用法了。至於比較特別的與未來事實不同的假設，因為使用狀況極少，在此先略過不談。建議大家也不需要刻意去記，只要理解前兩種用法，就很夠用了。

最後，助動詞 could / should / would / might 是拿來修飾語氣、輔助語意用的。有時候只需要助動詞，就有假設的意味存在。只要弄清楚這幾個助動詞之間的差異，假設法就不再困難了。

一般來說，國際溝通中，幾乎不使用假設法，因為在非母語人士溝通中，講究直接、清楚且明白地傳遞信息與事實，大都不使用這種過度修飾的用法。

◎ If women didn't exist, all the money in the world would have no meaning.

◎ If Steven had not dropped out of school 10 years ago, he would not have had a chance to start his business.

◎ We should stop letting unskilled laborers into Japan... （《紐時周報》）

◎ We could have deployed the full force of American power...（歐巴馬當選演說）

文法解析

★與現在事實不同的假設（If S + were / Ved, S + 助動詞 + V）

與現在事實不同的假設，意指「若是當下發生某事，則現在的某個事實就會產生改變」。

◎ If women **didn't** exist, / all the money in the world / **would have** no meaning.
　　　　　　Ved　　　　　　　　　　　　　　　　助動詞 + V
如果沒有女人的話 / 世上所有的錢 / 就沒有意義了　　（Aristotle 亞里斯多德）

※ 1. If 後方接的子句是與現在事實不同的假設情境。

　　因為是一種假設，所以用**過去式**（didn't exist）與現在的事實作區別。

　2. 後半段的子句 all the money...no meaning 則指出如果女人真的不存在的話，會產生什麼樣的改變。因為這改變也並非事實，因此用**助動詞（過去式）+ V** 再一次與現在的事實作區分。

　3. 助動詞 **would** 意指「就會」。不同的助動詞有不同的意義，舉列如下：

　　could（能夠）；should（應該）；might（也許）

◎ How dreary / **would be** the world / if there **were** no Santa Claus!
　　　　　　助動詞 + V　　　　　　　　　過去式 were
多麼無趣 / 這世界會是 / 如果沒有聖誕老人的話

※ 1. If 後方接的子句是與現在事實不同的假設情境。因是一種假設，所以用過去式（were）
與現在的事實作區別；在假設法中，即使主詞不是 you，Be 動詞也一律用 were。

2. 前半段的子句 How dreary would be the world 則指出如果真的沒有聖誕老人的話，會
產生什麼樣的改變。因為這改變也並非事實，因此用**助動詞 + V** 再一次與現在的事實
作區分。

◎ If we **used** more of this source of heat and light, / it **could supply** / all the

      Ved   助動詞 + V

      power needed throughout the world.   （99 年大學指考）

如果我們使用更多這種熱能和光能的來源的話 / 它就可以提供 / 世界上需要的
所有能源

※ 1. If 後方接的子句是與現在事實不同的假設情境。
因為是一種假設，所以用過去式（used）與現在的事實作區別。

2. 後半段的子句 it could supply...throughout the world 則指出如果我們多使用這種能量
來源的話，會產生什麼樣的改變。因為這改變也並非事實，因此用**助動詞 + V** 再一次
與現在的事實作區分。

★與過去事實不同的假設
（If S + had + PP , S + 助動詞 + have + PP）

與過去事實不同的假設，意指「若是在過去發生某事，則過去的某個事實就會產
生改變」。

◎ If Steven **had not dropped out** of school 10 years ago, / he **would not have had**

            had not + PP   助動詞 + not + have + PP

      a chance / to start his business.

如果十年前史提夫沒有休學 / 他就不會有一個機會 / 去開創他的事業

※ 1. If 後方接的子句是與過去事實不同的假設情境。
因為是一種假設，所以用**過去完成式**（had not dropped）與過去的
事實作區別。

2. 後半段的子句 he would not...start his business 則指出如果他以前沒有休學的話，會產
生什麼樣的改變。因為這改變也並非事實，因此用**助動詞＋完成式**（would not have
had）再一次與過去的事實作區分。

◎ Nancy **would have drowned** / if the torrential rain **had kept** raining then.
　　　　　助動詞 + have + PP　　　　　　　　　　　　　　　　　had + PP
南西大概會淹死 / 如果當時那場大雨持續地下

※ 1. If 後方接的子句是與過去事實不同的假設情境。
　　因為是一種假設，所以用**過去完成式**（had kept）與過去的事實作區別。

　 2. 前半段的子句 Nancy would have drowned 則指出如果雨一直下，會產生什麼樣的改
變。因為這改變也並非事實，因此用**助動詞 + 完成式**（would have drowned）再一
次與過去的事實作區分。

★沒有 If 的假設法（助動詞 + V / 助動詞 + have + PP）

有時候為了方便，我們也會省略 if 子句，直接用助動詞＋子句來表示假設。若是
指現在該做卻沒做，就用**助動詞 + V**（could / should / might）；如果表示過去該做卻
沒做，就用**助動詞 + have + PP**（完成式）。

◎ We **should stop** / letting unskilled laborers into Japan...
　　　　助動詞 + V　　　　　　　　　　　　　　　　　　　　　《紐時周報》
我們早就應該停止 / 讓無技術勞工進入日本

※ 助動詞 + V（should stop）表示我們現在應該要禁止讓無技術勞工進入日本，可是我們
卻沒有做到。因為與現在事實相反，所以是一種假設。

◎ I have these big piano-playing hands. / I feel like I **should be** / picking potatoes.
　　　　　　　　　　　　　　　　　　　　　　　　　　助動詞 + V
我有這雙適合彈琴的大手 / 我覺得我好像應該 / 摘採馬鈴薯

（Sandra Bullock 珊卓‧布拉克）

※ 助動詞 + V（should be picking）表示珊卓‧布拉克認為她現在應該要務農，可是她並
沒有這樣做。因為與現在事實相反，所以是一種假設。

◎ We **could have deployed** / the full force of American power...

助動詞 + have + PP　　　　　　　　　　　　　（歐巴馬當選演說）

我們原本可以布署 / 美國的所有兵力

※ 助動詞＋完成式（could have deployed）表示美國過去原本可以布署全部的兵力，但是
　卻沒有做到。因為與過去事實相反，所以是一種假設。

◎ I'm really bummed we didn't win Best Kiss. / We **should have rehearsed** /

助動詞 + have + PP

a bit more.　　　　　　　　　　　　　　　（Nicole Kidman 妮可‧基嫚）

我真的很失望我們沒有贏得最佳接吻獎 / 我們真的應該排練 / 再多幾次

※ 助動詞＋完成式（should have rehearsed）表示妮可‧基嫚過去應該要多排練幾次，但
　是卻沒有做到。因為與過去事實相反，所以是一種假設。

 重 點 整 理

◎ 英文的假設法是在時態上作變化。常用的兩種假設法為：

　與**現在**事實不同的假設：

　If S + were / Ved, S + should / could / might / would + V

　Ex) If women didn't exist, all the money in the world would have no meaning.

　與**過去**事實不同的假設

　If S + had + PP, S + should / could / might / would + have + PP

　Ex) If Steven had not dropped out of school 10 years ago, / he would not
　have had a chance to start his own business.

◎ 每個助動詞的意義都有所不同，而且會影響語意。常用的助動詞有：

　could（能夠）；**should**（應該）；**might**（也許）

◎ 助動詞 + V 也可以拿來用作假設！兩種用法如下：

　現在該做卻沒做：**should / could / might / would + V**

　Ex) We should stop the full force of American power.

　過去該做卻沒做：**should / could / might / would + have + PP**

　Ex) We should have rehearsed a bit more.

Grammar for Global English
附錄二
假設法

請依照情境判斷，填入適當的假設用法。

範例：If he sold the stone, he thought, he _____ enough money for
the rest of his life. (have) （97 年大學指考）
If he sold the stone, he thought, he **would have** enough money for the rest
of his life .

1. The car runs out of oil. We _____ the moment we saw the filling
station. (fuel up : 加油)

2. Republic of China _____ if Sun Yat-sen had never revolted.
(would not / exist)

3. Every restaurant was full on Christmas Eve. You _____ a reservation.
(should / make)

4. Yang Shu-juin（楊淑君）_____ the Asian Games in 2010.
(would / win)

5. If Nelson tried a little bit harder, he _____ the record. (could / break)

6. Lily could have avoided that car accident if she _____ . (drink)

第 1 題到第 4 題請依照括號內的提示，變換動詞時態；第 5 題和第 6 題請依照括號內的提示，填入適當的助動詞（could / should / might / would）變化。

範 例：Students _____ expelled from school if they misuse their computers, such as illegal downloads. (might)

Students **might be** expelled from school if they misuse their computers, such as illegal downloads.

1. Scientists find there is a close connection between these two species of bacteria. （過去該做卻沒做）

_____

2. You can improve yourself if you learn from those mistakes you made. （與現在事實不同）

_____

3. If Andrew doesn't enter the art school, he cannot reach such an accomplishment in sculpture. （與過去事實不同）

_____

4. Tom doesn't persuade Annie to go on a date with him. Now the chance is gone. （現在該做卻沒做）

_____

5. Sally will have a better future if she doesn't give up dancing. （與現在事實不同）

Grammar for Global English
附錄二
假設法

_____

6. Their marriage could remain well if the third party never interrupted.

（與過去事實不同）

_____

解答

文法解析篇
1. 主詞與動詞結構

文法解析篇
2. 肯定句、否定句、疑問句

練習

1. 主詞：Number of injured
   主要動詞：hits
2. 主詞：Newspapers
   主要動詞：tried
3. 主詞：The government
   主要動詞：works
4. 主詞：Making bread and washing cars
   主要動詞：are
5. 主詞：It
   主要動詞：is
6. 主詞：More than 150 people
   主要動詞：died

作業

1. Typhoons occur in the Pacific Ocean.
2. It isn't surprising to see him laugh.
3. Many animals and plants are under the threat of extinction.
4. Life is difficult for women in Afghanistan.
5. Bedbugs were wiped out in the 1950s.
6. It is troublesome to arrange so many refugees.

練習

1. 肯定；takes / took
2. 疑問；Do
3. 否定；can't
4. 疑問；Does / Did
5. 疑問；Is
6. 肯定；can

作業

1. isn't
2. Does / Can
3. Is
4. isn't
5. does
6. Does

文法解析篇

3. 十大句法

練習

1. 句法二：Ving(Ved)(to V)..., S + V
2. 句法六："...," says SB 或 SB says, "..."
3. 句法五：(Phrase), S + V
4. 句法九：S, Adj clause, V
5. 句法七：S + V + that + (noun clause)
6. 句法一：S + (...) + V
7. 句法十：Adv + V + S（倒裝句：Sentence Inversion）
8. 句法八：Adv clause, Main clause 或 Main clause, Adv clause
9. 句法四：With / Without + N + S + V
10. 句法三：S + V... (to V), Ving (Ved)

作業

1. In the cross-lake swimming race, a boat will stand by in case of any emergency.

   或 In case of any emergency, a baot will stand by in the cross-lake swimming race.

2. Tsai Ing-Wen, the head of DDP, had a debate with President Ma in 2010.

3. With the great efforts of the city, Ai River recovers its beauty.

4. Whenever a Dalai Lama died, a search began for his reincarnation.

5. People say that a Dalai Lama has the ability to identify his previous self.

6. Parodying Hollywood, Bollywood movies build its own features.

7. It is said that "Failure is the mother of success."

8. Stories about aliens, which are believed to exist, stir readers' imaginations.

9. Never did a person try to climb Taipei 101.

10. The news only tells part of the truth, leaving spaces for doubts.

解答

文法解析篇

4. 十大句法的實戰練習：閱讀報章雜誌

練習

段落一：

a. Now <u>France</u> <u>is pushing forward</u> with a novel approach: giving away papers to young readers in an effort to turn them into regular customers.

主詞為 <u>France</u>
動詞為 <u>is pushing forward</u>。

此句句法為 <u>S + V, with + N + (Ving or Ved)</u>，可切割為：

Now / <u>France</u> / <u>is pushing forward</u> / with a
　　　　 S　　　　　　 V

novel approach: / giving away papers / to young readers / in an effort / to turn them into regular customers.
現在 / 法國 / 正在推動 / （以什麼方式推動？）以新奇的方式 / 分發報紙 / 給年輕讀者 / 為了努力 / 將他們（年輕讀者）變為固定的顧客

b. <u>The French government</u> recently <u>detailed</u> plans of a project called "My Free Newspaper," under which 18- to 24-year-olds will be offered a free, year-long subscription to a newspaper of their choice.

主詞為 <u>The French Government</u>
動詞為 <u>detailed</u>

此句句法為 <u>S + V + O + 從屬結構 (which 子句)</u>
可切割為：

<u>The French government</u> / recently <u>detailed</u>
　　　　　 S　　　　　　　　　　　　 V

plans / of a project / called "My Free

Newspaper," / under which 18- to 24-year-olds / will be offered / a free, / year-long subscription / to a newspaper / of their choice.
法國政府 / 最近詳細地計畫 / （計畫什麼？）一項政策 / （那項政策）叫做「我的免費報紙」/ （在該政策之下）18 到 24 歲之間的人 / 將會得到 / 一份免費的 / 一年份的訂閱 / （訂閱什麼？）一份報紙 / （是什麼樣的報紙？）他們選擇的

段落二：

a. <u>Every celebrity Muggle in New York City</u> <u>showed up</u> for the Nov. 15 premiere of *Harry Potter and The Deathly Hallows: Part 1*, from Sarah Jessica Parker and Sandra Lee to Melissa Joan Hart, best known as *Sabrina, the Teenage Witch*, all of whom walked down the red carpet.

主詞為 <u>Every celebrity Muggle in New York City</u>
動詞為 <u>showed up</u>

此句句法為 S + V + 從屬結構 (whom 子句)
可切割為：

Every celebrity Muggle in New York City /
                    S
showed up / for the Nov. 15 premiere / of
    V
Harry Potter and The Deathly Hallows: *Part
1,* / from Sarah Jessica Parker and Sandra
Lee / to Melissa Joan Hart, / best known as
Sabrina, the Teenage Witch, / all of whom
walked down the red carpet.
每個紐約市的麻瓜名人 / 出現 /（為了什
麼場合出現？）為了 11 月 15 日的首映 /
（是什麼的首映？）《哈利波特：死神的
聖物（上）》/ 從莎拉潔西卡派克和桑德拉
李 / 到梅莉莎瓊哈特 /（梅莉莎以什麼作品
著稱？）*Sabrina, the Teenage Witch* / 所有
人都走上紅毯

註：Sarah Jessica Parker, Sandra Lee 和 Melissa Joan
Hart 皆美國知名影星。Sarah Jessica Parker 以演出《慾
望城市》著名；Sandra Lee 為美國知名美食節目廚師；
Melissa Joan Hart 以演出美國知名影集 *Sabrina, the
Teenage Witch* 著名。

b. As for the crowd of shrieking girls, they
just had one thing to say: "OMG OMG OMG
OMG OMG OMG!"

主詞為 they
動詞為 had one thing to say

此句句法為 (Phrase), S + V 和 S says, "…"
的結合
可切割為：

As for the crowd of shrieking girls, / they /
                                        S

just had one thing to say: / "OMG OMG
            V
OMG OMG OMG OMG!"
至於那一群尖叫的女孩們 / 她們 / 只有一句
話要說 /「我的天啊我的天啊我的天啊我的
天啊我的天啊我的天啊！」

c. Most of them also came carrying posters
that read MOODBLOODS ♥ EMMA, NYC
WIZARD ROCK, and I ♥ THE BOY WHO LIVED.

主詞為 Most of them
動詞為 came

此句句法為
S + V + Ving

可切割為：
Most of them / also came carrying posters /
    S   V
that read MOODBLOODS ♥ EMMA, /
NYC WIZARD ROCK, / and I ♥ THE BOY WHO
LIVED.
她們大多數 / 也來 / 帶著海報 /（那些海報
上寫著）/「麻瓜愛艾瑪」/「搖滾吧，紐
約的巫師們！」/ 還有「我愛那個活下來的
男孩」

d. "It always amazes me how enthusiastic
they are after all these years," says Rupert
Grint, who plays Ron Weasley.

主詞為 Rupert Grint
動詞為 says

此句句法為
"…," says SB 及 S, Adj clause , V 的結合
可切割為：

解答

"It / always amazes me / how enthusiastic they are / after all these years," / says / V

Rupert Grint, / who plays Ron Weasley.
　　　S

「這 / 總是使我感到驚奇 / 她們是如此熱衷 / 在這些年之後 」/ 說 / 魯伯特葛林特 /（他是誰？）扮演榮恩衛斯理的人

e. "It's really great!"

主詞為 It
動詞為 is

此句句法為 S + V 可切割為：

"It's / really / great!"
　S　V
「這 / 真是 / 太棒了！」

f. So are all these secrets that we plucked from the film's leading actors.

主詞為 all these secrets
動詞為 are

此句句法為 Adv + V + S 及 S, Adj clause, V 的結合

可切割為：
So / are / all these secrets / that we plucked
　　　V　　　　S
/ from the film's leading actors.
也是如此 /（什麼也是如此？）/ 那些所有的祕密 /（那些祕密是哪些祕密？）是我們挖出來的 / 從電影的主要演員們（身上挖出

來的祕密）

5. 主要結構與次要結構

1. 主要結構為：There was a time
次要結構為：when Whitney didn't have a lot of friends（副詞子句）
2. 主要結構為：
hair has had a special significance；
次要結構為：
In all cultures and throughout history
（副詞片語）
3. 主要結構為：
The idea of long hair is even mentioned in the Bible
次要結構為：
as a symbol of male strength
（形容詞片語）
4. 主要結構為：
The only person was Delilah；
次要結構為：
who knew his secret（形容詞子句）
5. 主要結構為：You will love；
次要結構為：
how you feel 和 after helping others
（名詞子句和副詞片語）

6. 主要結構為：

Camille and other children can fill in some of the gaps；

次要結構為：

volunteering thousands of hours annually（形容詞片語）

7. 主要結構為：

I just wanted to save some money and I always thought；

次要結構為：

the threat was just a scare tactic （名詞子句）

8. 主要結構為：

The organization states；

次要結構為：

that files lawsuits against illegal downloaders（形容詞子句）及 that suing students was by no means their first choice（名詞子句）

1. The NFW developed the project more than a decade ago to address the self-esteem problems that many girls experience when they enter adolescence.

分析：

The NFW developed the project <u>more than</u>
　　主要結構　　　　　　　　副詞片語
<u>a decade ago</u> to address the self-esteem

problems <u>that many girls experience when</u>
　　　　　形容詞子句
<u>they enter adolescence.</u>
　　副詞子句

主要結構：

The NFW developed the project more than a decade ago to address the self-esteem problems.

主要結構中的次要結構：

more than a decade ago（副詞片語）

句子的次要結構：

that many girls experience when they enter adolescence（形容詞子句）

次要結構中的次要結構：

when they enter adolescence（副詞子句）

2. According to research, kids who start volunteering are twice as likely to continue doing good deeds when they are adults.

分析：

<u>According to research</u>, kids <u>who start</u>
　　副詞片語　　　　　　　　形容詞子句
<u>volunteering</u> are twice as likely to continue
　　　　　　　　　　主要結構
doing good deeds <u>when they are adults.</u>
　　　　　　　　　　副詞子句

主要結構：

kids (...) are twice as likely to continue doing good deeds (...).

主要結構中的次要結構：

who start volunteering（形容詞子句）

主要結構中的次要結構：

when they are adults（副詞子句）

句子的次要結構：

According to research（副詞片語）

文法解析篇
6. 時態

練習

1. Inventors **are** always **looking for** ways to make our lives easier, greener and a whole lot more fun.

2. **Have** you **ever dreamed** of becoming a superhero?

3. The Hardworking Robot **will be** the perfect office helper.

4. Years ago, some foreign high-speed train producers **taught** China how to make a bullet train.

   或 Some foreign high-speed train producers **taught** China how to make a bullet train years ago.

5. Last Thursday, a new United Nations study **released** that the chemistry of the world's oceans is changing at a rate not seen for 65 million years.

6. "The new profile page **will enable** users to see all the things in common with a friend," Facebook CEO acclaims.

   或 Facebook CEO acclaims that the new profile page **will enable** users to see all the things in common with a friend.

G[D]U 作業

1. As a kid, Sally Ride **did not** think her dream would come true.

2. Sally Ride **is** the first American woman to travel into space.

3. Shanghai-Beijing train **has broken** world speed record.

4. **Will** this **impact** the information I choose to share on the internet?

5. All the buyers **are looking forward to** the release of iPad 3.

6. Last week(,) a Wikileaks spokesman **said** the arrest of their leader **was** an attack on media freedom.

文法解析篇
7. 連接詞

練習

1. but
2. Nonetheless
3. so
4. and
5. Because
6. or
7. Therefore

8. However

9. on the other hand

1. therefore
2. so
3. but
4. for
5. However
6. On the other hand
7. Neither, nor
8. Nevertheless

文法解析篇
8. 被動式

練習

1. am surprised
2. was opened
3. was warned
4. are / were asked
5. set up
6. is / was / will be built

1. My pink notebook **is / was filled with** my schedules.
2. My mom **is / was interested in** everything I told her, especially those happened in school.
3. Jack **was given** the rare privilege of using the president's office, which made others quite jealous.
4. Linda **is confused** and does not know in which part she should believe, for the two sides give totally opposite explanations.
5. By the end of the 18th century, all of Paris **was intoxicated with** coffee and the city supported some 700 cafés.
6. At first, the use of plastic for toy manufacture **was not regarded** by retailers and consumers of the time.

文法解析篇
9. 比較級

練習

1. the best
2. fluently

解答

235

3. the most popular

4. most important

5. better

1. The **most important** thing in life is to have a great aim, and the determination to attain it.

2. How **sharper** than a serpent's tooth it is to have a thankless child!

3. Living without an aim is **as aimless as** sailing without a compass.

4. Unbidden guests are often (the) **welcomest** when they are gone.

5. Victory belongs to **the most preserving**.

文法解析篇

10. 強調

練習

1. It was the young man's talent

2. do hope

3. It is Wang Tsai-Hua's song "Bobee"

4. It was deafness

5. does come from

6. does need to

1. **It is rapid advancement in motor engineering that** makes it technically possible to build a flying car in the near future.

2. Since our classroom is not air-conditioned, we **do have to tolerate** the heat during the hot summer days

3. Susan believed that the fragrance of flowers **did refresh** her mind.

4. **It is for this demanding math class that** I have to spend at least two hours every day doing the assignments.

5. My brother **does enjoy** having cold drinks, so he always puts his Coke in the refrigerator.

6. Jim grew up with many animals at home and **does know** well how to take care of pets.

應用篇
聽力

應用篇
口語訓練

練習與作業

Young people are perhaps better known for spending money than saving it. But some new banking websites are seeking to change that. These websites offer young people the information and tools they need to watch over their money. The websites also let the users share their financial experiences with other young people.

Nineteen-year-old Alix Scott has been working at a store this summer. She is saving money to pay for college next year.

ALIX SCOTT: "I have to save for all my college money because my parents, they can't afford to co-sign on loans. So, I have to rely on my own savings."

But instead of putting her money in a local bank, Ms. Scott began using SmartyPig, a Web-based banking service.

GEPT 中級預試 口說能力測驗－範例

1. I'm searching in my brain, in order to find an interesting event to share with my audience.
2. Like most of us, I was twelve when I went to junior high school.
3. I feel more relaxed at night because I usually finish all my studies during day time. I can enjoy TV shows with some bites of snacks at night.

練習與作業

範例一

I wake up at 6 but get up at 7.

I have bacons and eggs for breakfast, and I enjoy it a lot.

I put on my uniform, ready for school.

I plan to do my best on the exams.

I take the MRT to school as usual.

I feel confident, and am ready for any challenges.

範例二

Last weekend I had a wonderful experience of taking photos.

解答

I went to a photo salon for family salon pictures with my family.

We did this to celebrate my parents' twentieth anniversary. (anniversary: 周年)

(So) I wore a pink dress, with beautiful laces on it. My father was in a suit, and my mother was in a wedding dress, with red roses on it.

My parents took great pictures. Their pictures impressed me a lot because I could see happiness showed on their faces.

After that day, I felt really happy. My parent's love toward each other warms my heart. I was so glad that I have a happy family.

應用篇
閱讀

GLOBAL 練習與作業

Strange / is /our situation here / upon earth. / **Each of us** / **comes** for a short visit, / not knowing why, / yet sometimes seeming to / divine a purpose.

From the standpoint of daily life, / however, / **there is one** / this we do know / **that man is here** / **for the sake of other men** — / above all for those / upon whose smile and well-being our own happiness depends, /and also for the countless unknown souls / with whose fate / we are connected by a bond of sympathy. / Many times a day / **I realize** / **how much my own outer and inner life/ is built upon** / **the labors of my fellow men, / both living and dead, / and how earnestly** / **I must exert myself** / in order to give in return / as much as I have received. / **My peace of mind / is often troubled** / by the depressing sense / **that I have borrowed too heavily** / from the work of other men. /

To ponder interminably over the reason / for one's own existence / or the

meaning of life / in general seems **to me**, / from an objective point of view, / **to be sheer folly**. / And **yet everyone holds certain ideals** /by which /he guides his aspiration and his judgment. / **The ideals / which have always shone** before me / **and filled me with the joy of living** / **are goodness, beauty, and truth**. / **To make a goal of comfort and happiness** / has never appealed to me; / a system of ethics built on this basis / **would be sufficient only for a herd of cattle**.

語意與段落重點：

Strange / **is** / our situation here / upon earth. / **Each of us / comes** / for a short visit, / not knowing why, / yet sometimes seeming to divine a purpose.

奇怪的是 / 我們在這世界上的處境 / 我們每一個人 / 為了一場短暫的旅程而來 / 不明瞭原由 / 但有時似乎感受到 / 神聖的目的

（段落重點：Each of us / comes / ...seeming to divine a purpose → 每個人 / 來到世上 / 似乎是為了某個神聖的目的）

From the standpoint of daily life, / however, / **there is one** / this we do know / **that man is here /for the sake of other men** — / above all for those / upon whose smile and well-being our own happiness depends, / and also for the countless unknown souls / with whose fate / we are connected by a bond of sympathy. / Many times a day / **I realize /how much my own**

outer and inner life / **is built upon /the labors of my fellow men**, / both living and dead, / **and how earnestly / I must exert myself** / in order to give in return / as much as I have received. / **My peace of mind / is often troubled** / by the depressing sense / **that I have borrowed too heavily** / from the work of other men. /

從平日的生活看來 / 然而 / 有一件事 / 這件事我們很清楚 / 人來到世上 / 是為了其他人 / 尤其是為了那些人 / 我們依賴著其笑容與幸福而感到快樂 / 同時也是為了那些無數的不知名的靈魂 / 藉著那些人的命運 / 我們靠著憐憫之心連結起來 / 每天有許多次 / 我感受到 / 我內在和外在的生活有多大程度 / 建立 / 我同胞的勞動上 / 不論是活著的或是已逝去的 / 並且是多麼熱切 / 我必將竭盡自己的能力 / 為的是付出 / 與我所接受的一樣多 / 我內心的平靜 / 總是被擾亂 / 因為沮喪 / 我接受太多了 / 其他同胞的成就

（段落重點：there is one / this we do know / that man is here / for the sake of other men → 有一件事 / 這件事我們很清楚 / 人來到世上 / 是為了其他人）

To ponder interminably over the reason / **for one's own existence** / **or the meaning of life** / in general seems **to me**, / from an objective point of view, / **to be sheer folly**. / And **yet everyone holds certain ideals** / by which / he guides his aspiration and his judgment. / **The ideals / which have always shone** before me / **and filled me with the joy of living / are goodness, beauty, and truth**. / **To make a**

goal of comfort and happiness / has never appealed to me; / a system of ethics built on this basis / **would be sufficient only for a herd of cattle**.

總觀所有的理由 / 一個人存在的意義 / 或是生命的意義 / 大體上對我而言 / 從客觀的角度看來 / 是非常愚蠢的 / 不過每個人總有些理想 / 藉著那些理想 / 引導自己的抱負和判斷 / 有個理想 / 總是在我眼前發光的 / 並且讓生命的喜悅充斥我心的 / 是善,美,和真理 / 將舒適和享樂當作目標 / 從來都不吸引我 / 一個建立在這種基礎上的倫理觀 / 也僅僅能夠滿足牲畜罷了

(段落重點:The ideals / which have always shone... / and filled me with the joy of living / are goodness, beauty, and truth →有個理想 / 總是在我眼前發光的 / 並且讓生命的喜悅充斥我心的 / 是善、美、和真理)

全文主旨:
人來到這世上是為了其他人而活,才能創造人類共同的幸福。
"Man is Here For The Sake of Other Men," Albert Einstein

應用篇
寫作

GIN 練習與作業

An Unforgettable Scene

I go to school by bus every day, and go home by bus as well. The bus is always filled with students like me. Everyone talks aloud. The bus is noisy and crowded; I'm always in a bad mood. But today was kind of different.

On my way home a boy got on the bus, with shining golden hair. His looks aroused my curiosity. When the bus driver talked to him, he merely shook his head and smiled. It seemed he couldn't understand (what the driver said). Until he walked near me, I realized (that) he was a foreigner.

Other students looked at him with curiosity, and soon moved their eyes aside. That boy stood among the crowd, silently accepting people's curiosity. Suddenly the bus made a quick turn. That boy lost his balance and was about to fall...

應用篇
翻譯

練習與作業

1. Life was / is like a box of chocolates. You never know what you' re gonna get.
2. There' s some good in this world, and it' s worth fighting for.
3. Onion have layers. Ogres have layers! We both have layers.
4. With great power, comes great responsibility.
5. Keep your friends close, but your enemies closer.

考試篇
多益

練習與作業

Ms. Monica Eisenman
555 King Street
Auckland
New Zealand

Dear Ms. Eisenman:

I am <u> (1) </u> to confirm / our offer of part-time employment / at Western Enterprise. / In your role / as research assistant, / you will report to Dr. Emma Walton, / who will keep you informed of / your specific duties and projects. / Because / you will be working with confidential information, / you will be expected to / <u> (2) </u> the enclosed / employee code-of-ethics agreement.

As we discussed, / you will be paid / twice a month / <u> (3) </u> the company' s normal payroll schedule. / As an hourly employee / working fewer than twenty hours per week, / you will not be <u> (4) </u> / to receive paid holidays, paid time off for illness or vacation, / or other employee benefits. / Your employment status / will be

解答

241

reviewed / in six months.

If you have any questions, / please feel free to contact me. / Otherwise, / please sign and return / one copy of this letter. / You may keep the second copy / for your files. / We look forward to / working with you.

Sincerely,

Christopher Webster

Christopher Webster

Human Resources

Enclosures

Monica Eisenman 小姐

國王街 555 號

奧克蘭

紐西蘭

Eisenman 小姐：

很高興通知您 / 我們將雇用您為兼職人員 / 在 Western Enterprises / 身為 / Emma Walton 博士的研究助手 / 您必須向她報告 / 她會告訴您 / 具體的職務以及專案 / 由於 / 您的工作內容具高度機密 / 我們期望您 / 遵守附件的 / 公司員工倫理規定

誠如我們討論過 / 您將領薪水 / 每個月兩次 / 根據本公司一般的發薪日 / 您是時薪員工 / 一週工作時間少於二十小時 / 您不適用於 / 享有有薪假日以及病假與休假 / 或其他員工福利 / 您的工作狀況 / 會再檢視 / 六個月後

若有任何問題 / 請儘管與我聯繫 / 若無 / 請簽名並寄回 / 此封信的其中一份 / 您可留存另一份 / 備份 / 我們期待 / 與您一起工作

Christopher Webster

人力資源部 謹上

有附件

題 1

pleased 是形容詞，be pleased + to V 是書信所常用的尊敬語，有「樂意～」的意思。(B) 是形容詞，「令人舒適、愉快」。(C) 是形容詞，將事物當作主語是「令人愉快的」，人當主語是「討人喜歡的」。(D) 是名詞，表「高興、樂趣」。故答案選 (A)。

題 2

選項全部是動詞，接下來的「附件的公司成員倫理規定」是受詞，適當的動詞由前後文來判斷，應為 follow「遵守（規定等）、依照～」。故答案選 (A)。

題 3

according to ～是「依照～、根據～」，本文的 payroll schedule 為「薪資支付時間」。(A) accords 是「一致」的名詞複數形，以及「一致」動詞的第三人稱單數形，這個選項不符合文法。(B) according 並不能單獨使用，應為 according to。(D) 若是 in accordance with 才是「依照～」的意思。因此，答案為 (C)。

題 4

空格之後有不定詞，由文意來看，eligible 是最適當的，be eligible to ～ 是「有～的資格」。(A) 是形容詞，表「可忍受的」。(B) 是形容詞，表「心胸寬大的」。(D) expressed 是動詞的 express「表達」的過去分詞。最適合的答案為 (C)「有資格……的。」

GEPT 練習與作業

Because / the beautiful lake country of central Canada / has few roads but thousands of lakes and streams, / __(1)__ is best explored by canoe. / All the lakes are connected to __(2)__ by trails, / called portages, / and most lakes have one or two camping areas to choose from. / Visitors can start their __(3)__ on one lake, / paddle their canoe __(4)__ lake. / In this way, / they can __(5)__ from lake to lake / while they enjoy the fresh air, / clean water / and quiet surroundings of this beautiful area.

因為 / 那座加拿大中部的美麗湖城 / 有少少的道路但（也）有數千湖泊和溪流 / 獨木舟是探索它（那座城市）的最佳辦法 / 所有的湖泊間都有路徑連接彼此 / （那些路徑）叫做陸路 / 而且大部分的湖泊都有一、兩個露營區可以選擇 / 觀光客可以從一座湖開始他們的旅程 / 乘獨木舟划向另一座湖泊 / 這樣 / 他們就可以遊遍每一座湖 / 當他們享受新鮮空氣 / 乾淨的湖水 / 還有這個美麗地區安靜的環境

題 1

1. 判斷句構為「連接詞＋S＋V, S＋V」。

2. 選項觀察得知本題在考「S＋V」這個概念，因此可輕鬆選出 (B) it 這個答案。

題 2

根據選項，可知此題在考 another / the other / each other / other 這四個代名詞的語意。依據文意判斷，本題應填入「彼此」，因此選 (C) each other。

題 3

根據選項，可知此題在考 journey / flight / hike / course 這四個名詞的語意。依據文意判斷，本題應填入「旅程」，因此選 (A) journey。

題 4

根據選項，得知此題在考 beside / within / across / toward 這四個介系詞的語意。依據文意判斷，本題應填入「橫跨」，因此選 (C) across。

題 5

根據選項，得知此題在考 drive / begin / ride / travel 這四個動詞的語意。依據文意判斷，本題應填入「旅行、遊遍」，因此選 (D) travel。

解答

考試篇
指考

GD 練習與作業

Signs asking visitors to keep their hands off the art / are everywhere in the Louvre Museum, Paris. / But one special sculpture gallery / invites art lovers / to allow their hands to __(1)__ the works. / The Louvre's Tactile Gallery, / targeted at the blind and visually __(2)__ , / is the only space in the museum / where visitors can touch the sculptures, / with no guards or alarms to stop them. / Its latest exhibit is a __(3)__ of sculpted lions, / snakes, / horses / and eagles. / The 15 animals exhibited are reproductions of famous works / found elsewhere in the Louvre. / Called "Animals, Symbols of Power," / the exhibit __(4)__ animals / that were used by kings and emperors throughout history / to symbolize the greatness of their reigns. / The exhibit, / opened in December 2008, / __(5)__ scheduled to run for about three years. / During guided tours on the weekends, / children can explore the art / with blindfolds on.

要求民眾不能碰觸藝術品的標示 / 在巴黎的羅浮宮隨處可見 / 但是有一個特別的雕塑藝廊 / 邀請藝術愛好者 / 允許他們用手碰觸作品 / 羅浮宮的觸覺展廳 / 特別為了視盲者和視障者而設 / 是羅浮宮內唯一的場所 / 開放參觀者碰觸雕像 / 沒有警衛或警告標示阻止 / 它最新的展覽是一系列的雕塑獅子 / 蛇 / 馬 / 以及老鷹 / 這十五件展示品是有名作品的複製品 / 可在羅浮宮的其他區域發現 / 名為「動物，權力的象徵」 / 這展覽以動物為特色 / 在歷史中被國王和君主使用 / 象徵他們領土的廣闊 / 這項展覽 / 2008 年 12 月開幕 / 計畫展出三年 / 在週末的導覽中 / 孩童可以探索這些藝術品 / 戴上眼罩

題 1
根據選項判斷本題在考動詞片語語意，再依照上下文，可知本題應選擇與「碰觸」有關的片語，因此選擇 (B) run over，有雙手在展示品上下滑動撫摸之意。

題 2
根據選項可知本題在考詞性。因為先前的 the blind 為集合名詞，泛指所有盲人，因此此處選擇 (C) impaired 最為恰當。visually impaired 意為「視覺障礙者」。

題 3
根據選項可知本題在考名詞語意。配合本文主旨即可選出 (A) collection（展覽品）。

題 4
根據選項可知本題在考動詞語意。配合主詞 the exhibit 即可選出 (D) features（這項展覽以～為特色）。

題 5
1. 判斷本句句構為「S + ,..., + V」。
2. 由主詞 The exhibit 和動詞 scheduled「這項展覽（被）安排～」，可知本題在考被動 (Be V + PP)，故選 (A) is。

GO!!! 練習與作業

Many people like to drink bottled water / because they feel that tap water may not be safe, / but is bottled water really any better?

Bottled water is mostly sold in plastic bottles / and that's why it is potentially health __(1)__ . / Processing the plastic can lead to the release of harmful chemical substances / into the water contained in the bottles. / The chemicals can be absorbed into the body / and __(2)__ physical discomfort, / such as stomach cramps and diarrhea.

Health risks can also result from inappropriate storage of bottled water. / Bacteria can multiply / if the water is kept on the shelves for too long / or if it is exposed to heat or direct sunlight. / __(3)__ the information on storage and shipment / is not always readily available to consumers, / bottled water may not be a better alternative to tap water.

Besides these __(4)__ issues, / bottled water has other disadvantages. / It contributes to global warming. / An estimated 2.5 million tons of carbon dioxide were generated in 2006 / by the production of plastic for bottled water. / In addition, / bottled water produces an incredible amount of solid __(5)__ . / According to one research, / 90% of the bottles used are not recycled / and lie for ages in landfills.

很多人都喜歡喝瓶裝水 / 因為他們覺得自來水也許不安全 / 但是瓶裝水真的比較好嗎？

瓶裝水大多都裝在塑膠瓶裡販賣 / 而那就是為什麼它們對健康有潛在的威脅 / 處理塑膠（的過程）會導致釋放有毒的化學物質 / 到瓶內的水中 / 這些化學物質可能會被人體吸收 / 造成身體不適 / 像是胃痙攣和腹瀉

瓶裝水的不當儲存也會導致健康風險 / 病毒會繁衍 / 如果水被放在架上太久 / 或是水被暴露在高溫下或直接接受日曬 / 因為儲存和運輸的知識 / 並不總是能完全傳遞給消費者 / 瓶裝水也許並不是自來水更好的替代選擇

除了這些安全問題之外 / 瓶裝水也有其他缺點 / 它造成溫室效應 / 2006 年大約產生了兩百五十萬噸的二氧化碳 / 生產裝瓶裝水的塑膠瓶 / 另外 / 瓶裝水製造驚人的垃圾量 / 根據一個研究 / 百分之九十的瓶子都是不可回收的 / 而且在垃圾掩埋場埋了很久的時間

題 1

根據選項，得知此題在考 frightening / threatening / appealing / promoting 這四個詞的語意。根據文意判斷本題應填入「對……有威脅的」，因此選 (B) threatening。

解答

題 2

1. 判斷句構為「S + V + and V, phrase」。

2. 從 The chemicals can be absorbed... 可知 and 後面省略了助動詞 can，必須接原形動詞，故選 (A) cause。

題 3

1. 判斷句構為「連接詞 + S + V, S + V」，得知前後兩個句子之間有邏輯關係。

2. 根據文意判斷前後文有因果關係，因此本題應填入「由於」，故選 (C) Since。

題 4

1. 判斷句構為「Phrase, S + V」。

2. 根據文意判斷，issue 應是指前文所談論的健康問題，因此選 (D) safety（安全），與健康較為有關。

題 5

1. 判斷句構為「Phrase, S + V」。

2. 根據文意判斷此處仍然延續前文的垃圾問題，因此選 (A) waste（廢棄物），較符合語意。

考試篇
統測

GOAL 練習與作業

The tiger may be more ancient and distinct than we thought. / Tigers are less closely related to lions, leopards and jaguars / __(1)__ these other big cats are to each other, / according to a new study. / The genetic analysis also reveals / that the tiger began evolving 3.2 million years ago, / and its closest living __(2)__ is the equally endangered snow leopard. / __(3)__ the popularity / and endangered status of tigers, / much remains to be discovered about them, / including how they evolved. / It has long been known / that the five species of big cat /— the tiger, lion, leopard, jaguar and snow leopard — / and the two species of clouded leopard / are more closely related to each other / than to other smaller cats. / But it has been difficult to pin __(4)__ / the exact relationships between them. / So to find out more, / scientists __(5)__ an analysis / of the DNA of all these species.

老虎可能比我們認為的更為古老和獨特 / 老虎與獅子、獵豹和美洲虎的血緣關係

較不親近 / 比起這三種大型貓科動物彼此之間的血緣關係 / 根據一項新研究 / 此遺傳學的分析也顯示 / 老虎在三百二十萬年前已經開始演化 / 並且現存關係最為親近的動物是一樣瀕臨絕種的雪豹 / 儘管老虎如此受歡迎 / 和面臨瀕臨絕種的處境 / 牠們還是有許多地方有待探索 / 包括牠們如何演化 / 這是長久以來都知道的事實 / 五大類貓科動物 / 老虎、獅子、獵豹、美洲虎,以及雪豹 / 以及兩種雲豹 / 彼此的血緣關係是更為親近的 / 比起其他小型貓科動物 / 但很難徹底查明 / 牠們之間的精確關聯 / 因此為了找出更多(證據、事實等)/ 科學家們進行一項分析 /(分析)這些物種的 DNA

題 1

此句為比較用法 (less closely related to A than B),故選 (A) than。

題 2

根據選項可知本題在考名詞用法,再根據文意,可知此處談的應該是同類的動物,因此選擇 (D) relative。

題 3

根據選項可知本題在考連接詞用法,而且 popularity(受歡迎)和 much remains to be discovered(仍有許多地方有待探索)有些微的矛盾,因此 (B) Despite(儘管)是較為恰當的選擇。

題 4

本題在考搭配動詞 pin 的介系詞,根據文意,可知 (C) down 為最適合的答案。pin down 意為「徹底查明」。

題 5

根據選項可知本題在考動詞用法,再根據文意得知科學家正在「進行」新的研究 (an analysis),因此選擇 (A) conducted(執行)。

考試篇
基測

〈克漏字測驗〉

A small town has a good chance of (1) / that can bring in a lot of money, / if it has something special to be proud of. / One example is Gukeng town of Yunllin, Taiwan. / Gukeng has long been famous for growing good coffee, / but the town didn't start to make much money from it / until some years ago. / As more and more people have visited Gukeng for its coffee, / the coffee farmers have begun to open their farms to the public. / At these farms, / people can have the fun of finding out where coffee comes from. / (2) , / coffee shops are opened all over Gukeng, / and people can take a rest / and taste delicious coffee on the sidewalks / in or after a day's visit. / The new businesses make a better life possible / for those who (3) the town. / They don't have to leave the town / to find jobs in other places.

一個小鎮有好的發展機會 / 能夠吸引大量錢潮 / 如果那小鎮有讓人驕傲的特點 / 臺

解答

灣雲林縣的古坑就是一個例子 / 古坑一直以來以出產好咖啡聞名 / 但是那小鎮並沒有開始因咖啡賺許多錢 / 一直到幾年前 / 當愈來愈多人為了咖啡造訪雲林 / 咖啡農就開始開放大眾參觀咖啡田 / 在那些咖啡田裡 / 人們可以開心得知咖啡是來自哪裡 / 而且 / 古坑到處都開了咖啡店 / 而且人們可以休息 / 並在人行道上品嘗香醇的咖啡 / 在一天的參觀中或參觀後 / 這個新興產業（讓人們）有機會過更好的生活 / 讓那些住在鎮上的居民 / 他們不必離開小鎮 / 到別處找工作

題 1
根據文意，可判斷本篇重點在談論古坑的特色產業，因此 (B) starting a new business 是最好的答案。

題 2
根據選項可知本題在考 First / Also / However / For example 四個連接詞的用法；再根據文意判斷本句應該是在呼應並補充前文，因此選 (B) Also 最為恰當。

題 3
根據下文文意，可判斷本句所談論的應該是當地居民；因此可選出 (A) live in 為最佳答案。

〈閱讀測驗〉

Read Cindy's diary and answer the questions.

Nov. 13, 1990 /

Today I got a letter from Jenny, / my new friend in America. / I wrote her last week, / and it was my first time to write a letter in English. / I was worried / that she wouldn't get my letter. / But she did, / and she wrote back a nice long letter. / She told me a lot / about her family, / school life, / and the things she likes to do on holidays. / I found we both love watching basketball games / and think of Michael Jordan as the greatest player ever.

I can't wait / to get a letter from Jenny again. / It's so much fun / to share things with a foreign friend. / In my next letter, / I will tell her some interesting things / about my school.

閱讀辛蒂的日記並回答問題

1990 年 11 月 13 日

今天我收到珍妮的信 / 我在美國的新朋友 / 我上星期寫信給她 / 而這是我第一次用英文寫信 / 我很擔心 / 她收不到我的信 / 但是她收到了 / 並且回了一封很棒的長信 / 她告訴我許多事 / 關於她的家人 / 學校生活 / 還有她假日喜歡做的事 / 我發現我們都喜歡看籃球比賽 / 並且認為麥可‧喬登是有史以來最棒的球員

我等不及 / 收到珍妮的下一封信 / 這真的好好玩 / 和一位外國朋友分享事物 / 在我的下一封信裡 / 我將告訴她一些有趣的事 / 關於我的學校

題 4
根據上一句可知辛蒂擔心珍妮收不到信，從連接詞 But 與 and she wrote back a nice long letter.，可知肯定助動詞 did 代表珍妮其實有收到信，所以選 (A) Jenny got the letter。

題 5
根據選項可知本題在考文意理解，根據 I found we both love watching basketball games，可知答案為 (A) She is a sports fan.

附錄二
假設法

練習

1. should fuel it up
2. would not have existed
3. should have made
4. would have won
5. could break
6. had not drunk

作業

1. Scientists **could have found** there is a close connection between these two species of bacteria.
2. You **could improve** yourself if you **learned** from those mistakes you made.
3. If Andrew **had not entered** the art school, he **could not have reached** such an accomplishment in sculpture.
4. Tom **should persuade** Annie to go on a date with him.
5. Sally **could have** a better future if she **didn't give up** dancing.
6. Their marriage **could have remained** well if the third party **had never interrupted**.

解答

附件：重點整理

★ 1. 主詞與動詞結構

◎ 先抓出句子中的主詞及動詞
◎ 抽象概念（如片語等）和虛主詞（It）也是主詞的一種
◎ 動詞是句子的靈魂，動詞的變化決定了句子的不同意義。
◎ 一個句子裡只會有一個動詞！主詞所採取的動作就是主要動詞； 　 其它動詞皆會以弱化形式（**Ving, Ved, to V**）出現。

★ 2. 肯定句、否定句、疑問句

肯定句	表達事實、情境、觀念的句子即為「肯定句」
否定句	表達否定的概念即為「否定句」 ＊ **am / are / is / was / were + not** ＊助動詞 + **not** + 動詞
疑問句	詢問他人意見（表達心中疑惑）的句子即為「疑問句」 ＊ **Am/Are/Is/Was/Were** + 主詞 + 名詞（或修飾主詞的字詞）**...?** ＊助動詞 + 主詞 + 動詞 ...?

★ 3. 十大句法

句法一	**S + (...) + V**
句法二	**Ving (Ved) (To V)..., S + V**
句法三	**S + V...(to V), Ving (Ved)**
句法四	**With / Without + N + (Ving or Ved)..., S + V** 或 **S + V, with / without + N + (Ving or Ved)**
句法五	**(Phrase), S + V**
句法六	**"...," says SB** 或 **SB says, "..."**
句法七	**S + V + that + (noun clause)**
句法八	**Adv clause, Main clause** 或 **Main clause, Adv clause**
句法九	**S, Adj clause, V**
句法十	**Adv + V + S**（倒裝句：Sentence Inversion）

★ 4. 十大句法應用要訣

1. 觀察句型，找出主要結構與次要結構，並找出相對應的十大句法

2. 找出主要結構中的主詞及動詞

3. 依照語法結構將長句切成小單元，有助於了解語意

4. 依照英文句法邏輯理解語意，不要硬從中文邏輯去理解

★ 5. 找出主要結構、次要結構的三步驟

1. **找出主要結構，理解句子的主要涵義**

（依邏輯判斷哪一組主詞和動詞構成的子句決定了句子的主要涵義，就能夠分辨出主要結構和次要結構。）

2. **判斷次要結構是片語還是子句**

（如果次要結構不能單獨成句，稱為「片語」；可以單獨成句的話，則稱為「子句」）

（根據用法的不同，即可判斷某次要結構為「名詞片語／子句」、「形容詞片語／子句」或是「副詞片語／子句」。）

＊次要結構是可以不斷增加的！在主要結構和次要結構之內，亦可以穿插更多的次要結構。

＊用標點符號，尤其逗號、破折號，來與子句作區隔的片語或子句，通常是次要結構。）

3. **理解次要結構的涵義，再與主要涵義作結合**

★ 6. 五大時態

1. 現在式	**V, V-s, V-es 或 V-ies**
	描述事實或狀態；第三人稱動詞要加 -s, -es 或 -ies
2. 過去式	**V-ed 或不規則變化**
	描述過去的事件或狀態；動詞分規則變化及不規則變化
3. 未來式	**will / shall + V 或 am / is / are + going to + V**
	描述未來發生的事件或狀態
4. 現在進行式	**am / is / are + Ving**
	強調當下正在發生的行為或狀態
5. 現在完成式	**has / have + PP**
	強調事情或狀態由過去持續到現在，並暗示可能延續到未來

重點
整理

★ 7. 連接詞

(1) 對等連接詞

and	暗示兩個連接的字詞或句子彼此相關
or	暗指每個選擇重要性相等，選項間彼此可互相代換，可能有多重選項
either...or...	強調選項的互斥性，只能二選一
neither...nor...	否定兩個選項，強調「兩者皆不」
for / because / so	皆表示因果關係 ＊for 和 because 強調原因，so 強調結果，三者可視情況互相代換
yet / but	強調對比作用，只是 yet 較為口語

(2) 連接副詞

連接副詞指的是具有連接詞功能的副詞，通常用作語氣轉折，以凸顯上下文的關係
「A 子句 . 連接副詞 , B 子句」
「A 子句 ; 連接副詞 , B 子句」

However	通常強調前後文互相駁斥的情境，表示「然而」
Therefore	表因果關係，暗示前句（原因）造成後句的結果
On the other hand	以另一個新角度看待同一件事情時用
Nevertheless / Nonetheless	表示讓步，暗示在某種條件之下，有特例發生

★ 8. 被動

◎ am / are / is + PP (+ by + N)
  ＊視情況使用 by + N 進行補充

◎ 以「人」為主詞時，某些被動式形式的動詞表達亦可用來表示主動含義。
  ex) He is exhausted... / I am surprised...

重點
整理

★ 9. 比較級

自我的比較	A + am / are / is + Adj-er + than + B
	A + V + Adv-er + than + B
自我與他人比較	A + am / are / is + Adj-er + than + B
	A + V + Adv-er + than + B
	A + am / are / is + as Adj as + B
	A + V + as Adv as + B
自我與多者比較	A + am / are / is / V + the best (+ N)
	A + am / are / is + V + the most + Adj / Adv
	A + am / are / is / V + the Adj-est / Adv-est

★ 10. 強調

◎ **It + be + 強調部分 + that ～**
＊通常用來強調名詞
◎ **S + do / does / did + 原形 V**
＊通常用來強調動詞
◎倒裝：Adv + V + S

★ 11. 假設法

與現在事實不同的假設	If S + were / Ved, S + 助動詞 + V
與過去事實不同的假設	If S + had + PP, S + 助動詞 + have + PP
沒有 If 的假設法	助動詞 + V
	＊ 現在該做卻沒做
	助動詞 + have + PP
	＊過去該做卻沒做

Global English
全球英語文法

2011年11月初版　　　　　　　　　　　　　　　　定價：新臺幣360元
有著作權・翻印必究
Printed in Taiwan.

著　　　者	陳　超　明
發　行　人	林　載　爵

出　版　者	聯經出版事業股份有限公司	叢書編輯	李	芃
地　　　址	台北市基隆路一段180號4樓	文字整理	郭　惠	菁
編輯部地址	台北市基隆路一段180號4樓	校　　對	林　雅	玲
叢書主編電話	（02）87876242轉226	封面設計	江　宜	蔚
台北忠孝門市	：台北市忠孝東路四段561號1樓	內文排版	江　宜	蔚
電　　　話	：（02）27683708			
台北新生門市	：台北市新生南路三段94號			
電　　　話	：（02）23620308			
台中分公司	：台中市健行路321號			
暨門市電話	：（04）22371234ext.5			
郵政劃撥帳戶第0100559-3號				
郵撥電話	：27683708			
印　刷　者	文聯彩色製版印刷有限公司			
總　經　銷	聯合發行股份有限公司			
發　行　所	：台北縣新店市寶橋路235巷6弄6號2樓			
電　　　話	：（02）29178022			

行政院新聞局出版事業登記證局版臺業字第0130號

本書如有缺頁，破損，倒裝請寄回聯經忠孝門市更換。　　ISBN　978-957-08-3896-1（平裝）
聯經網址：www.linkingbooks.com.tw
電子信箱：linking@udngroup.com

國家圖書館出版品預行編目資料

全球英語文法/陳超明著．初版．臺北市．
　聯經．2011年11月（民100年）．256面．
　18×26公分（Global English）
　ISBN　978-957-08-3896-1（平裝）

　1.英語　2.語法

805.16　　　　　　　　　　　　　100020187

聯 經 出 版 事 業 公 司

信 用 卡 訂 購 單

信 用 卡 號：□VISA CARD □MASTER CARD □聯合信用卡

訂 購 人 姓 名：_____

訂 購 日 期：_____年_____月_____日　（卡片後三碼）

信 用 卡 號：_____ _____ _____ _____ _____

信 用 卡 簽 名：_____(與信用卡上簽名同)

信用卡有效期限：_____年_____月

聯 絡 電 話：日(O)：_____夜(H)：_____

聯 絡 地 址：□□□_____

_____

訂 購 金 額：新台幣_____元整

（訂購金額 500 元以下,請加付掛號郵資 50 元）

資 訊 來 源：□網路　　□報紙　　□電台　　□DM □朋友介紹
　　　　　　　□其他

發　　　　票：□二聯式　　　□三聯式

發 票 抬 頭：_____

統 一 編 號：_____

※ 如收件人或收件地址不同時，請填：

收 件 人 姓 名：_____ □先生　□小姐

收 件 人 地 址：_____

收 件 人 電 話：日(O)_____夜(H)_____

※茲訂購下列書種,帳款由本人信用卡帳戶支付

書　　　　　　　　名	數量	單價	合　　計
	總　　計		

訂購辦法填妥後

1. 直接傳真 FAX(02)27493734

2. 寄台北市忠孝東路四段 561 號 1 樓

3. 本人親筆簽名並附上卡片後三碼(95 年 8 月 1 日正式實施)

電 話：(02)27627429

聯絡人:王淑蕙小姐(約需 7 個工作天)